An Eighth of August

Also by Dawn Turner Trice

Only Twice I've Wished for Heaven

An Eighth of August

A NOVEL

Dawn Turner Trice

Crown Publishers

New York

To Faith and the power of Prayer

Published by Crown Publishers, New York, New York.
Member of the Crown Publishing Group.

Random House, Inc. New York, Toronto, London, Sydney, Auckland
www.randomhouse.com

CROWN is a trademark and the Crown colophon is a registered trademark of Random House, Inc.

Printed in the United States of America

Design by Leonard W. Henderson

Library of Congress Cataloging-in-Publication Data
Trice, Dawn Turner.
An eighth of August / by Dawn Turner Trice.—1st ed.
1. United States, President (1861–1865: Lincoln), Emancipation Proclamation—Anniversaries, etc.—Fiction. 2. Women—Middle West—Fiction. 3. Afro-American women—Fiction. 4. Female friendship—Fiction. 5. Middle West—Fiction. I. Title.
PS3570.R453 E34 2000
813'.54—dc21   00-043219

ISBN 0-517-70589-3

10 9 8 7 6 5 4 3 2 1

First Edition

Acknowledgments

To William H. Wiggins Jr. for his book *O Freedom! Afro-American Emancipation Celebrations.*

To James Mellon for compiling *Bullwhip Days, The Slaves Remember, An Oral History.*

To Rhonda Racha Penrice for directing me to *Exploring the Illinois Countryside.*

To the *Chicago Tribune* for heartrending news articles that plant seeds.

To the Illinois Arts Council for its financial support.

To my agent, Denise Stinson, for her foresight and dedication.

To my editor, Kristin Kiser, for her utter calm, keen vision, and direction in the eye of the storm.

To my family and friends, within whose love I take refuge.

Day One

J. Herbert Gray

From the start . . .

From the very start, them women on the Mothers Board say they saw her coming up the shoulder of the road, half dressed and walking scatter-legged 'long the side that hugs the river.

Them no-seeing women on Greater Faith's Mothers Board say they knowed it was her even when they was looking straight ahead up toward the pulpit at young Delaware Matthews, the assistant pastor, and she was merely caught up in their side glance. Them women say they knowed right off who it was just as soon as they saw all that pretty yellow coming toward the church. Yellow set 'gainst green country-side and the clear blue sky. 'Gainst newly laid black asphalt with a fresh white seam painted straight up the middle, so ain't no mistaking which side for heading east and which for heading west. One woman say yellow that pretty used to belong only to the sunflowers in the patch on the other side of town. But that was before Sis moved to Halley. Folk liked to intuit that women with skin that dark couldn't, or shouldn't, hold claim to such a vibrant color. But Flossie Jo never cared 'bout such particulars. Wore it without shame or sorrow, like she owned it and the sun, too; walked—when she wasn't walking scatter-legged—like she had wings and could show it off finer than any bird or butterfly of the same hue.

Them women on the Mothers Board say they was standing right here in this front pew, looking out this window, when they saw her. Never mind that the day was hazy and you could hardly see for the heat waves making everything ripple and blur. Heat beating down from the sun and rising up from that black asphalt, meeting in the middle in a steamy crease. Them women say they saw her, never mind them black fringes on the window's awning. Them fringes always hang long like scrappy thin pickaninny braids and nearly block the view. Still, them women say them fringes wasn't making no difference that morning. Neither was their wide and cocked, colorful Sunday hats or their rheumatized joints or their bad feet, which taken together made them stand stooped over and made seeing straight even more of a chore. They say when they saw Sis coming toward the church, everything sorta moved out the way; sorta opened up or eased up to let her through. They remember the exact moment she deboarded the bus under the last of all them fine houses on the hill. They remember 'cause them propane cannons sounded, nearly jarring the deafness out of them. They even recall when she crossed the Jefferson bridge, officially entering the downtown, and not long after that, stepped under the

WELCOME TO THE 1973 HALLEY'S LANDING EMANCIPATION FESTIVAL

banner that stretched between the cornices of the old glass company and the taxi place.

Them five women say by the time she made it halfway to the church and was hovering 'bout the Mercury Filling Station, they had done finished Communion—had gulped down double portions of that potent elderberry wine—and was up clapping and singing, swaying, though they couldn't recall the song. They did remember sorta that the choir was standing, too, and so was the young people up above in the loft area, and so was young Delaware and Pastor hisself—who, standing next to Delaware, always lost some of his handsomeness, what with that good-sized hole eating into his Afro. You noticed Pastor's hole only 'cause Delaware had a head full of that curly hair. And with Pastor's head and Delaware's head bowed over the empty Communion vials, Pastor's hole gaped wide open and shined, too, on account of the sweltering heat. So many people had done arrived for the goings-on that every seat in the sanctuary was filled to overflowing and everything running water: the walls, the floors, the pews, the people, and naturally, Pastor's head.

At one point, them women say, the big fat organist grabbed their attention 'cause he jumped up from his bench and screamed hallelujah. The music fell off as he hot-footed it down the center aisle toward the rear of the sanctuary. He turned the corner, smacking into the last row of pews—pews that don't offer much in the way of comforts for sitting, let alone for smacking into them—and rolled back up toward the pulpit 'long the outside aisle by the windows.

Them women was certain he ain't seen nothing outside that window, or 'round them fringes, or through the haze, what with his eyes squeezed shut the way they was, which explained why he smacked into them pews, bruising and welting up his stumpy legs. Windows may as well have been pushed down, showing off the stained glass, rather than propped open, beckoning a breeze. Especially since there was no breeze to speak of and the onliest thing coming in through those windows was a few of them forehead-kissing horseflies and, every now and then, a whiff of that good ol' barbecue pit smoke from the fairgrounds behind the church. Air was so thick and smelling so good that every time Pastor shook his tambourine and said "Somebody say Amen," you said "Amen" and tasted hot tangy sauce and soft white bread.

When the organist reached the front of the church again, the rest of the congregation and the choir had returned to their seats and was dabbing at the sweat behind their knees and grabbing their cardboard James Funeral Home fans, hoping to stir something. Them women say that when the organist hisself finally sat back down, the room was so quiet they could hear the crunch sound his wide butt made plopping down on the padded red bench, then the squeegee sound the padded red bench made scooting 'gainst the sweaty floor.

Them women say that organist started thumping on that organ again when Pastor motioned for Delaware to sing. Delaware stood and walked over to the microphone through a veil of incense smoke floating over the altar. He was wearing the hell out of a cream-colored cotton suit that set him back a ways, price-wise. They say you could tell 'cause the suit resisted a shine at the elbows and under the ass area and the jacket didn't start to crawl up his back as he eased into his song.

That Delaware wasn't only good-looking. He could sing, too. I could hear him all the way down in the basement, in the church's kitchen. That's where I was sitting, finishing up a plate of scrambled eggs, ham fat, and grits. Delaware sang "O Freedom" in a baritone so sweet my glass began to shudder at the pitch. And I had to stop eating for a second to sit up straight and rub on this gut of mine. I knowed from past experiences that from the moment he throwed his head back and dragged out the *O,* a freshet of sound would flood the sanctuary. He placed his hands on his hips and rocked from side to side the way his mama used to while perched on the opening float in the parade. "O Freedom." That there thing always brought everybody in the congregation to their feet, just cheering. I could hear it from the basement. But people didn't cheer long on account of wanting to hear the words. So instead of cheering, James Funeral Home fans took over, batting up cardboard kisses to him. Aunt Cora stopped rolling out her dough and smiled, thinking on his mama. May Ruth kept measuring flour and nodding her head. Even though she wasn't 'round to really know his mama, she knowed him and knowed how good he could preach and sing, and how that smile of his could set afire a whole pew row of young women (and some old enough to sit on the Mothers Board, truth be told). Even some white folks like our May Ruth saw Delaware and got happy.

Delaware always took his time with that song. Sang it nice and slow so everybody could get a good understanding about what it meant. So people could think on freedom for a while. That boy always took his time.

But then all of a sudden—all of a sudden, I'm telling you—Delaware started to jumble up on his words. It sorta took me, Aunt Cora, and May Ruth by surprise. I stopped rubbing on my gut. Aunt Cora stopped rolling out her dough again. It was like Delaware's words had done jammed up in his head and he couldn't get them out right. We all knowed he'd sung that song too many times to lose the words. The music started to skip 'round the wrong way. Then there was this long screech from the microphone falling to the floor, then all that cracking and popping coming 'cross the loudspeakers. All you could hear was O. You heard O over and over and no *Freedom* at all to speak of. It was like everything had done turned upside down. And nobody could right it. Them women who was up there say Delaware could hardly sing on account of how he was staring at the back doors of the sanctuary. The organist swiveled his hefty self 'round so he faced the back, too. One by one, all them hats in the congregation angled into turning; people in the loft crowded the rail to see better, but they couldn't see what was beneath them.

In the same time it took for everything to get all jumbled, it got stark, stark quiet.

Them women say everybody was frozen solid. Frozen solid was what come to mind even in that heat. Them women say nobody moved till the creaky doors in the back swung open wide, crashing into the wall, shattering the glass portions, and sending tiny pieces scattering here and there. They say nobody had time to duck. Them no-seeing women say the glare from all that yellow hit the walls, and the way the light splintered and fell over the pews made it difficult for most people to see who was responsible for blinding them. That was at first. But soon thereafter, Sis clearly came into view. For the longest, she stood under the threshold, leaning 'gainst the door frame, like she was collecting her thoughts and rear-ranging the sights before her. Didn't take much looking to see she was drunk beyond all Saturday-night expectations, which, truth be told, caused more of a commotion than that broken glass. Or, at least, just as much.

Back then, Sis was still new to Halley, and by the way she dressed and carried herself—talking that educated talk, words lining up all nice and neat—you sho' didn't take her for the sloppy-drunk type. Sis was quite a looker, with a fine shape, too. So, naturally, nobody could have guessed that on the busiest Sunday of the year, she'd be standing in that door-way with her skin holding a shine rivaling Delaware's shoes and with her blouse clinging to her bosom, showing off far more than what was respectable for a Sunday morning. And right after the point in the service when everybody's mind was on the Sacrament. Blood and all.

Before you knowed it, them women say, she was walk-ing—still scatter-legged—down the center aisle. She had her big satchel pocketbook snug-tight in her arms, cradling it like she was carrying a baby. She got to the pulpit and dropped her bag. And when she bent over to rummage 'round in it, the entire congregation—Delaware, Pastor, them women, the organist—everybody leaned with her.

Sis dug through that purse, and dug and dug, and when she finally pulled her hand out, all you could see was the glowering steel of a barrel, first peeking up from the folds of cloth, then in full view when she took it up in both hands and pointed it right toward Delaware's head.

Them women on the Mothers Board, behind her, started shouting, "Oh Lord, Sister Flossie. No, Sister Flossie. No, baby."

Delaware took two steps backward. He held his hands up in a shield, trying to keep her at bay. They say Pastor just outright hit the floor. Then Delaware had the good sense to jump behind the stoop wall separating the choir and the pulpit. The organist and drummer ducked behind their instruments. Lost chords hung in the air. People started screaming and gasping.

The sight on Sis's pistol bobbed as she pointed it down toward the wall where Delaware was squatting.

"Come on and show yourself, you no-good bastard." Her words slurred bad, kinda crawled out over the loudspeaker. And, they say, she blinked hard as she wiped at her forehead, trying to stop the sweat from running like raindrops in her eyes. "Come on out before I shoot you right there."

"In God's name," Delaware say. "What in God's name have I done to you?"

"Nothing in God's name, if I recall correctly. It's what you've done behind his back." They say Sis ran her hand 'cross her nose and her mouth; she then took two steps backward as she set her feet. "I'm going to count to three, and if you haven't shown your face, then I'll just aim where I think is best. And after I hit you square in your ass, I'll tell everybody what you did."

Delaware say, "What, tell everybody?"

"I'll tell everybody. Tell God. The church. The minister. I'll tell it."

One somebody from the loft yelled down, "Tell it, Miss Flossie. Tell it!"

But Sis didn't hear. At least I don't think she heard, since she didn't speak toward it. Her pistol just wavered every which way, despite the fact that her eyes, them steel black eyes of hers, was stuck on Delaware, who was still hunkered down behind that wall. She was so fixed on him, she ain't noticed my wife, who had done made it to the back of the church. My wife, Thelma, who was just as drunk as Sis and was holding on to the broken door for dear life.

Thelma steadied herself and pointed down the aisle, yelling, "Don't y'all mess with Flossie Jo!"

Them women on the Mothers Board say they dropped to their seats and started praying, calling on Jesus. As good fortune would have it, all that praying distracted Sis and she didn't see them ushers coming up behind her. So she didn't have time to pull the trigger before them ushers tackled her. They say when that first usher got hold of her, the pistol flew clear from her hands and skidded 'cross that wet floor under the Amens of them old women, who—even though old as black pepper—quickly craned their legs to get out of the way. Finally that pistol reached the metal grate by the baptismal font and clanked inside.

By the time me, Aunt Cora, and May Ruth got upstairs to the sanctuary, we'd done sweat so much en route that we didn't have no more sweat to speak of. Sis had been carted out. But Thelma was still trying to pick her way down the aisle. My wife was walking bent over a bit, latching on to the backs of the pews with them suction cup hands of hers. She had to grab hold of one pew before she could let go of the other. I took Thelma up 'cause she don't weigh nothing and I carried her over near the window. I couldn't make it to the front of the crowd, but I could hear that siren and eventually saw the police car driving off down Old Riley, turning at the street leading to the courthouse.

People in the loft area milled 'bout trying to peek out them high-up windows. But them windows was too high and offered nothing more than shafts of light and wavy dust streams that crisscrossed below the rafters.

That was thirteen years ago. Already, thirteen years.

This morning when Sis walked down this here center aisle, it was probably the first festival church service in years that people ain't whispered mouthfuls 'bout Sis and all that commotion. Probably the first time in years that they ain't looked forward to pointing a finger, neither.

And then this afternoon as everybody started setting up—hanging them Mylar balloons and that tinsel from the trees and street posts; draping yards and yards of that red, white, and blue bunting from the storefronts—the talk up and down Old Riley for the first time in ages probably had little to do with what them Mothers Board women claimed they saw way back then.

Quite possibly the talk was centered on them Halley's Comet statues situated 'round the downtown. Or them street vendors setting up their tables, getting ready for hawking everything from "official" Halley T-shirts and telescopes to cocktails, sky charts, and comet medallions, with the inscribed lie:

HALLEY'S LANDING, WHERE THAT COMET LANDED IN AUGUST 1910 AND THIS YEAR CAME BACK AGAIN

I s'pose when people couldn't find enough interest in that comet, the focus then turned to the tour buses and the semitrailers and flatbeds rolling into town. Seem like more coming this year than ever before. Them buses tote people arriving from all over; them trucks carry watermelon, meat, and other perishables, not to mention portable toilets, bedrolls, pieced-together circus rides, and more souvenirs. In between, Porter cabs dash in and out of the garage, heading to the train station and back down here, looping God knows how many times 'round that river. People always got a lot to say 'bout them Porter cabs.

This evening I'm standing in the quiet and the stillness of this sanctuary, looking out the window onto the fairgrounds behind the church. The fairgrounds is where the festival is held.

Out on the baseball field, way off from the hullabaloo of commerce, our Halley's Comets Little Leaguers are busy practicing. On account of the celebrations, their hair has been clipped so low that their little round heads shine like ball bearings in the waning sun. They keep hitting those balls and hitting them, until one boy connects with the electronic scoreboard in the back, accidentally making it shoot sparkles and colored smoke like it do when our team hit a home run.

I raise up now 'cause I see Sis and May Ruth giggling and walking arm in arm, coming toward the back of the church. Sis hold a bunch of sunflowers, which show up bright as anything, even in this light. The two pass through the wrought-iron gate to the cemetery beside the church. As they kneel before my nephew's grave, I don't even care to look. Aunt Cora say that's the awful, awful thing 'bout losing somebody during a celebratory time of the year. You got to learn yourself how to separate the celebration from the sadness. In a few days we'll come up on the one-year anniversary of that boy's passing, and it's no easier separating the sadness now than it was one year ago.

Instead of looking down at El's grave, I fix on the gold metal Jesus on the wall behind the choir stand, on his glimmering outstretched arms. I can't help but wonder how Sis would've dealt with El's birth had she knowed he wouldn't be long for this world. I don't believe she would've been so 'shamed of him early on if she'd knowed how much she was gone love that boy. No matter how he consumed her thoughts back then—made her show out on the busiest Sunday of the year—I know it ain't nothing compared to how he consume her thoughts now. All of us feel that way. And not only this family. Maybe in some respect the whole town feel that way.

Everybody's getting ready.

As for me, I'm just stealing me a few minutes of quiet in this sanctuary. Even though I know it won't be quiet for long.

Something bound to happen.

The simple truth is you just can't cram this many folk into one little town—get them eating real good and laying back, talking 'bout who they are, where they come from, the hard times behind them and beyond—and expect things to remain the same.

Sho' is hard to put a finger on right now when everything's getting started. Lord knows, ain't nobody looking for a repeat of what happened this time last August. But as God is my witness, something bound to happen.

Always does this time of year.

2

Herbert
The Festival
THE YEAR BEFORE

We was sitting in the parking lot of the mini-mall east of town.

That mini-mall that got the king-sized purple fiberglass cow sitting on top of ALL-RITE LIQUORS. That cow and them translucent bubbles flying 'bout his head lure all kinds off the interstate. Some come for the liquor; some come to take a gander at that cow and her one lone udder that point to the OPEN 24 HOURS sign above the entrance door.

We was sitting in that parking lot, watching the sun go down. We being myself, my nephew, El, and my youngest boy, Pepper. Them boys was in the backseat. El was flipping through them baseball cards of his. Flipping through them like a gambler, shuffling the deck, fanning them out, checking his figures. His favorite, Ernie Banks, was stuffed in his back pocket. You always saw that one separated from the other and sticking out of his back pocket.

I was sitting in the front next to the basket of fried chicken and coleslaw we'd just bought from the Kentucky Fried in the mini-mall. That good smell was getting wedged up in our noses, only we didn't have time to think 'bout that good smell after we started hearing that song, "Take Me Out to the Ball Game," coming from the interstate.

The top was down on the car and we could hear the music getting louder and louder. El jumped up and started pointing toward them trucks rolling off the ramp. Rolling single file, hissing and bouncing.

El sat on top of the seat to see better. Pepper was sixteen and just learning how to drive. The car was king and Pepper was too cool to let a eleven-year-old see him jumping up on the top seat on account of some trucks. So Pepper just leaned forward to grab a strawberry Nehi soda pop, like leaning forward alone didn't give him a better view. Which, naturally, it did.

Wasn't no ordinary festival trucks El was gawking at. These was real spiffy, big ol' tractor trailers. White in color with bold red letters that read, PAUL'S CLASS A GROUNDSKEEPERS INC. Lightbulbs flashed like merry-go-round lights 'round the top cabins. That song, "Take Me Out to the Ball Game," played from the loudspeaker of the first one. That first one was little and squat, half the size of the three trucks that followed. Followed like they was being led by a little pied piper. Them three trucks hissed when the first one hissed, squealed when the first one squealed. Single file, them trucks crossed the railroad tracks and hit Old Riley, heading toward town and playing that song. "Take me out to the crowd."

El say, "Them the people coming to set up the baseball trivia exhibit."

"Uh-huh," I say, studying more on my chicken wing than on that boy.

El say, "If Sweet Alma ever brings herself out of the store, we can go watch them unload. Right, Uncle Herbert?"

I say, "I don't think Sweet Alma gone want to watch nothing on no baseball. She too busy baby-sitting Rena Davies's baby."

El say, "We can drop her off at home, Uncle Herbert. Sweet Alma ain't got to go."

Pepper leaned forward again, this time for a chicken leg. El loved to copy Pepper, but El didn't bother with that food.

That boy's eyes was greedy more for them trucks and for baseball rather than for that good chicken.

Them gulls sitting on the canal wall 'long the river saw them trucks, too. And as the trucks rode pass, something musta spooked them birds. Their nerves was already bad from the noise of them propane cannons, which was sounding all the time to scare them birds out of the infield grass. Without one word from them cannons, though, them birds heard that song and saw them lights and flew off that canal wall. Hundreds of them, it seemed, flew off that wall with their wings above their heads like white capes, splashing into the water.

El glanced at them birds, then kept on watching them trucks wend their way 'round the river pass the sunflowers at The Famous Johnny Weston Hunt Club, pass the houses on the hill and on toward the sunset. Me and Pepper watched, too, on account of El being our little pied piper.

Throughout the whole thing, that song kept playing. Kept playing all over the place. Echoes of it rang throughout town, bouncing back and forth over the water.

"Buy me some peanuts and Cracker Jacks, I don't care if I ever get back. . . ."

Day Two

Cora Riley Hoskins
MONDAY, AUGUST 4, 1986

My kitchen normally has order. My life normally has order.

This morning neither has any. Pots and pans are strewn hither and yon. My Bolbei wedding china has been cast asunder and sits sprawled across the kitchen counter near the heat of my stove. But I try hard not to utter one word just yet. Especially not one about disorder and how, at my age, the sheer notion taxes the nerves and can be downright deadly. I keep working my crossword, looking up every now and then, expecting my niece to return my personal belongings to their proper places.

A saucer slips from her grasp and teeters on the edge of the counter. Thelma grabs the saucer just before it hits the floor.

"Thelma, honey," I say, catching my breath, "why don't you take a break for a minute?"

She doesn't turn around. She just keeps on stacking china, oblivious to my existence.

Herbert and I are still seated at the table. I'm finishing up the nice breakfast he has prepared. Unlike me, Herbert isn't paying his wife one bit of attention. He still has a paper towel tucked into his collar and he's busying himself by fiddling with May Ruth's bag of jewelry beads on his lap. Herbert bothers with those beads because the sheer rhythm of the stringing helps regulate his nerves. Not surprisingly, being married to Thelma has put him on the high-strung side.

"What you working on, Herbert?" I ask him. "A bracelet, a necklace for your wife?"

Like his wife, he doesn't answer. Course, it's taking all of his energy just to get his stubby fingers to pinch the beads right.

I may as well be dining alone and talking to myself.

Sunlight from the three-quarter windows above the sink lands in thin slices across the kitchen. One in particular meets Herbert across his suspenders and midsection, warming his wide, gurgling girth. As he threads those beads, every now and then staring off into his wife's untouched plate, I notice how his third button seems on the verge of popping—and zinging me right in the eyeball for concentrating on it so much.

Over by the sink, Thelma now fills a bucket of ammonia water. The windows open out, allowing a faint breeze to carry the ammonia smell into the garden. Despite the harsh odor, those greedy little mourning doves flutter about the window, waiting on one of us to throw them pieces of stale bread. But I can't study on stale bread right now.

I'm studying on Thelma as she stands on that wobbly step stool, scrubbing the glass on my upper cabinets. I've long wondered where she stores all that energy. She has no hips to speak of, no breasts, no rear, no bulge in her stomach. To look at her pale skin, she seems rather on the anemic side. Yet she's strong as any mule and somehow, miraculously, ten children, all boys, have passed through her tiny frame. (Herbert's belly, on the other hand, seems quite capable of holding a fleet of youngsters.) Thelma's been busy fussing over things all morning. First, at the crack of dawn, I could hear her sweeping the gallery steps. The sound broke my rest, so I just lay there listening to her for a while. *Swish, swish, swish. Swish, swish, swish.* In just the time it took for me to walk from my bed to the second-floor balcony, she was in my room, pulling back the curtains, taking my fresh towels from my bathroom, and stripping my bed linen. She didn't dare grab May Ruth's or Flossie's linen because they remained asleep; but she did sneak into their rooms for towels along with stray pieces of foundation garments, carting the entire lot down to the laundry room. Working like she's working to the coat, as my father used to say.

Herbert sucks his teeth before stretching behind him to grab a toothpick from the counter. He reexamines his wife's plate, squinting. There's gold laid out before him and the glare is at once stinging and inviting. "Thelma, girl, you ain't ate one bit. Look at all this here good food going to waste. Ain't no steam left on it at all, and it'll loose all the good flavor I worked into it once it's lukewarm. Thelma? Thelma, you listening to me?"

Finally, Thelma turns away from the cabinet, returning to the land of the living. She reaches behind her back to fix at her apron strings, which the oscillating counter fan keeps slipping undone as she stretches from one cabinet to the other. "Why don't you just eat it for me, then, Herbert. Since when do you need an invitation to anything I got?"

Without further hesitation, Herbert, bless his soul, plops May Ruth's beads onto the center of the table, then slides Thelma's plate atop his and starts to pour maple syrup over the French toast and three plump sausage patties. He removes a pile of grapes and sets them on the table, off to the side. Then he scoots the scrambled eggs over to the sausages and pours more maple syrup. Soon everything on that plate has breathed its last breath. Sweat bubbles up on his forehead and over his top lip as he hunches over, elbows just as square on my table, and starts to plow through in utter silence. He's perspiring so much that the witch hazel he's slapped on his face for aftershave now has the distinct smell of lighter fluid.

All is fairly quiet and still peaceful enough, until Flossie Jo comes barreling down the front steps, running down the hall toward us. I pull my glasses up so I can see her better. Her cigarette hangs sideways in her mouth. The buttons on her dress are misaligned and she's mumbling to herself, words— knowing Flossie—nobody cares for her to repeat. Her black patent-leather purse and sandals straddle her arms and her purse is wide open, showing the books of U.S. postage stamps she steals from the post office.

"Why didn't somebody have the decency to wake me?" She looks up at the clock. "You all know good and well that I was up there oversleeping."

"Well, good morning to you, too, Miss Flossie Jo Penticott." I shake my newspaper out and fold it in half. Herbert nods and lifts his fork. "Too bad you didn't have the decency to wake yourself."

Flossie sets her purse down on the counter and immediately turns on the black-and-white set over by the fan. The sound of static fills the room as fast as her cigarette smoke. She fixes at the rabbit ears atop the set, trying to make the picture come in straight. When it doesn't, she solves the problem by muting the volume, which is typical of Flossie Jo. "You all hear May Ruth up there? All over Halley's Landing bread is trying to rise and can't because our houseguest snores. She should pack a muzzle. Listen to her."

"Didn't seem to disturb your sleeping," I say.

Flossie rolls her eyes at me.

Thelma wipes her hands on her apron and takes Flossie's hand so she can balance herself as she slips into her sandals. Flossie reaches into her purse for her lipstick. Her reflection shows through the kitchen window. She nudges Thelma out of the way, puckering her lips. When her lipstick is on, she glances over at Herbert before tunneling under her dress to hike up her stockings. Course, Herbert can't see beyond his plate of gold.

"It's only seven o'clock," Thelma says. She starts to align Flossie's buttons properly, but Flossie slaps her hand away. "You've got a lot of time, Flossie. Yes, indeedy. Enough time

to stop off somewhere if you had to. All it takes is ten minutes to get to the post office. You've got more than enough
time." Thelma wipes her hands across her apron again. "Herbert's got some more batter. You want him to fix you breakfast? He doesn't mind. Do you, Herbert? It won't take but a
second, considering you got more time than you think. All
the time in the world. Even to drop me off somewhere."

"Honey, I don't have time to sit, let alone eat or drop you
off somewhere." Course, this doesn't stop Flossie from
pulling the chair out and sitting down next to me. "That old
man is always looking for any excuse to complain, and I
don't feel like hearing it this morning."

She looks up at the clock again, then picks at the balled-up
napkin beside my plate. She flubbles her hand about her lips
to signal to me that I've forgotten my partial (as if I can't tell
on my own when my mouth has one too many vacancies and
is collapsing in on itself). I reach for the napkin and fasten my
teeth into position.

Herbert's attention drifts from his plate long enough for
him to get up to fix her a cup of coffee. He places it before her
and sits back down.

"Mr. Otha has been complaining for the past ten years
about old Flossie here," I say. "It's a mystery to me how she's
lasted this long at the post office. Flossie Jo takes orders as
well as a greasy pig fresh out of the lot gate."

"A pig?" Flossie says, trying to sound insulted.

Herbert says, "You still spend your first two hours on
counter duty?"

"Yes, sir," I say. "And the line still snakes out the door.
Mrs. Florence Johnson Penticott takes her time and gossips
when she wants, though she's under strict government regula-
tions to keep the line moving. Folk also complain about their
correspondences winding up in the wrong boxes; certified
and registered mail being delivered past deadlines; mail-order
fruit being picked at through the cellophane."

"Cora is not truthful," Flossie says into her coffee.

"And just for sport, she's been known to purposely misdirect her share of process servers, repossession men, bill collectors who have come to the post office looking for directions . . ." I look at Flossie over my glasses. "I just figure she endures Mr. Otha because delivering the mail gives her an opportunity to snoop in detail on folks' yards in the afternoon when they aren't home. And snooping is the mainstay of being Halley's Landing's Beautification Committee president, the job for which she does feel a calling. Only drawback is that it's voluntary and provides no real source of income. Flossie still leaves her little yellow notes attached to folks' correspondences, pointing out how patches of weeds could stand to be pulled or sideboards could stand a few coats of fresh coloring. It's a wonder somebody hasn't shot her down for trespassing on their property."

"At the end of each year," Flossie offers, "the committee member who makes the most significant contribution to the overall enhancement of Halley is honored with a plaque and a nice write-up in the *Halley Daily*."

"And, most importantly, a twenty-five-hundred-dollar check, bearing the village seal and the treasurer's signature."

Flossie mushes her temples, then eyes May Ruth's Thermos, which sits right soldierly over in the corner on the floor next to May Ruth's tote. A box of Toni perm sticks out of the tote along with a bag of red licorice. "I don't know what in the Sam Hell May Ruth keeps swishing around in that Thermos," Flossie says, "but last night will be the last time she and I sit up late sipping from it."

"According to May Ruth, it's sassafras tea," I say.

"Sassafras tea, hmpf. My head is about to pop clear off my shoulders, thanks to that Thermos. That's why I had such trouble waking up. I bet she has some kind of illicit narcotic in there."

"May Ruth seems to be doing okay with her tea. Perhaps it was something you ate."

"Perhaps my hindside. I remember sassafras from when my aunts used to mix it into a poultice to quiet a bad tooth. What May Ruth has in there is whiskey. Pure corn whiskey. That tea is just a part of her conversation."

"By the way, I forgot to mention your ex-husband called for you last night," I say. "It was late and by then you were already passed out from those illicit narcotics. Which reminds me, you don't have to count my blood pressure pills this morning. I've already taken today's dosage. Haven't I, Herbert?"

"Solomon didn't call for me," Flossie interrupts, trying to sound indignant. "Maybe he called for his sister. And I couldn't care less whether you take your pressure pills or not, old lady."

"My brother called?" Thelma says.

I've been so caught up with Flossie Jo that I didn't notice when Thelma left the kitchen. Neither one of us did. So it's a bit unsettling when we all look up now and she's standing in the doorway wearing the same long navy blue dress that she wore yesterday for the church service. The same solemn black pumps, scuffed around the toes, and the navy straw hat that even after a full twenty-four hours still sits funny on her head. Also, above her eyes, there's a dusting of that shimmery yellow-green eye shadow of hers, which gives her lids an eerie lighthouse glow. The only difference in her outfit is that now she's wearing a gold-plated, good-luck Halley's Comet medallion necklace, about the size of a half dollar. It's worn under her dress, but the polyester is thin enough so that I can see the medallion through the fabric.

"Something you liked so much about that getup that you had to do a repeat, Thelma?" Flossie walks over, lifts Thelma's hat so she can see her eye shadow. Flossie gently swipes her finger across Thelma's lid, then sniffs her finger. Thelma checks her shadow, too, now wondering if it's rancid. "You'll remember yesterday I told you that in my humble opinion this eye color went out with lime green go-go boots of the sixties and that dress looked better wrapped up in tissue paper in your suitcase."

Thelma pushes her hat forward over the shadow. She grips the straps of her pocketbook tighter since there isn't much she can do about that dress.

"All it needs is the hem raised." I scoot back from the table and walk over to Thelma. "See here, the bias is off. Cuts her in half at the wrong place, which makes her look slight."

"And a shorter hem won't make her look slight?" Flossie says to Herbert.

I grab Thelma's dress in several places, lifting it, tucking it, to give the effect of a sewing job.

"I'm going into town," Thelma blurts out. Blurts it out like somebody just stuck her with a stickpin. And I know I'm not using pins. She pulls away from me and once again her dress engulfs her. "I called me a cab since Flossie can't find the time to drop me off."

"What you need in town?" Herbert asks.

"I need to get more salt pork for tonight's party." She turns to Flossie. "And I needed *you* to drive me, Flossie, since I was going on your behalf. You need more salt pork for your collards, don't you, honey? That's why I'm going. How many people we're expecting tonight?"

"Freezer downstairs full of salt pork," Herbert says, wiggling the toothpick around in his mouth. "Flossie could patch together a whole hog if she had to, Thelma. Ain't that right, Flossie?"

"I ain't in it," Flossie says.

"Thelma, baby, you don't need to go nowhere. Besides, most of the party is being catered."

"I know what I need, Herbert." Once again Thelma turns her attention to her pocketbook. Rearranging his fork and knife crossways on his plate, Herbert studies his plate for a second as he draws his napkin up to wipe his mouth. He rides back in his chair so that his girth expands sideways and his entire weight now balances on just two of my poor chair's legs. "Thelma, baby," he says. "I meant what I said last night about our boy. You heard me, didn't you? Let Pepper stay his li'l ass right where he is. You hear what I say, don't you? Let him stay right where he is."

Herbert looks at me, then over to Flossie. "Me and Thelma ain't said nothing on account of some things needing to pass without comment. Especially considering all the effort being made for the celebrations. Don't make no sense if you ask me to put more of a damper on spirits than what is already in place." Herbert takes a breath; Thelma lets out one. "When me and Thelma come in the other day, we stopped over at June's apartment first. Where is Pepper? He ain't been home for two days. And June so round with that baby, she can hardly find comfort in her own skin, let alone wasting worry on Pepper. Then, last night, we get a call. It's Billy, the dispatcher, from the cab station. Said he was listening in on the police frequency when he heard them deputies sending a car over to June's place. Turns out Pepper came home, finally. Then had the nerve to come in with some noise. I hear told he even shoved on June some. Not only did he shove a woman, but a pregnant one, no less. One he still ain't found the decency to marry. I hate to be the one to tell y'all that my son's in jail for disorderly conduct. Now, that's the first part of the story. After we found all this out, I went over to check on June, and come to find out she done whooped his head pretty good. June ain't the type to stand for no mess. But the second part of the story is that June was fool enough to scrape together bail money for that boy. But when she tried to bail him out, he said it's his constitutional right to refuse bond. Pepper say he ain't up for no *indentured servitude* and, consequently, won't accept bond on account of not wanting to be beholden to the person posting it. Craziest mess I've ever heard. So what do I look like going to see a fool who ain't got sense enough to leave jail? The new officer down there say he ain't never seen nothing like it. Ordinarily, people don't want to spend any more time behind bars than they have to. Especially during freedom week. Nevertheless, we gone let him sit right there. You hear me, Thelma? Let that boy be. It's high time he learn that he ain't the onliest person in this world with some hardship on him. It's high time he start looking forward to that baby coming, 'stead of looking over his shoulder. I ain't trying to make light of El's passing. You hear me, Sis? I know Pepper will always have that on him. But it's time we all start putting one foot in front of the other."

The room is too quiet, except for faint sounds of piano lessons next door at the Millers' place and deep-throated sputtering from May Ruth upstairs. Course, there's the whir of the counter fan, which has gathered up enough strength to make the rabbit ears on the television set break their V. Now the horizontal hold needs adjusting and the picture is drifting in and out on quick bursts of white light.

Herbert gazes back down at his plate. Clearly it's lost all its appeal.

"Before me and Thelma left Pittsburgh the other day, I called all our boys and told them I wanted them to be here this year for the goings-on. They done got too high and mighty for these festivals, but I told them I wanted them here for this one. I told them that, if for nothing else, we needed numbers on account of this being the first year after. I called Sweet Alma, too."

"I could have told you not to waste your dime calling my darling daughter," Flossie says.

"Each of them hemmed and hawed so bad, especially my boys, that I just hung up. I said to hell with them. At least Sweet Alma said she'd try to make it. Sounded like a lie to me when she said it. But at least I can give her the benefit of the doubt. Naturally I didn't call Pepper. Pepper's already living here in town. Onliest thing is, I didn't expect him to lock his fool self up. Sho' didn't anticipate that."

Herbert had wanted to stop after son number nine. Most of the conversation that swirled around Pepper had always seemed to remind me of that. But it was Thelma who insisted on one more. Insisted because she had wanted a girl. The first nine boys had come without even thinking about them, Thelma said. Had come with Herbert barely touching her. "All I have to do is dream of fish, Aunt Cora," she had said over and over.

"Unless I don't recollect properly, honey, you're doing more than thinking on fish."

We would just laugh and soon Thelma's belly would grow, and with her being so thin, she'd look ready to topple forward. And the next thing we knew a child was popping from her. The first nine tended to grab the good from both parents: a medium brown that wasn't the deadly white skin of Thelma's or the tar black of Herbert's; a medium build that wasn't the stocky box of Herbert's frame or the rail-thin lanky pole body of Thelma's. A handsome grade of thick wavy hair that didn't at all resemble the knot peas that occupied Herbert's skull before he went bald or that straight stringy mop of Thelma's.

Course, Pepper, the baby, was a different story. Everything on him tended to the extreme. He was pale like Thelma, maybe paler, with her long hair. He was short like Herbert, even shorter, with his crooked bowlegs and high forehead and broad shoulders. I suppose one thing he did get of both was their temperament. He was at once flighty and good-natured; yet as stubborn and, at times, as cantankerous as a two-dollar mule.

Pepper also had the distinction of being the most difficult in coming. He required Thelma to carry charms and rub them in places I didn't want to know. Then she wished on more stars than any universal law allows. With him, she craved chalk, of all things, and she bled so much she could hardly hold him. But she did, and finally delivered at about seven months. Course, he still come here just as spare. Never did seem to catch up with himself. Sure enough, the runt of the group.

Maybe the reason Pepper and Herbert never seemed to see eye to eye on much had to do with that undue burden Pepper put on Thelma's body. I don't know for sure. Maybe there was some resentment that even Herbert couldn't name. Something that Pepper picked up on and as a result the two couldn't seem to get the right footing. Pepper was always running away from home for one reason or another. Wouldn't stay away very long, just long enough to rile Herbert and to send Thelma's heart into spasms.

I could look back and find numerous examples. One that immediately comes to mind was the summer when Pepper was fourteen and El was nine. Those boys spent their summers together and were inseparable.

On an afternoon just before the festival got under way, Deacon Alan, who was also a sheriff's deputy, drove over to tell Herbert that somebody saw two boys over in the Lexington Heights neighborhood blowing up mailboxes with firecrackers. He said the description the residents gave of the culprits sounded a lot like our Pepper and El. What residents saw was a little *Caucasian* boy with long hair, and a big-boned, dark-skinned chocolate drop of a boy who was wearing a baseball jersey. They both were riding ten-speeds.

Herbert said he couldn't imagine why they would get into such foolishness, considering Flossie worked for the post office and this would reflect poorly on her. But he told Deacon Alan that he would see what was what. By the time Pepper and El made it back to this house and hopped off their bikes, Herbert was waiting for them on the front gallery. He was pacing up and down it. His hands were jammed in his pockets and he couldn't stand still.

Pepper got off his bike. El got off his. They both walked up to the bottom step.

Herbert said, "I hear told y'all been blowing up mailboxes in the Heights. Them expensive mailboxes, too, the ones set in them nice bricked-in encasements that cost heaven and earth to replace. Y'all know anything 'bout that?"

"El don't know nothing 'bout them mailboxes," Pepper said, looking Herbert dead on in the eyes. Course, El would have been better off looking at Herbert, too, rather than turning around to his bicycle, drawing attention to the burnt-up mailbox he had strapped to the back of his seat. Pepper must have forgotten about that little piece of evidence when he fixed his mouth in his lie.

Herbert stopped pacing and stood with his hands on his hips, staring at them, giving them every chance in the world to tell the truth. When all they could do was search the sky, the trellis, the veranda, Herbert unbuckled his belt. That's when Pepper started inching backward over his feet.

Cocking his head, El said, "You ain't gone beat us, are you, Uncle Herbert?"

"What I'm gone do is teach y'all a lesson 'bout recompense." Herbert stopped with the belt and they just watched it dangling from his pants hooks, the buckle shining like new money. "Y'all need to know there's a price for destroying other folks' property, but an even bigger price for not owning up to the truth and to your responsibility. Y'all 'bout to learn how to stand up and be men."

"That mean you gone beat us, Uncle Herbert?"

By the time Herbert pulled that belt from his pants and it snapped like a static pop in the wind, Pepper took to running down the drive. El got his answer mighty fast and decided to follow after his cousin. Now, El didn't have many fears. He was a big child, not stocky but built solid, muscular. Those types of children tend to grow up faster since they look older and more is expected because of their size. This, too, tended to close the age gap between El and Pepper.

We didn't think much of the boys' running off until well into the evening when they were still gone. We searched and searched for Pepper and El. Thelma was sick with worry. Thelma and Flossie, to be truthful. Both cursed Herbert. Flossie, mostly. Herbert kept saying, "Them boys all right. Ain't a thing gone happen to them."

Sometime during the middle of the night it began to rain and Viola Miller's dog next door started to lose his mind, barking all over Creation. Dog was scared to death of thunder. And so was El. El must have come in through the back when we were up in the front, and the next thing we knew, El was in his bedroom, under his covers.

Flossie heard the floor creaking overhead and went upstairs to give him what-for and to tell him to reveal his cousin's whereabouts. But he wouldn't say a word. Herbert threatened to beat it out of him. And that boy wouldn't tell on Pepper for the world. Just wouldn't do it.

The next morning, Herbert was fixing breakfast, stirring like it was any ordinary day. He happened to look out the window and noticed a flimsy white thread of smoke rising from behind a wall of wisteria out back. He went out there to see what was what and found Pepper sitting cross-legged while smoking a cigarette under a tent he'd constructed.

The next thing we knew, Herbert was yanking Pepper by the collar of his T-shirt, across the thickets and brush back up to the house. As Pepper tried to keep up with his father, he stumbled, he slipped; you could easily feel sorry for him from afar.

Thelma ran outside. But Herbert made her keep her distance. They continued coming with Herbert dragging Pepper so that the boy struggled on his tiptoes, arms dangling beside him. Thelma followed closely, pleading with Herbert to turn loose her son. In deference to Pepper's plight she herself pulled up on tiptoes every time Pepper yeowed. "I ain't gone run away again. I promise. I promise."

"Or be a bad influence on your cousin?" Herbert asked.

"Or be a bad influence," Pepper screamed.

This morning Thelma's entire body sags as she stands in the middle of the kitchen floor. Her fingers are wrinkled and white from all that ammonia water, and her straw hat once again has her looking like she's pointed in no particular direction. Though we all know that's a lie.

There's a tap on the screened door and it startles me because I didn't even hear the car pull up, though I hear it now idling in the driveway.

"Somebody here phone for a driver?"

Everything is too, too quiet. Before I know it, I poke at May Ruth's bag of beads with the tip of my newspaper. Two sudden jabs against the plastic and beads rain down onto the kitchen floor, scattering about until the bag flattens and lies limp.

"Oh my, May Ruth is going to kill me." I turn to Herbert, showing him my palms. "My hands sometimes get the palsy. Be a dear and help me with this mess I've made, will you? My eyes, too, have taken to watering. Being aged is such a bother."

Flossie elbows Thelma and she finally gets the hint and scampers down the hallway. The door opens, slams, and Thelma grabs the man's arm and pulls him down the steps.

Flossie fiddles with that wristwatch of hers. She takes her time as she lowers her cup and saucer into the sink. "Well, I guess I'll be leaving now. Going to meet the Post Massa." She plucks a few grapes off the vine, then saunters down the hallway.

Herbert's feet are as flat as boat oars, and when he runs he rocks a bit. Still, he's fast enough and could go after his wife if he wanted. Instead he expels a long, deep sigh as he lowers onto all fours. The *Halley Daily* sports section coiled in his side pocket pushes out onto the hardwood. He folds his legs under him and scoops handfuls of beads into his chest pockets until they bulge out round and heavy.

"Words I speak ain't worth the air I breathe into them, are they? Palsy, ha!" He shakes his head. "Aunt Cora, I've seen you thread a needle in half the time it takes most of us to find the eye. You, Sis, and Thelma, y'all women ain't no good. That's the matter here. Not a one of you. Just ain't no good, is all."

When the ignitions on the taxicab and Flossie's pickup catch, Viola Miller's dog next door starts to hooping and carrying on. Flossie adds to the chaos by blowing her horn in a staccato rant that mimics the barking.

"Funny thing about that dog," I say to Herbert. "No matter how Flossie Jo goads him, he stays in his yard just fine. Viola says he's spent so much time tied up that she doesn't have to tie him up for real. All she has to do is throw that frayed string of hers around his neck—and that string doesn't have to be connected on the other end, either—and he runs out only so far before he stops right about the place where the rope used to jerk the bejesus out of him."

By the time Herbert makes his way over to the counter to adjust the fan speed to high, the dog stops his barking. He doesn't even offer up the least bit of a whimper. Neither does Herbert.

Now both of those girls must be gliding down the hill toward Old Riley, completely out of his sight.

4

Cora

I'm standing out here on the gallery with the sense being cooked out of my skull as I wait for May Ruth. At the foot of the hill, the river seems calm and sociable, inviting even, but that's always a lie. In August, the river sets the entire town on a slow boil. Only that doesn't concern our May Ruth any.

The morning fog has disappeared and from up here on this hill the downtown lays wide open and exposed. It's as though an old knotty blanket has been lifted. Greater Faith's three gold spires rise into the heavens and can be seen for miles. The same with the blue and white dome of the municipal waterworks; and the top half of the tallest building in all of Halley, the village hall, whose new wing holds copies of the property deeds, probate records, and birth, marriage, and death certificates. After all these years, nobody still trusts the county annex in Jaspar to keep colored folks' records right.

Ordinarily I'd have asked Herbert to drive me into town so I could run my errands. But this morning it's best to leave him off to himself, way back in the kitchen, where he's trying to get cooking on some of the food for our party tonight.

"May Ruth!" I call over my shoulder. "You coming before nightfall? You know, honey, I can take a bus or call Billy down at the cab place. It's no bother at all. All I want to do is get to the market before everything's picked over. And before my head explodes."

For the longest, silence, until I hear the jingling of May Ruth's earrings and her arm bangles coming down the stairs. I wonder why such a flourish doesn't give her a nervous condition.

"Picked over or not," she says, now standing behind the screen in a fuzzy haze, "you know Flossie would simply kill me if I allowed you to go out in this heat unchaperoned."

"Since when do I need a chaperone? And since when do you have to answer to Flossie Jo in regard to me? Worry rubs off too easily in a house full of women. I only gave up my license a couple of years ago. That doesn't mean I've forgotten how to drive. Herbert!" I call over her head. "Where are your car keys?"

"Listen, dear heart, I'm coming in two seconds. I'll be just one moment more, I've got to ring a friend." May Ruth's strawberry blond hair is stuffed beneath a white straw hat with a red bow. A thin layer of zinc oxide stripes the bridge of her nose. She's wearing a long white sleeveless dress with an olive-colored shawl that keeps slipping down her shoulders, exposing skin that's badly sunburned.

The other day when May Ruth arrived in town, the first thing she wanted to do was go sunning out back, and she convinced her cohorts to join her. Thelma, I can understand wanting, and maybe needing, a little color. But there's no reason on this earth why a woman as black as Flossie thinks the sun can bleach her color up a notch to tan. Just putting on airs is what I say. Somehow May Ruth convinced them both to go far out back so they could tan the *German* way, by taking off all their clothes. Then they could take a dip in the pond. I watched the three of them heading off after lunch. Thelma carried the blankets and May Ruth's incense sticks; Flossie had her transistor and their towels; and May Ruth held her Thermos and a red-and-white-striped parasol that matched her outfit.

They were out back for a good hour when the three of them came running up the draw. Only thing was, by then, they were stark naked and dripping wet. In broad daylight. Breath rushed out of me fast as life leaving when I saw them, and I had to look twice before I could even believe my eyes.

Thelma came first, so that if Herbert had returned from the cab garage early, the eyeful he got was of his wife and nobody else. Luckily for Herbert, he was still away. Thelma had two fistfuls of moss grass, with which she tried to conceal her unmentionables as she ran. She stopped every now and then, tucking herself behind lilac bushes and oaks, to see who was looking and to summon up the gumption to keep going. Course, the grass was no help, and her little thin body was more than anybody, especially somebody my age, could stomach while eating the cold chicken salad sandwich Herbert had prepared. Suddenly I felt light-headed and the sandwich slid from my grasp. Thelma finally got to the back gallery, leaving a trail of grass along the planks, and ran inside the kitchen. She grabbed the frilly pink apron she keeps beside the refrigerator, flinging it across her hindside as she darted up the back stairs. Then May Ruth and Flossie Jo came gloppety, gloppetying up behind her. Though Flossie held nothing but her cigarette, May Ruth had her parasol spread out over the both of their heads, covering the wrong parts if you asked me. They were proceeding at a good clip, but not fast enough.

Just as the two of them were coming down a shallow slope, one of those little Cessnas roared overhead. Cranes ran wild as a gauze of mist fell from the plane. Flossie and May Ruth huddled in the middle of the yard, shielded by the parasol. With it being the last Thursday of the month, the Mosquito Abatement men were spraying the countryside for larvae.

Course, this meant that the surprise I got was nothing compared to that of the county workers up in that airplane. I imagined them and Providence looking down on two grand behinds (one more wrinkled than the other) running a good ways through a wide-open field. I don't know if I should have felt more sorry for them or for me.

When the mist had settled and the plane was gone, Flossie and May Ruth started coming again. May Ruth, looking shorter and squatter than I'm used to, started to laugh, which slowed her down. She could hardly catch her bearings, if she had any left. Then she noticed one of those birds of hers flapping overhead. She lowered the umbrella, shaded her eyes to see it, and began to twirl like some certified looney who'd just scaled the state mental health facility's shortest fence. Course, Flossie, on the other hand, had the good sense to keep coming. She doesn't take to bird-watching.

"I am convinced that white folks are crazy, especially the British," Flossie said, tossing wet hair in May Ruth's direction. "I don't care about being naked, but poor Thelma. For the longest, she wouldn't even stick her head out of the water. She forced us to close our eyes when she did. Like we haven't seen her whatnots before. You can let the Queen of England fill you in on why I'll be taking a belt to little Bailey Rogers's ass." Once inside the kitchen, Flossie threw her cigarette into the sink. As she continued on up the back stairs, I chose to watch the fizz from the dying cigarette rather than watch Flossie pull away from behind.

When May Ruth finally made it inside, she took a few seconds, standing in my kitchen, mind you, to give me a tour of her body, showing me a slew of bug bites as well as her sunburn splotches. One in particular bothered her; it was on her left butt cheek just a ways from her red and black parakeet tattoo, which, after years of wear and tear, has toppled over on itself, the way birds do in death. Because she lingered longer than Thelma or Flossie Jo, I could smell the mixed odor of corn whiskey, incense, and algae mud.

She pointed outside, up to the sky. "An African gray parrot, did you see it? It's quite extraordinary if that's what it is. Must be someone's pet." She scratched the pinkish, translucent scars on her chest where her breasts used to be. (Not that May Ruth's the least bit bothered by the fact that she no longer has breasts. When she's fully clothed, we've known her to whip the two flabby prostheses out of her bra—Flossie says, "as easy as eggs popping from a chicken's ass"—right on the front gallery, scratch the scars, and return the two without comment.)

As to whether I'd seen the bird, I could only shake my head.

"Remind me to jot down that I do believe it was an African gray, will you, love? There's a grove in the village of Ikodi in Nigeria where the people gather and wait for the parrots to roost and shake loose their red tail feathers. The people sell the feathers for a pittance, sometimes as low as ten naira, or five cents apiece, to survive. I sent you a feather a couple of years ago, do you remember, dear heart?"

Again I shook my head. "May Ruth, honey, Flossie suggested you tell me what happened. But why don't you go get dressed before you proceed any further?"

May Ruth collapsed her parasol and leaned it against the table. She grabbed a few paper towels to wipe her face, then her feet.

"We were in the water when we noticed a remote-control toy jeep hurtling by." She took another paper towel and laid it on the chair seat before sitting down. Course, I gasped out loud. But that meant nothing to May Ruth. "I daresay I didn't think much of the jeep at first. In fact, the first time I saw it, I thought it was a mirage or a swift-footed opossum or something. But I do believe opossums are nocturnal, are they not? Never mind that, we continued swimming. It wasn't until the jeep slammed into a large rock and got stuck, with the tires whizzing and whizzing to no avail, that we put two and two together. That little Bailey Rogers and a couple of his Little Leaguer friends shot out from behind some bushes to grab their toy, and in one fell swoop, they also grabbed our clothes and blankets, and ran like gazelles. Flossie called those boys everything but children of God. And vowed that as long as she lived she would never again sponsor their Little League team. One boy yelled back that they hate the sunflower decals she makes them wear on their jerseys, so they didn't care."

May Ruth got comfortable and I didn't think she'd ever leave my kitchen until finally we heard Herbert, bless his soul, whistling as he was coming up the front gallery.

Now May Ruth's shawl slides down her red and splotchy shoulders as she pulls her telephone book from her tote. "I don't know why you have to worry yourself about going to the store, Cora. I'd be more than happy to go for you. You could perch right on your gallery with your puzzle and enjoy the fresh air and the beautiful songbirds. No traffic. No crowds. No bother."

She walks down the hall to the phone table, which is midway between the main door and the kitchen door. Herbert, still in the kitchen, has the black-and-white set on. I hear snatches about the PLO's Yasser Arafat and that bombing last month that killed thirty people. Then I hear the music to that *The Price Is Right* show. Herbert's sitting at the table with a bowl of pole beans on his lap. But he's not thinking about the beans. He's got his pencil and notepad out, for logging the show's items and their prices, so he can check them against the prices at the grocery store. Herbert also listens for word on the trade deficit, oil price hikes—like what comes when the PLO and the Shiites get to fighting too much—and increases in interest rates, which are all tied together and eventually linked to prices at the grocery store, and to that *The Price Is Right* show. It's all one big cycle, he says.

The back door is open, so there's a nice breeze in the hallway that grabs May Ruth's shawl some more. She stands over the phone, tugging on her bottom lip like she's waiting on a call, when I distinctly remember her saying she was the one making the call.

"Before you get a connection, you got to dial, May Ruth," I offer, through the screen.

She looks out at me, then back at the phone like she's about to steal it. "What?" she says into clasped hands.

"Phone doesn't work that way," I say again. "Staring at it will do neither of us any good."

After a few more seconds of watching May Ruth look lost, I begin to wonder if she's taken by Flossie's new phone table and chair—both avant garde, Flossie says. It's just like May Ruth to have been here for four days already and to just now take notice.

"You know how Flossie gets before the festival," I say. "Just goes on an all-out decorating binge. She saw both the table and the chair in the Sunday magazine last week. Though they were outlandishly priced, she couldn't get them out of her head. So she went to that little furniture place in Justin she goes to where she can barter, and just happened upon the same set. We come to find out the reason it was *reasonably priced* is because the chair's *slightly imperfect*. The two front legs are shorter than the rear ones. So it leans forward. You don't notice it when you come in from the front door. Course, it's clear when you sit down." May Ruth sits down. "Flossie says the trick to not inching forward is to sit real straight and grip hold with your toes. I tell her if I have to do all that, there's no sense in me trying it out. At my age, I grip hold well enough in the process of standing. Don't need to have such worries when I'm sitting, too."

When May Ruth still doesn't pick up the phone, I take it that it's privacy she wants. So I step away from the door and walk over to my chair where I can hear her, yet it just gives more of the appearance that I can't. I pick up my newspaper and start to flip through it for the umpteenth time this morning.

"Sweet Alma, dear heart," she says finally into the receiver, her back toward the door. "You must come, dear. Your aunt Cora looks a sight. You haven't seen her for nearly a year. I'm afraid she's not getting any younger, you know. And she's not doing well a'tall. Who knows how much time she's got remaining. Her hair is thinning something awful." I reach up to pat my hair to check and it feels fine to me. "She's quite gaunt, you know. Her eyes are jaundiced; and her complexion pasty and ashen, I'd say. We think it's her sugar or her blood pressure. Well, certainly no one can be sure until she sees a doctor. But she won't listen to us. I know that if you came, she would listen to you. Why, she always listens to you. But she won't listen over the phone. She'd only listen if you come. What? I didn't say anything last week because I hadn't seen Cora yet. You do understand, don't you, dear heart, why you must come as soon as possible."

I get back up and open the screen door. I let it slam to get May Ruth's attention. May Ruth looks up at me. "Sweet Alma, I'll look forward to seeing you. I must get off the tele now. Good day, dear heart."

As she walks back down the hall, she dabs at her brow with a tissue and shakes her hands as though something gooey sticks to them. I'm still standing in clear view. "All righty," she says, opening the door, brushing past me. "Really, Cora, eavesdropping is so beneath you."

She walks over to sit for a second in her chair. Lifting her glasses to her eyes, she pulls her hat off and fans herself briskly with it.

"Well, look at this," I say, unfolding my newspaper, snapping it loudly. "That Father Lawrence Jenco had his first big

Sunday back home in church yesterday. Nineteen months of that man's life spent in bondage, all the way in Lebanon. What a crying shame that was."

"Oh, come out with it, Cora." May Ruth dabs again at her brow. She throws her sandals onto the gallery floor and shuffles into them. "Don't be so bloody coy."

"And look here, in the midst of all this war, death, and destruction, prime rib's on sale for a dollar twenty-nine a pound."

"Avoidance is about as becoming to you as silence. Come out with it, I say."

"Few things in nature like to be lied to, May Ruth, and lied on, for that matter. Who gives you the right to say such awful, disparaging things about me like that? And practically in front of my face."

"Oh, Cora, it was for a good cause," May Ruth says. "Besides, you have been looking quite peaked to me. I've been meaning to comment on it and just haven't gotten around to it. Have you lost weight?"

"May Ruth, you know dang well I've been a size four all my life." I brush my dress around the stomach area and hips. "Size four, ninety pounds. Hardly ever has my weight vacillated. Even during the Depression."

May Ruth's face tightens. She walks over to the banister and stands next to me. She's forgotten to remove two hair clips, one above each ear. They keep her side curls from jutting out like horns. As she nears me, the metal catches a piece of the sunlight and the glow stabs me right in the eyes. "Sometimes, and I quote, 'when we can't rely on a person to do what is just or right, we must rely on her to do what is practical.' And that's from you yourself, Miss Cora Hoskins. I didn't mean to hurt your feelings. I simply believe Sweet Alma should be here with her family."

"You think you're the only one with such a bright idea? Herbert called her, too. That's what he said this morning. I've called her and sent letters—not once commenting on my impending death, I might add. Back in April, I made Flossie call her. I threatened Flossie that if she went another day without speaking to her child, I was going to make her move out of my house. I've never said anything like that to her in all the years she's lived here. But right is right. There are days, more than I want to think about, when I hear Flossie crying. She doesn't think I can hear her. But I hear her. She tries to muffle it or she'll run for cover in between those rows of weeds, acting like they need more tending than they really do. Anything to get out of this house so she can let herself go. Some of those tears are for El, the rest are for Sweet Alma. So I made Flossie call her. The problem is, during the phone call, Flossie and Sweet Alma had yet another falling-out. I'm sure Flossie hasn't tried again. She says she's done with the matter. I tell her she can't be done with it. That's her daughter. How can she be done with her daughter?"

May Ruth reaches into a front patch pocket on the sundress and pulls out two strips of red licorice. She stares out into the garden. "Sweet Alma and Flossie need a giant push in the right direction."

"Everybody needs a push. Pepper needs a push. The problem is, we're all just as stubborn as mules. Maybe everybody except Thelma, and sometimes she's like a wind sock, ready to go whichever way the wind blows." I grab one of May Ruth's licorice pieces and point to the clips in her hair. I start down the gallery steps.

May Ruth gets her tote and catches up with me. She reaches for my arm to assist. I pull away.

"I sincerely apologize if I hurt your feelings, Cora. You know I believe you're the most beautiful woman on this earth. Are you still cross with me, dear heart?"

"I'm not cross. I'm pissed, May Ruth. I'm in tip-top shape, I'll have you know. Why, up until five years ago, I used to stand on my head every morning out here on this gallery, including in the summer. I only stopped when the doctor told me I was liable to wind up blind or cross-eyed. I'm old, but I have preserved a goodly portion of my vanity."

"Here's my hand to the patron saint of forgiveness, who-ever she is. I solemnly swear never to lie again."

"You're lying now, May Ruth. I can hear it in your voice. Will lie fast as look at you."

Once we get inside Herbert's car, May Ruth places her tote between us, then scoots the bench up a notch until it locks into place. May Ruth's about to turn the ignition when she stops to reach inside her tote for her driving glasses, which are different from her walking and reading glasses, and yet still different from her bird-watching glasses. Placing the glasses on, she looks over at me and smiles assuredly. I smile back into her magnified circus eyes and stare straight ahead so as not to disturb her.

When the car starts, the radio is tuned to WHVN and some minister with a heavy voice is preaching. "Sometimes you got to stop and take inventory," he says. "When your house falls apart, you got to figure out how the bricks are laid; you got to determine if there's a crack in the foun-dation."

May Ruth wags her forefinger. "Preach, Reverend Minister."

I turn him off so May Ruth can concentrate. She grips the steering wheel so tightly you'd believe she'd fall backward forty feet if she lets go. Her bangles start to slide down toward her elbows. And she battles with them for a second, trying to make them stay around her wrists, as though gravity doesn't have a say. When May Ruth throws the car into gear, there's utter silence. I sit back and try not to look her way. It has been my experience that the worst thing you can do is stare at May Ruth while she's driving. It makes her too jumpy, which serves neither of us well. Slowly the car begins down the drive. Alongside Flossie's quarter-acre sunflower patch, pollen hangs thick as yellow confetti in the air. And further east, the white bedsheets Thelma washed earlier this morning and positioned out of the pollen's reach wave how-do's to a gathering of butterflies.

At the bottom of the drive, May Ruth brakes short of the driveway's entrance. A couple of romance novels with satin bookmarkers and her Thermos roll out of her tote onto the floor. I don't pay them any never mind. She doesn't either, which speaks to how she's concentrating. May Ruth lunges a few paces and brakes again as she looks left, then right to see how traffic is flowing along Old Riley.

Soon as she gets a turn, she ekes out into the westbound lane, the way a chicken sticks her head out to gauge if her neck is next on the block.

All is fine so far and she's zooming on up to her customary twenty-five miles per hour, when Earl Watson pulls his Porter cab into the eastbound lane to pass us. But he slows for a conversation and to show off the shine on his car.

"Miss May Ruth, Miss Cora," he says, half looking into the lane and half looking at us. He smiles and tips his hat. "Heard y'all ain't doin' too well this mornin'?"

May Ruth waves quickly before reattaching her hand to the steering wheel. "We're doing just fine, Mr. Wilson, and you?"

"It's Watson," Earl says. "I'm okay, all right. One of the boys dropped Miss Thelma off at the jail earlier this morning. Everything all right with you all? They say Robert's in jail again, is he? Heard he caused quite a fuss down along his way."

"Everything's just fine," I yell at him. I'm staring into the eastbound lane, looking out for oncoming traffic, as our car veers into it, which pushes Earl over into the gravel that precedes the riverbank. He keeps yelling over because he's a damn fool.

"What does this make, the fifth or sixth time Robert's been in jail in how many months?"

May Ruth turns to me, still smiling. "I dreamt this once, you know? This exact scenario. I really did. In the dream, however, I ran what's-his-name over there off the road. Shall I run him off the road now, dear heart? I'm fortyish, middle-aged, and it's a wonder the New York State Department of Motor Vehicles renews my driver's license every year, considering my mild vision impairment. Who would blame me?"

"'Mild vision impairment,' my foot," I say, laughing at her. "And 'fortyish,' my ass."

"Such language, Cora." May Ruth and I both laugh, ignoring Earl.

Eventually he realizes he won't get much grist for his gossip mill from us. "Anything we can do down at the cab place to help, let us know," he yells over. His voice trails off as he speeds on down the road.

May Ruth and I wave and smile at him.

My nerves are doing just fine until I see a Greyhound in the side mirror plowing up behind us. I grab my seat cushion. He flashes his lights and honks loud enough to wake the dead. Doesn't make May Ruth move faster, though. She honks right back at him, takes her hand off the steering wheel to flip him the bird, as the young folks say.

"You can just bugger off!" She readjusts herself, and her hat, and begins to hum some tune ("Camptown Races," I believe, but my nerves are too shot to be sure).

May Ruth and I cross the bridge into the downtown. Here the road widens into four lanes and all of Creation is happy and speeds around us. Finally May Ruth pulls up in front of the Krogers. Cars are piled into the side lot. She has a time trying to get me close to the entrance, which I tell her isn't necessary. But she keeps trying, anyway, pulling forward and backing up several ways before the car is safely stopped. She shakes the tightness from her hands and hones in on her Thermos, which has rolled under the seat.

"I'll be in shortly," she says, returning the Thermos securely to her bag.

"You have to come in so soon?"

"All right, then, dear heart. I'll wander over to the hill to determine whether anybody's spotted that comet this go-round. There're at least fifty telescopes up there, at my last count."

"They're all looneys," I say.

"You must wait here for me when you're done, all right, dear heart?"

"Cross my heart and hope to die from the heat," I say under my breath.

When I'm safely positioned on the curb, she flips on her right-turn signal (even though she's going left) and crawls back out into traffic. I watch her as she makes her way down toward the park. The car fishtails over toward the sidewalk rather than the center of the lane. Her hat flies back, unfurling her fog curls, whose red dye in the bright sun takes on a pinkish cast. And that old Cadillac couldn't move slower sitting still. Drivers lean on their horns as if that would push her ahead faster. Course, they don't know she enjoys shrill tones.

Once inside the Krogers, I dislodge a cart and start down the produce aisle. I spy Viola Miller, my next-door neighbor, over by the parsnips. I plan to navigate around her, and not because I'm being rude, but because she can't hang a period on a sentence in a reasonable amount of time.

"Yoo-hoo, Cora Hoskins." She speeds over and parks her cart in front of mine, hemming me against wilting endive and romaine. Viola's in her forties. Her face is heavily plastered with makeup, with those painted-on eyebrows that hold a wicked arc. Make her look like she's on the verge of asking a question. "Cora, I am appealing to your good sense of decency and honor . . ."

She pauses, distracted by two women in tight shorts over by the apples, five varieties.

"Look at them," Viola whispers.

"The McIntoshes?" I say.

"No, those women," Viola says. "Look at how their behinds are stuffed into their shorts. They're whores, Cora. Imported, no less, for the festival. I remember them from last year. I remember them slinking up to the park area and stealing our good Christian men, leading them to the awful Hallelujah tents beyond the hill."

"I don't remember those good Christian men putting up much of a struggle about being stolen," I say. "And whores deserve to be able to shop in peace, too, Viola, without being spied on. If one of them comes over, hauls off, and punches you in the nose for staring at them, you'll have only yourself to blame." *Yourself and those wicked eyebrows.*

Viola doesn't listen. She keeps staring until the two women realize they're being scrutinized and leave the produce area. They join the line at the butcher's counter, where women over there turn up their noses; the men, however, don't seem to mind.

"I don't mean to impose," Viola says, "but it is important that you talk to Flossie and Thelma. Are you aware they chose my portion of Thursday's beautification day events to skimp on? They've cut my time in half. My time for giving tips on beautifying your boudoir. Can you believe Flossie's allotting only thirty minutes this year?"

"No. Can't say I can."

"As president, Flossie's vote counts for two. And Thelma always arrives in town voting with Flossie without any regard to anybody else's needs. I do sympathize with Flossie and all she's been through over the last year, but my feeling is that Thelma should resign her membership in both the Victuals and Beautification committees since she hasn't lived in Halley in God knows how long. This year is especially important since we're expecting so many visitors with this being a comet year." She takes a breath. Barely. "Thirty minutes. Why must I be the one to compromise on my time? Nobody's asking those nasty hookers to compromise on their time."

I look down at my watch, but this means nothing to Viola.

"Cora, you remember the crowd I had last year? Cora?"

"Honey, you'll excuse me, won't you? My mind slips a bit. This matter is something you'll need to take up with Flossie and Thelma. I don't interfere with how they coordinate the ceremonies. This way it keeps the peace. All I concern myself with is our Victuals table and making sure we have enough food to feed the masses—which includes whores, hookers, prostitutes, the criminally insane, and thieves, too, if they get hungry."

"The evil on that Flossie Jo is rubbing off on you," Viola says.

I step away from my shopping cart. Viola isn't counting on the cart being a mere prop. So, when I walk away from it, completely unencumbered, it's as disconcerting as seeing some old cripple suddenly pick up and leave without his cane.

She calls after me, but I get away with pretending I don't hear. Still, so that I'm cordial, I look left and right as though a fly is buzzing around my temples. It gives the impression that I'm disoriented by the noise.

As soon as I pass the first aisle, I realize how much time Viola has eaten up when I see May Ruth all the way down at the other end looking for me. The red bows on her hat fly back and the hat itself bobs like it's riding an ocean wave and nobody's under it. (May Ruth says her birds manage from place to place so easily because they have built-in compasses in their heads. Not true for May Ruth. Ain't a compass for miles in that head. She probably couldn't find the hill.) I duck behind a stack of canned goods so she doesn't mess with my plans to visit Pepper. Then I realize there's no need hiding from her, due to her nearsightedness. I pass aisle two, and so does she, all the way at the other end. We keep in step, seems like, until frozen foods, where I lose her. I don't see her again until I'm at the front of the store and I look around and she's standing in line. She's chosen the longest one so she can read the *National Enquirer* without having to purchase it. May Ruth is hankty that way, won't be caught plopping down good currency for it; but she *fancies* it so much that with each step closer to the checkout counter, she waves people in front of her so she has more time to read it from cover to cover. She's also nibbling from an unpurchased bag of bulk licorice. That, too, will be gone before long. Pure thievery.

I'm about to leave the store when I happen to look out the window, around the broad white advertising sheet nearly blocking the view. Lo and behold, I notice Flossie strolling down the sidewalk, pushing her mail cart like it's a baby buggy and she hasn't a care in the world. She's already passed the barbershop, Ely's Deli, James Funeral Home, a new real-estate office, and First Republic Savings and Loan, having portioned off letters like she's delivering tea party invitations, while smiling that phonied-up smile.

Having finished the south side of the street, she sits on the bench in front of the cabstand at Porter Cabs before crossing over to the north side. I hesitate to leave, fearing she might see me and try to stop me. The courthouse is a stone's throw from the cab place and the Krogers, just around the corner.

Luckily, a bus pulls up in front of the store. It's nearly empty because this is near the end of the line. I board and ride a few blocks west to the front of the church. The bus circles around, beginning its trip back east. After we pass Flossie, the driver turns right at the corner, letting me off directly in front of the courthouse.

5

Cora

Pepper leans against the cinder blocks, looking out the little peep window onto the foot traffic along the sidewalk.

His mother hovers over, brushing back frazzled and matted hair, picking lint from his scruffy beard. No matter how she fawns, she can't smooth the fact that he looks older than his seventeen years. But not simply older, the beaten-down type of old.

Neither bothers with seeing me just yet.

"Oh, did I mention I'm taking some more classes at the community college?" Thelma tries her damnedest to sound cheery. "Yes, indeedy. Two to be exact. I'm taking another astronomy class. And this time I'm taking a pedicuring class, too. Daddy said he couldn't get too excited about the pedicuring class. He said he doesn't think I have the right *constitution* to work with people's feet. You know how Daddy is. The truth is, he's always more concerned about the up-front expenses, which were quite exorbitant since I had to purchase ten shades of polish, five loofah scrub pads, at least four slosh tubs, and enough cotton balls to absorb a whole lifetime. I'm just drowning in cotton balls."

Pepper spits into the blue water of the commode, then turns his attention back up toward the peep window.

"I bet you don't know how to get rid of foot fungus. Not that I think you have foot fungus. Normally you can tell by the putrid smell, and I don't smell nothing, anything, really I don't, what with all these lemon stick-ups all over the place. But if you did have foot fungus, you could soak your feet in a solution that's half water and half bleach. The regular kind you get from the grocery store, nothing fancy. We learned that the first day. Or was that three-quarters water, one-quarter bleach, and one-quarter of Epsom salts?"

"That don't add up, Ma," Pepper says finally. He turns but only halfway and not enough to face her. He looks down at the tray of oatmeal, orange juice, water, and buttered toast that's sitting on the floor. The oatmeal has crusted over.

"What?" she says.

"You got five quarter-parts. That don't add up."

"Oh, you're right," Thelma says.

"Something else doesn't add up," I offer. They both turn around. "Most people leave this place once bail has been posted. You do know you're free to leave?"

"I'm free to stay if I want, too," he says to me in a gruff voice, like he's snatching something away. "I know my rights."

"I've heard enough about your rights. And you'd better watch your tone, son," I say.

"I need some peace of mind. That a crime? If so, maybe they should tender some new charges against me. I need some time to sort stuff out. I got a lot on my head."

"Son, please," Thelma says. "You can sort it out at home, can't you? You've got a baby coming."

"Ain't got no home, Mama. That's June's home now that she's paying the bills and I ain't got no job. And I'm sick of her reminding me of it. And I ain't so sure that's my baby. 'Specially if she plans to horde that baby the way she hordes her apartment. They say possession is nine-tenths the law, and since that baby is growing inside her, seems to me it's all hers."

"Well, this certainly is no home," I say.

"Good as any. Let's call it subsidized housing. It's mine for tonight and tomorrow night and the next. Until they kick me out."

He leaves the little window and yanks his pants up as he shuffles over to his bed. He bends to place a sock ball in his boots, those old ragged combat boots. They sit side by side with the tongues hanging over the tops and the strings lying splayed. Now that he's turned around, I can see his entire face and the purple ringing his left eye. I suppose it's courtesy of June.

He sees his mother staring at his eye and says, "Yeah, man, it hurt like a motherf—"

"Please, Pepper," Thelma says, stopping him.

"Now, Pepper," I say, "boy, don't you get so beside yourself that you consider using language unbefitting present company. You understand me? I was the first person to wipe your hindside right after you come into this world too soon. Make no mistake, you disrespect me or your mother and you'll have hell to pay."

He looks away.

Thelma walks over to the food tray and reaches inside a plastic cup of water. Two little tired ice cubes float to the top. She wraps the two in tissue that she's been using to dab at the tears in her eyes. She places the tissue over his eye. He leans away. He leans so far that he lies back on that stiff little dingy pillow. Then he folds his arms behind his head and stays there. Throughout his contortions, she continues to press the tissue against his eye.

"Son," she says, "did I tell you Sweet Alma might be coming after all?"

"Sweet Alma and her mother is stuck-up," he says. "I don't want to have nothing to do with either of them. She can come or not. Don't make me no durn difference. I'm tired of kissing their"—he pauses—"butts. With their high-and-mighty selves."

"They're not acting that way, Pepper," Thelma says. "You're just not seeing things clearly. Everything is going to be all right, son. Everything is going to be just fine."

"Mama, I have a thought. I'll leave if you can tell me how to make everything all right. I'll leave right now. Right at this very instant, if you can tell me how to make everything all right, so to speak."

Thelma doesn't say anything.

"Nothing's free, Pepper," I say. "That includes peace of mind. Neither your mama nor your daddy nor anybody else can give it to you. If they could, you know they would do it in a heartbeat. You think everybody's against you. That there's a war going on and you're the enemy. Nobody blames you, Pepper. For El. We can say that a thousand times. But you've got to believe it for yourself. We can't make you believe it."

"To hell they don't blame me."

"Nobody blames you, son," I say. "You've got a lot to consider. And if you need to stay here to do it, then so be it. We'll be back to check on you."

He sits up. "Mama, say y'all going ahead with the party tonight."

"It's an annual event and we're going to keep it that way. We're going ahead with setting up our Victuals table, too. Your aunt Flossie will make her fine collards, as she has for years, and your mama will slop the pot liquor, as she has for years. Only hindrance before us is that your mama's got my china dishes sprawled all over Creation. I reckon if she can put my things up and return my kitchen to near presentable, we can go forward with the cooking."

Pepper turns back toward the cinder blocks.

"You just stay as long as you need until you figure things out. That's why we pay taxes, I suppose."

"Jail is quite liberating, to tell the truth about it," he says, his voice now muffled. "I got all the time I want to read and think. I ain't got to hear June's big mouth or my father's. I can control each minute of my twenty-four hours. Don't have to worry about clipping them help-wanted ads or nothing. Like I said, don't mind me. Y'all go'on and have a good time at your party and your festival."

I leave the cell and begin heading down the corridor. Thelma follows me out the door. Shakily, she extends her hat over my head to block the sun. I gently take her hand and place it to her side.

"Maybe we should cancel the party," she says.

"We'll do no such thing."

"He's been like this all morning, Aunt Cora: feeling down. He's been just pacing around that room, throwing his socks up toward the ceiling. When I first walked in this morning, he looked over at me and didn't say a word to me. Me, his own mama. It was like I wasn't even there. Like he could see straight through the bars without the least bit of an impediment. Now, imagine that. You'd think your boy would be excited to see you. I said, 'Son, is that how you greet your mama?' He said, 'Hey, Dorthula Jane.' Dorthula is what he called me. And he knows I hate my name. Falls too hard on the tongue and makes me sound mean, which I'm not. After he called me by my real name, he just looked away and kept messing with those socks. Now that I think about it, that's why I went on and on too much about my pedicuring class. Because of those blasted socks. I did ramble on like a fool before my son, didn't I, Aunt Cora?"

"Thelma, honey, are you going to be okay?"

Thelma nods, rerouting the blood flow to her nose and making it turn beet red. She sits on the bench in front of the courthouse, slumping forward. I stand next to her. Halley's Comet commemorative flags wave and snap in the breeze. They show a white burst of light with a fuzzy tail on a navy background and hang from nearly every light post in the downtown. The flags catch Thelma's attention, which, I suppose, is why she remarks, out of the blue, "The closest it ever got to us this time was thirty-eight million miles, and that was back in the fall when it was near the Pleiades star clusters." She turns to look up at me, pointing to the flag beside us. "Years ago, that comet drifted as close as fifteen million miles. My instructors have said that it could be seen clearly back then, sometimes even during the day. That's why it's plausible that it may have touched down here in Halley."

"Never touched down here, Thelma," I interrupt her. "I've been telling you that for years. It was always just a town gimmick. Pure propaganda."

"But this time the comet was too far away from us to perform its miracles. Even the moonlight got in the way of seeing it this time."

The cannon sirens shoot off five blasts, and the gulls scatter as they cackle to high heaven.

Instead of studying on those flags, I lock on the birds flying over the courthouse, out toward another section of the canal downstream. "May Ruth has a notion," I say. "But, I warn you, it's important to remember May Ruth drenches herself in that corn whiskey way too much, so you never know what to believe about what she believes. But May Ruth says those birds fly one behind the other like that because it gives them lift. So when they all flap together, something about the aerodynamics or some such, that makes it easier on the ones flying behind. The ones flying behind don't have to work so hard and they can go for miles and miles. We just have to find a way to create some more *lift*, is all."

Without even looking up, Thelma nods just to be doing something. From where she's staring, you'd think she's looking right at those birds, or at the people ambling about Eva's House of Beauty across the street, scurrying with their sequined bags and newly fried hair. But then upon closer inspection, it's plain to see that her vision's gathering nothing in particular. Course, that blue dress can't help her concentration much. Navy is deadly in this kind of heat and tends to bake the senses.

I lay my hand on her shoulder, then head down the street. A bus pulls up, slows to open its doors for her, but keeps going when the driver realizes she's not getting on.

When I get to the corner across from the Krogers, I see Flossie Jo still sitting on her bench. The taxi drivers who are waiting for their cars to be overhauled stop to flirt with her. She pretends to work, sorting through the stack of correspondences that are lined up on her lap.

She holds one envelope up to the sun, trying to glimpse its contents; another she shakes next to her ear. After years of delivering mail, she's become expert at snooping around even the most obscure or discreet packages. A magazine wrapped in brown-paper-bag-like covering is pornographic material, that's easy. She has a smattering of such deliveries along her route: a couple of cabdrivers down in the "bottoms," a seedy section of Halley; and a woman librarian, or a woman Libertarian (I can't remember which Flossie says), on Fifth and Green.

An ice cream truck comes up behind me and takes my breath.

It's playing that silly song, "Take Me Out to the Ball Park." It's a different beat, a different tempo from that no-good Mr. Paul's truck, but the same song nonetheless. By the time I hear it, the truck has already passed the courthouse. I turn to look down the way at Thelma. She's now coming toward me. Flossie looks around, almost disoriented at first. She looks and looks until she sees the truck, which has stopped in front of the Krogers, flooding the street with its song.

Flossie still looks distracted, but she doesn't leave the bench. And she doesn't stare at the truck overlong. Or the people waiting in line. Seeing me, she waves. "Cora, what are you doing down here this time of day?"

I grab Thelma's hand and we walk over to Flossie. She smiles her phonied-up smile and goes on and on about nonsense: insufficient postage and revolving credit-card accounts.

Anything but that boy.

Soon the ice cream man has served his last customer and he pulls away toward the fairgrounds. He pulls away with a different song, a different lure for those down the street. I watch the truck until I can't see it anymore. Its chrome and white panels cast a blinding glare all the way down to Greater Faith, so much so that it makes my eyes water.

When I see May Ruth coming out of the Krogers, I head over to meet her. Flossie and Thelma remain seated on the bench for the moment, leaning against each other, laughing and fumbling through Flossie's stack of mail.

Overhead two half-naked young men stand on scaffolding, hanging bunting along the second floor of the taxi place. Lawn sprinklers mist the air. Cabdrivers hover. The comet flags wrestle on the breeze and pop like firecrackers.

Placed in the middle of it all, Flossie and Thelma look deceptively as though neither has a care in the world.

Cora

APRIL 1973

Before the Krogers squeezed the Canady Glass Company off the lot and moved it to a nondescript hovel a couple of doors down from Greater Faith, that glass company took up nearly the entire block.

When Thelma was a little girl—oh, I'd say about nine or ten—she and I would window-shop in the downtown after church. Invariably, she'd hurry me along, tugging and pulling, until we got to the glass company, where she'd just stop and stand starry-eyed looking at the offerings in the big picture window. I always warned her against going inside because of how excited she got, and I was afraid Thelma, who was a little on the clumsy side, would break something and we'd have to buy up the store.

Something about that window made her troubles move off to the side. While standing before it, she'd forget about her Sunday dress, which by the end of services had turned sideways on her, and her hair, which never held a plait or a bow like the other girls' hair. Thelma's hair always unraveled, like so many things in her life.

Thelma would stand there watching Halley's Landing reconstructed in miniature. Here you saw Old Riley, when it was just an old plank road, rolling toward what would become the downtown. The road wound along the river and under the hill into a swampy valley. You saw the trough that was the canal and the mountains of fossilized limestone piled up on either side. You saw the slave figures. They were men and women brought up on a lease to work the canal, who would return later, after the Surrender, to build the community, using that limestone. And, of course, you saw *our* comet. That old dusty dirt ball that the glass company had transformed into the prettiest crystal figurine you'd ever want to see. Dangly stars and blue chunks hung over the comet's tail, and the whole thing was suspended over the hill behind the fairgrounds.

Course, Porter Cabs was on the other side of the street. It could have been a million miles away from Canady Glass. At first glance, you could find little going for the taxi place. The scabby corrugated-tin door made an awful noise as it rolled up when the cabs honked to enter the main garage. The dispatcher busied himself in a smoke-filled office with a thick opaque window. Right outside the window, Buster, Jones, and Russell—old-timers with wide girths and ashy legs—often sat in their folding chairs, no matter the weather, waiting on fares. Above them, on the second floor, T-A-X-I was scrawled in fat white letters on four oblong windows—one letter per window. The windows were dull and had been broken and replaced countless times following impromptu ball games.

Kids weren't allowed to get a game going on Canady's side because of the company's glass. Canady always called the cops. The cabdrivers never did.

The day Thelma learned Flossie was coming to town, she dragged me over to the glass company. We stood in the middle of the tinging chimes, staring at the windows across the street. It was the first time I'd ever known her to stand on that block and concern herself more with what was on the south side rather than the north.

Across the street, Herbert and the boys sat crunched together in their little Chevette, which was parked in front of the garage. Thelma paced, pulling on her lip, while little Pepper followed behind.

"Oh, it's a mess, Aunt Cora. Just a mess. That brother of mine told me we had until the end of the summer before Flossie and my niece were coming. That's what he said. I got the letter right here in my pocket to prove it. He said Sweet Alma and Flossie were coming later, after he'd done all the groundwork." Pepper's pacing made Thelma edgy, so she made him sit on the curb.

She dug into the pockets of her cut-off blue jeans. Wads of tissue for noses spilled over the sides. She pulled out a wrinkled piece of stationery and, her cheeks flushed, began reading:

"'I'll arrive on April eighteenth. I'm coming for the sole purpose of replenishing my coffers before I move the family to St. Louis for a business deal. As I have run into some hard-ass luck in Chicago and need to get away. Flossie and Sweet Alma will finish the school year and follow sometime in the summer. By then I'll have everything in order. So for now, I'll just need arrangements made for me. Nothing special, as we are cutting costs. Just a place for me to lay my head. And I appreciate you offering to let me stay with Aunt Cora or you, but I'd like a little privacy. You understand, don't you, Thelma?'

"He said he didn't need 'nothing special,' Aunt Cora. Ain't that, isn't that, what he said? He told me not to worry about Flossie and Sweet Alma because they would come much later. . . . Don't you know that brother of mine called a few minutes ago to tell me there's been a change in plans? Now Flossie and Sweet Alma are packing their things to come with him. Not more than thirty minutes ago, I picked up that phone and he told me. How was I supposed to know he was going to change his mind? I got Felix to let us rent the apartment over the cab company. I thought that would be the most suitable place, figuring it was for Solomon only and he was concerned about cutting costs and he didn't want to stay with family."

Lowering her voice, she looked down at Pepper and twirled a lock of hair over her ear. "Did you know that those drivers had been using that apartment to sneak up there with those women from the bottoms to do"—she jerked her head—"you know what? I didn't know that. The smell of the place was something wretched before Herbert and I got up there with some bleach water. In my wildest dreams, I hadn't considered that place for Flossie. I thought we had time to find something nice for her. Aunt Cora, she's from up North, from Chicago. She's got them funny ways, I know she has. I've visited her place only twice. And neither time could I find a strip of clothing just sitting around in the living room, waiting to be folded. No dust at all. She pretends to be friendly because that brother of mine is always standing nearby, tending to her every whim." Thelma started pacing again. "Did I mention the wide-buckled shoes she flaunts in front of me, with the high heels? And the patent-leather purses that match? Everything's lined up all neat in her closet. Bet she doesn't have to buy one thing secondhand." She leaned against a parking meter and slapped her forehead. "Bet she talks about me behind my back, too. All because I didn't have sense enough to finish high school before I got married. Bet she also comments on why I birthed so many babies. Not one set of twins. I bet she thinks I'm a lowlife."

"Thelma, who has time to study on you that hard? Honey, you're getting yourself worked up for nothing."

"Miss Florence Johnson Penticott is a college graduate." *Graduate* took a long *a* at the end because Thelma wanted to sound proper. "She wouldn't even marry my brother until she finished school. And he begged her. That's how much sense she's got. She must think I'm three hundred and sixty degrees backward. Or is that one hundred and eighty degrees? That's why she never comes to visit Halley. That's why she *sends* Sweet Alma every August for the goings-on but doesn't come herself. Solomon would never tell me all the mean things she says about me behind my back."

Course, at that point, Herbert had had his fill of all those boys piled in that Chevette. He went inside the garage and got a Pepsi. When he came back out, he stopped to talk with Buster, Jones, and Russell.

"I got a feeling is all," Thelma went on. "A deep-down feeling. That's why I know that apartment's not going to be good enough for her, Aunt Cora. And who do you think will be blamed? Me, that's who. It's too cramped. It's dark and still smells like you know what, even though I scrubbed everything down hard as I could. Herbert and me just came back from looking at it again, trying to picture Flossie standing in the door. And the flaws slap you right in the face. Lord, soon as you walk into the living room, you see that hole as big as Herbert's head under the fireplace. And the wallpaper in the kitchen is black with mold from the radiators and won't stay glued to the wall no matter how much glue you use; the windows are painted shut. I thought if Solomon needed fresh air, he could go downstairs. But not Flossie. I wasn't thinking it was for Flossie. Not in a million, billion years."

She flopped down on the curb next to Pepper and really started to cry. Pepper looked over weakly, patting her back. Meanwhile, Herbert sighed or moaned. From across the street, the sound was indistinguishable. When he noticed her crying, he was on the verge of placing the Pepsi bottle to his lips. He stopped and called over. "Thelma, honey, didn't I tell you I'm gone get the place in order? Words I speak ain't worth the air I breathe into them, are they?"

Ashamed, Thelma looked down into her lap. "Early this morning something told me this day wouldn't be worth a dime. I should have turned over and allowed it to pass without me. I just hate this little backward town."

"Town wasn't backward before you got that call, Thelma." I looped my purse over my wrist and began walking across the street to see the apartment for myself. "Town's not backward now. Let's go see what type of magic we can work on this apartment. You fret too much, honey. It's a wonder you have any sense at all."

Until the day Flossie arrived, one of the church deacons and Herbert plastered and painted, nipped and tucked—it seemed, around the clock. They hung new wallpaper in the kitchen, an icky lime green that Thelma matched with the appliances, so that the colors offered consistency if nothing else. They fixed the plumbing in the back bathroom, allowing the drain to empty down pipes rather than in a bucket. They fixed wiring and fuses so that both were ample. They set traps for rodents and other vermin, cleaning up droppings and patching holes. Thelma threw away all the yellowing Norman Rockwell prints and replaced them with plain, landscape scenery. She placed glass trinkets around the house, on the mantel over the fireplace, on inset moldings at odd places in the walls. When all was said and done, the place still looked like only a stopover place. But it was greatly improved and would have to suffice.

On the day of the Penticott family's arrival, Thelma assembled the entire family, including myself, on the sidewalk outside the cab company. Herbert and the boys milled about waiting for direction. The boys kept their distance from one another so their crisp suit jackets wouldn't wilt or crinkle and their clip-on plaid ties wouldn't accidentally pop off on impact.

I sat on the bench watching Thelma sweep down the sidewalk in her sky-blue two-piece dress. It was too short for her, and as she swept, she kept tugging on the hem and the smocking, which seemed to make her itch.

Herbert sat down next to me, wiping sweat from under the fedora Thelma shoehorned his head into. I tried to readjust his hat. He said, "This hat is just half my worries, Aunt Cora. These here shoes is pinching my toes worse than this hat is pinching my head. Thelma done made such a fuss. Nothing hanging in either of our closets was suitable enough, so I had to drive her over to Jaspar. Blue is her lucky color. She saw that dress and nearly knocked another woman off her feet trying to grab hold of it. I told her, Seems to me, it's too short. Look at how she keep yanking on it. Dress done withered up and fit 'bout as well as these shoes she bought me, if you ask my corns."

As last-minute trimmings, Thelma used the stick part of the broom to dislodge Buster, Jones, and Russell from their chairs. She prodded the boys into line, according to height.

We were all waiting. Cabs rolled in and out of the garage; the wind chimes across the street at the glass company let loose, making us forget about the clankety noise from that garage door. We were waiting for a good fifteen minutes before one of the boys spotted his uncle's black car coming across the bridge.

Solomon was waving and honking his horn. Several of the cabdrivers came out of the garage and even passersby simply turned toward the noise. Thelma smoothed her dress and grabbed a bunch of flowers she'd bought earlier that morning. When the car passed Mercury Gas, everybody began to wave and cheer at the brand-new Chevy coming down Old Riley. Solomon was, oh I'd say, a good six feet tall, but in Thelma's eyes, her brother stood nothing short of ten.

The car eased to a stop. Solomon ran over to Flossie's side to open the front and back doors. Sweet Alma stepped out first. Then Solomon extended his hand to Flossie, who has always been quite, quite good looking for a dark-skinned girl. She flipped her big pretty legs out one after the other. Her right hand extended to meet Solomon's. She wore dark sunglasses, a wispy thin scarf, and a white-and-yellow-striped overcoat. Ordinarily, Solomon's high yellow skin and gray eyes was the kind that made most women feel they'd struck gold. I didn't get that sense from Flossie. Clearly, Flossie Jo thought she was the star of this show.

Buster, Jones, and Russell never talked about much of anything, but rare was the day when you can hush them up. They hushed for Flossie Jo. And it took all that was in them to poke their chests out, suck in their gibbous guts, and stand tall as she walked pass them, toward Thelma.

"Morning, sirs," she said.

"Morning, Miss Penticott." They nodded.

Lowering her sunglasses, she turned back to Thelma and stretched her arms wide. "Thelma? Did you pick those flowers for me?" Because Thelma was too nervous to offer them, Flossie gently scooped them from her hands, making sure to sniff each dahlia, petunia, and marigold, even though they weren't truly the fragrant variety. "How lovely."

Thelma nodded sheepishly as Flossie took her arm and started walking away from the car. At once, everybody behind them was forced to fend for themselves. There was the car that needed unpacking; and Sweet Alma, who was chasing Pepper; and Pepper, who was running because he didn't want her treating him like a little doll, braiding his hair and cuddling him. There was Herbert, whose tight shoes had him standing in the soft grass; and Solomon, who was talking to Buster, Jones, and Russell while eyeing the new girl working the dispatcher's radio.

"I'm depending on you to be my guide and show me the entire town," Flossie said to Thelma, eyeing Solomon.

"At this very moment?" Thelma asked.

"Not all of it," Flossie said. "You can take me on an abbreviated tour right now. Solomon once told me that some comet touched down here just after the turn of the century. On a hill behind a baseball field. I'm sure you're well aware of how your brother stretches a story."

Thelma stopped walking and, for the first time since word of Flossie's coming, must have felt like she was on solid footing. This was Thelma's terrain: the sun, the moon, the stars, seventy-six-year comets. "Whether it happened," she said, "depends on whom you ask and whom you believe. Near the baseball field? There's a promontory. As soon as you clear the trees, there used to be a sign up there that read, 'Halley's Landing, Where That Comet Sprinkled Down in August 1910 and Is Destined to Come Back Again.' Beats me what happened to the sign. Old folks say the land is the luckiest piece of property for miles. Lucky, they say, because when the comet visited, more crystal blue chunks of it were found up there than any other place in Halley. They say one year all the squirrels up there turned red and each skunk that wandered up lost his stripe. Another year a group of barren women went up there for a revival and all came down with wombs made capable of bearing armies of babies."

Thelma turned to me.

"This is Aunt Cora. She's not really any relation, but she's one of the women who helped raise me when Mama died. She attended your wedding."

"I remember, Miss Cora," Flossie said. "Lord, has time stood still? You must have one of those Dorian Gray pictures in your attic or something that wards off aging. Has it been fifteen years? Very nice to see you again, ma'am."

"And you, too," I said. "We say that the comet landed here in our town. But keep in mind all kinds of crazy things went on that year. Some folk considered sacrificing virgins. Others locked themselves in root cellars. Six in one hand. Half dozen in the other. All pure insanity."

Not allowing another word between Flossie and me, Thelma looped her arm through Flossie's and continued: "Vegetation never grows right up there."

"Course, some people say it's the clay soil," I offered as another modicum of reason. "Never has been that hospitable to seeds."

"My Herbert was told when he was little that he probably wouldn't be able to father a child. Result of a bad case of the influenza, followed too closely by smallpox. Anyway, his mama took him up there during sap season, and look at him now. Defies all manner of pills, coils, and Delfen foams."

Before I motioned for Mr. Defiant himself to drive me back home, I watched Thelma and Flossie Jo walking down the street together. Every now and then Thelma's arms flailed as she told her story. Flossie leaned into it like leaning into a great wind.

Course, Thelma wasn't around the last time that comet made its orbit. But, by the way she talked about it, you'd swear she saw it with her very own eyes. She stopped to show Flossie the top of the water tower, where a light was said to have appeared in the sky before the comet chunks allegedly fell. She slowed to point over her shoulder back at the glass factory, whose windows were said to have blown out one after the other. I've told Thelma over and over that I was there. I was ten years old and in complete use of my faculties—even though others may not have been. There were nights when my father and I stood on the highest point of our land, staring up at the heavens. Each time I saw that thing, I remember holding my breath in awe of the largest, most brilliant shooting star I'd ever witnessed. I've told Thelma that as far as I can tell it hung up there on a steady course, never once falling. I've told her that for three months the entire town watched it arc across the heavens. And it only fell when the town learned the railroads would soon make our canal obsolete and New-port, as Halley was called back then, needed something more than our Emancipation Festival to hang its livelihood on. Pure propaganda, it was. Still, enough people believed, or at least came to see about it, all plopping down good currency.

The bells in the campanile began to ring that afternoon. Thelma and Flossie continued walking down the street. When they got to Greater Faith, young Delaware Matthews's car pulled up in front of the church. Thelma made him slow down, I supposed, to introduce him to Flossie. The next thing we knew, Flossie and Thelma were jumping into Delaware's car.

Course, the whole thing was odd to me. Less than an hour into town and Solomon was in the dispatch office hitting on the new girl; his wife was jumping into the car of the young assistant pastor. Yes, to look at it, quite odd indeed.

Delaware's fine car passed us. Flossie sat in the front seat, holding her flowers like a bridal bouquet. Thelma was in the backseat, yelling out of the window.

"We'll be back soon," she called. "Reverend Delaware and I are going to show Flossie the historical markers where the canal wall meets the river. It won't take long. We're just going for a little ride."

Cora

By late afternoon, I've weathered the ride back to the house
with May Ruth and I'm sitting on the gallery nodding off.
The white Christmas lights have been strung throughout the
trees in the front yard and the yellow-and-white-striped tent
stands off the driveway. Under the tent, ten wrought-iron
tables are arranged in a circle and hold Flossie's sunflower
bouquets. In the center of the circle is a setup of period pieces:
an old spinning jenny, a Martha Washington–style dress made
of calico and domestic, a cat-o-nine-tails whip, a horse collar,
a corn broom with marriage bows, and iron leg shackles. A
long table for the buffet and a small platform for the band sit
off to the side.

I'm half asleep when May Ruth comes flying out of the
screened door dressed in Herbert's rain slicker and duck
boots. She teeters on the top step, then swings from left to
right, licking her finger and holding it up to the air until she
finds a north wind.

Seeing me, she says, "My instincts tell me a molly of a
storm is coming, dear heart."

"Got a feeling, do you? Never mind the fact that the sky
has turned in on itself and has just clapped thunder. And
never mind the fact that in August rain comes nearly every

day around this same time. But you go on reading your own signs."

"Not merely any storm, dear heart. One that's right for watching my little loves. Now that I'm done watching those muscular young men who were raising that tent. Muscles bulged from every inch of their taut bodies as they pushed and pulled on those wires. They had my undivided attention, they did. These binoculars have far more uses outside of birding." She kisses her binoculars before pulling them over her head and folding her bird book into her pocket. "The rain slows the birds down, giving me a wonderful opportunity to get a good look at them. Especially the yellow-billed cuckoos and red-eyed vireos. When they're moving extremely fast, I sometimes don't have time to focus and I miss far more than I care to. I'll be back shortly, dear heart."

"Suit yourself, cuckoo," I say under my breath.

After finding the wind turned right, May Ruth starts out toward the river.

Soon as she's out of sight, the rain pours like ninety-nine to a hundred. Course, the heat tries to snatch it up before it hits the ground. The river has feigned calm all day. But now it nudges gently at the canoes and the sailboats lined up along the piers and in the middle of the water. People start to scatter every which way up and down the riverbank. I assume May Ruth is getting a good soaking.

I'm enjoying the sound and the smell of hot summer. My eyes are getting heavy when I hear a bus stopping down along Old Riley. Not long afterward, I see a woman with a black raincoat covering her head running up my driveway. She clears the trees and she's slipping and sliding through the mud puddles, looking over her shoulders like somebody's behind her. Only, as far as I can see, nobody follows. She's alone.

I lean forward to see better. *May Ruth? What are you doing running like that? Take your time, honey. Take your time.*

Nobody's going anywhere. The rain sounds like it has mustered strength enough to punch through the veranda. Dark clouds collect over the river and lightning flashes leave white streaks hanging, then fading along the horizon. Those raucous mourning doves fly over to the gallery, seeking refuge from the storm. When I turn to take a look at them, I notice Thelma, Herbert, and May Ruth standing behind me, each in a different window. They're beckoning for the woman to run faster. I wonder if they can see what's on her heels. And if they can, why can't I?

Midway up, even with the rain needling like it is, the woman slows to study Flossie's sunflowers. They bow and sway under the force of the water, barely able to stand. The woman only studies them for a brief moment, and as the rain picks up, she starts running again. That black raincoat flies back like a head full of hair.

By the time I make it over to the top of the steps, the woman rests at the bottom.

"Afternoon, honey," I say, voice sounding unused, too unused to greeting company. "Can I help you find something?"

She runs up the gallery steps, dripping wet, and peels back that coat. "I'm home, Aunt Cora," Sweet Alma says. "I've decided to come back home."

Wet strands of hair fall into her face, her eyes, and I can't tell if the water streaking her cheeks is solely from the rain or from tears.

"Sweet Alma, baby? Is that you?" Course, I know right off who it is. But my eyes fix on her face so long that to an outsider it would seem I can't place her. I grab her tightly. I can feel her bones in my arms. I knit her fingers through mine and her hands feel cold and slick. "We need to warm you up, child. What're you doing taking the bus? You know your uncle Herbert would have picked you up from the train. Why didn't you call?"

Sweet Alma smiles again and turns to face the driveway. After a few seconds, those two boys appear through a curtain of rain. El and Pepper are dressed in their Halley's Comets uniforms. El's suit fits tight as always; Pepper's swims around him as they run up the drive.

"What in the world?" I say. Sweet Alma looks at me and smiles.

Seconds later, Flossie Jo bursts through the front door. She slows to kiss Sweet Alma. The balloons that are tied to the porch railing pull against their strings, trying to chase after her. And Flossie runs as fast as I've ever seen her toward those boys, grabbing El up and twirling him around. They're spinning in the joy of each other. And, this time, he doesn't pull away. He lays his head real gentlelike on her shoulder.

Then that old dog, Mr. Paul, drives up in his truck. El jumps down from Flossie and runs up here to him.

Mr. Paul walks over to the porch step and sits, leaning forward on his elbows. He says to El, "Way I see it, you're the man of the house when your uncle Herbert and your cousins go back home. You're the only man in a house full of women. You got to be the protector. You got to protect these women in case of danger. That's the way I see it, since you don't have no daddy around. That's a big task for a little boy. You still up for it? They're in your charge in case something bad ever happens. You sure you can handle such responsibility?"

"I'm up for it," El says. "I ain't no sissy."

"Ain't saying you're a sissy, boy. I want to know whether you're up for it?"

"I'll show you I'm up for it," El says. He starts to run down the hill, waving over his shoulder at us. This time he passes Flossie like he doesn't even see her. She falls down to her knees weeping for that boy. Pepper keeps coming toward the house and to Thelma, who's now out on the gallery with her arms ready to catch him.

The near and far sound of both of those boys' cleats digging into the gravel carries the rhythm of somebody hitting a tin drum. It reverberates so in my chest and soon replaces the thumping of my own heartbeat.

The horn blasts and I awake like I'm tossed in the air.

I see May Ruth walking alongside the drive as Flossie's blue truck comes flying up the middle. Two yellow-and-green signs—BUY FLOSSIE'S SUNFLOWER SEEDS—hang above the words U.S. MAIL. The yellow swirling light atop the truck flickers off as she stops at the edge of the gallery, nearly slamming into my azalea bushes.

"Flossie Jo, you're coming too damn fast," I yell down toward her.

As Flossie climbs out of her truck—ass-first like she's getting off a horse—Herbert hollers, "Is that my wife?"

"No, it's your sister-in-law," I say.

Herbert grunts and returns to his baseball game.

"Can you believe this?" Flossie bellows. "Look at me!"

Her hair drips wet and frizzes about her head. The navy blue violets on her cheap little utilitarian dress have faded into a light purple and smudged into dagger-shaped stripes.

May Ruth sloshes over to Flossie's aid at the foot of the steps and pulls up short. "I hate to tell you this, dear heart, but something on you has woefully expired." May Ruth cups her hand over her nose.

"Dog shit," Flossie says, leaning on the banister. "I stepped in it at the VanMusels' place. I was delivering a good-sized box, certified, when I heard that bitch of theirs yelping. I went around to the back to try to find out where all that noise was coming from, and don't you know those nasty people haven't made one effort toward repairing that side garage of theirs. The garage burned down last spring. Theirs is the worst-looking house on Third Street, and the parade passes right in front of it."

Flossie begins to mount the steps. Her feet and legs are caked in mud, and it looks like old turkey buzzards have puked on her entire lower half. One splat on the gallery step reminds her of the dog shit and she turns toward the hose under the porch. She hooks her purse around her neck before rinsing down her shoes.

"Well, I was in the back, and wouldn't you know, the sky unleashed a torrent. No warning at all. That idiotic dog Lucinda had caught her leg in a stack of two-by-fours. I lifted one of the boards up to free her and the ingrate started to growl at me. So I started running. And she came tearing behind me like some rabid fool."

May Ruth says, "Why did you run, dear heart? That's the absolute worst thing to do."

"I don't know exactly why, May Ruth Albee. Next time you encounter a dog frothing at the mouth and growling, let's see what you do." To me, Flossie says, "Lucinda is the one that has those fainting spells. She's got some kind of heart condition. But of all days, she wasn't bothered by it today. Nearly scared the hell out of me."

"Not quite," I say.

"I heard that." Flossie rolls her eyes at me. "After flopping around in that mud back there, I finally made it to a patch of weeds and sticker bushes over along the side of the house. Then I remembered I had my pepper spray. I hit her square in the eyes. She ran off crying, sounding all sorry. But look at me. Look at my dress. And now, I swear, I can feel it starting to shrink right around my very body. I tell you, those Van-Musels are some nasty people. And the next time that Lucinda needs a helping hand, she'll have to chew her damn leg off before she'll get some help from me."

Flossie tries to sit on the step, but jolts back upright due to a clump of mud that has fastened her dress to her thigh. She yanks it out and eases back down on the step like a pregnant woman in her final turn. She pulls blades of grass from her brassiere and tosses them over the side of the gallery.

"When I ordered this dress, they flat-out lied and said it was machine washable. There's no way this old mess would have survived a washing."

"Did you get a good price?" asks May Ruth.

"Price doesn't matter now," I say. I reach over for my newspaper and my eyeglasses. I'm irritated because I hate nodding off in the middle of the day.

Right about now, I'm so angry with Miss Sweet Alma. I'm angry that as each day passes during this week, every time the doorbell rings or some taxi driver makes a wrong turn into the driveway, our hearts will fill with hope that she's decided to mend her rift with her mother. And even though May Ruth probably will be the only one who runs to the door or starts down the drive, a piece of us will follow along with her.

Meanwhile, Flossie Jo makes me even madder. As is customary, she busies herself by making a commotion over nothing.

"Look at these stockings," she says. "I bought them for five dollars, and now they're in an awful state. And my shoes . . . stretched to high heaven. You'd think my—"

"My this, my that. Damn it, Flossie Jo, is *my* the only word in your vocabulary? Why don't you march your black ass on in the house and take a bath. This is not a tragedy, for God's sake. There are far more important things in life than a silly little dimestore dress that never was all that flattering in the first place. The whole world's not about to come to an end because you got rained on. And take Tweedle Dee here with you. I'm sick of all this foolishness."

They swirl around to look at me, faces askew. Course, if I could, I'd swirl around to look at me, too. Flossie tucks her chin and gives me the evil eye before going inside. May Ruth sees fit to walk over to me. I'm straightening, fingering mostly, the stack of newspapers and magazines that I keep out here next to my chair.

"Why, Cora Hoskins, I do believe you've gone stark mad. This won't help matters, you know."

"I don't feel like helping matters right now, May Ruth."

"I know things are tense, but aren't you feeling well otherwise? Perhaps you'd like to lie down, dear heart?"

"I feel just fine. No thanks to you, cursing me the way you did earlier with Sweet Baby."

May Ruth doesn't say anything. She simply looks out over the garden. The wind is drying everything and making the fastener on the flagpole clank loud against the metal. Most of those sunflowers have returned to normal, standing with their chests poking out, looking no worse for the wear; yellow petals of the battered ones dot the driveway; and, over the river, the clouds are becoming sparse, so that blue sky overtakes them in places with white shafts bending into the river.

May Ruth rubs my arm, then heads back over to the door. "I'm going up to see how Flossie's coming along. I do hope you'll be in a better mood for the party."

"Suit yourself," I say.

Flossie's bedroom faces the front yard. I hear the water running as she prepares for a bath, shower, or some such. A soft breeze of lilacs from her primp table floats down, tickling my nose. Even though I'm not ready for tickling just yet.

The catering truck pulls up in the driveway, followed by a Porter cab. I walk to the edge of the gallery. I motion for the driver in the truck to pull around to the side so the driver in the taxi can pull up closer. My heart starts to beat fast and I start down the steps. The taxi driver gets out and opens the back door. It's only Thelma.

"This has been one of the longest days of my life, maybe longer," she says, walking up the steps. Her face, her eyes, look like she's been in the middle of a storm, though the rest of her is completely dry.

"Is that my wife I see coming up those stairs?" Herbert says from the kitchen.

"Hey, Herbert," she says to him. To me, she whispers, "I've got something to tell you, Aunt Cora. After you left, I went back to see my Pepper, and he told me some mean and hurtful things about Flossie Jo. Sounds like she's been smiling in my face and treating my son like a no-count behind my back."

"Honey, there's so much confusion right now. We have to temper everything we hear and say. Before we rush to judgment on any of this, we have to be careful first. Okay, honey? Let us all stop and take a deep, deep breath."

She curls her lip, staring at the spiderweb hanging from the veranda. Water droplets cling to it like diamonds. "I'm beginning to wonder whether we all should have passed on coming together this year. Maybe that would have been best."

Herbert starts clapping and hollering at the baseball game. He turns up the volume on the television set. We can hear the crowd cheering.

"A grand slam, Thelma," his voice booms. "Whew, buddy! Hey! Thelma, a grand slam! Baby, you got to see the replay on this one. Come here, baby, before you miss it."

"I'll tell you about Pepper and Flossie later," Thelma says.

As she scuttles back toward the kitchen, I notice she's tracked a few of the sunflower petals onto the gallery. The caterers clamor about, unloading bags and boxes of food, small crates of liquor. They trek back and forth through all that yellow and pay it no never mind. Back and forth and it doesn't make the least bit of difference to all their bustling.

Neither they nor Thelma have any idea those petals are all that remains of my dream and Sweet Alma's rain.

Cora ·

The organist from Greater Faith, the drummer, a horn player, a fiddler, and one of the choir members make up a band called Jacob's Ladder.

While they tune up and practice under the tent, Herbert ties the remaining balloons and globelike paper lanterns to the gallery. "They sho' can sing," Herbert says, snapping his fingers and bopping his head.

"Herbert," I say, "where's your wife?"

"Thelma's sleep come down on her hard and she decided to go up and get some rest before the party. She just like a child that way—ever since them babies, she been napping at nearly the same time every day."

When Flossie Jo slams her bedroom window shut and turns on the house's lone air-conditioning unit, the lights in the house surge.

Herbert looks down at his watch. "Time sho' is flying faster than I can get a handle on it," he says. "I'm gone make sure everything's set up under the tent. Then I'll check on the grill and make sure our meat is coming along fine. We better get a move on, Aunt Cora. You gone be late for your own company."

"People don't come to see me, Herbert. Not anymore. They come to eat and dance and tell a few lies. They won't know if I'm here or not. Course, when Arthur was alive, they came to see him shoot off his gun, scattering those poor mourning doves clustering in the trees."

"Used to remind me of a sho' 'nuff cowboy," Herbert says, "the way he grabbed that gun off his hip and twirled it 'round his fingers before shooting that thing."

"And never hit one bird, either. He prided himself on that. Course, folk also came to watch him nail those big fat pigs to our most stately catalpa or oak. The men would stand around and watch Arthur gut old porky, slit him wide open and clean him up real good. Then he'd take the meat and place it in the pit; he'd take the lard, hog jowl, and chitlins and push it off to the side. It all had its place. Every year the spring litter on the hog farm had an odd way of knowing that as soon as they were fattened up real well with all that corn and the weather crept above ninety degrees and remained, Mr. Arthur Hoskins would be on his way downstream with his rope and mallet."

"You g'wan 'way from here," Herbert says. He comes over and kisses me. "You're the sole reason people come every year. We all miss Uncle Arthur, but it wouldn't be the same without you, Auntie."

I wait until Herbert's under the tent and I slip back in the house. I stand on the bottom step so I can hear upstairs. Course, I can't hear a thing over that air-conditioning unit.

May Ruth laughs and I hear footsteps coming down the hall up there. I dash back outside.

After a few seconds, May Ruth joins me on the gallery, holding two glasses of liquor. She's changed into her powder-blue sari with the Navajo bangles and the Princess of Egypt falcon earrings. Her hair is greased back and the ends are curled up.

"Aren't you going to freshen up, Cora?"

"I'm fresh enough," I say. "Besides, you've freshened enough for the both of us."

"Thelma's up in her room asleep," May Ruth says. "Flossie's up in her room, half naked. She can't decide what to wear. She's got five outfits spread across her bed. She says she's so hot she's about to pass out."

"As long as she doesn't come down naked, any outfit will do."

Taking into account my earlier outburst, I don't comment further. I go to sit back down when I notice Viola Miller struggling up the driveway with her two dogs. One pulls her sideways and causes a commotion, the other is gimp-legged, half blind, and dragging behind. So she's pulling him along.

"Yoo-hoo!" Viola calls.

"Oh, Lord, here comes the devil and her gimp imps," I say to May Ruth. "I know a quick secret, you want to hear it?"

"Do tell, dear heart."

"I hear told Jack Spencer, our mail carrier, delivered Kyle Miller's ashes about a week ago. Viola and Kyle had been *estranged* for much of their nearly twenty-five-year marriage, so why she wanted his ashes remains a mystery to us all. As much of a mystery as why she also decided at the last minute to take out a full-page ad in this year's festival book and dedicate the ad to his memory." A ream of fireworks go off down by the river, scaring the hyped-up dog so bad that he leaps over into a row of sunflowers, taking Viola and the gimp dog with him. A flock of birds shoot out, sending pollen every which way. May Ruth covers her ears. "These things come to light after a while, though. Course, it could be guilt, since right about the same time the ashes arrived, Viola's lawn began to outshine everybody's on the hill. A much, much younger fellow who'd come initially to tend her garden also started receiving piano lessons. Flossie says he now comes by twice a day to uproot Viola's crabgrass, fertilize dead patches, and break up *every* inch of her fallow ground."

"You're such a delicious gossip, Cora. I just love you for that."

"I don't gossip," I say while waving at Viola because she's waving her dogs' leashes up at us. "Look at her. Mark my words, you can't trust anybody who waves at you with both hands. That's what I said all along about Tricky Dick Nixon."

"Baby, I just got the news!" Viola yells over her dog's protestations. I now can see she's got that jug of voodoo wine she concocts tucked under her arm. "Here I am going on and on about my time being cut in half, and that poor, poor nephew of yours is back in jail, I hear. I must beg your pardon, Cora. That's why we came a little early. We were wondering if we might be of some help. Can we wash dishes or anything?"

"Do the dogs rinse or dry?" May Ruth mumbles to me.

Viola stops. She takes the leashes one at a time and throws them atop my azalea bushes. She fiddles with them as though she's tying them. But she's not. She's only making like she's tying them. The idiot dog minds immediately, lying down and resting his head on his front paw. The other dog is on a longer leash and sniffs around in circles before hunching on his hindquarters. She takes a bowl from her bag and goes over to the hose under the gallery to fill the bowl with water. Then she brushes her short sequined dress off and smooths her hair back.

I lower my voice.

"I tell her every year that she doesn't have to dress up so much for this thing, and to leave those dumb dogs at home. Look at them, they're too stupid to know they aren't even tied up. Anything that stupid should be left at home. And Viola really doesn't want to help. She can spot work a mile away and will find the most efficient detour around it."

"Now, Cora, you should really try to have fun." May Ruth smiles and offers me a glass. "Perhaps you need a balm for your nerves."

"Did it come from your Thermos, May Ruth? Course, if it did, that means you're conspiring to kill me straight off, aren't you? My system is not made of cast iron like yours. You must be in cahoots with that Flossie Jo."

May Ruth leans over the banister, watching Viola. But in all actuality, she's zeroing in on that jug of wine, as though concentrating on it can telepathically assure Viola doesn't lose one drop while fooling with those beasts.

"How can we make things better, hmm?" Viola asks her dogs.

I open my mouth to tell her to get the hell off my property when May Ruth interrupts me. "Viola, dear heart, you're the belle of the ball tonight. Come, love, let us sample your gift. I hear the grapes are extraordinary this year. Those grown in California and locally." She turns around to me. "You should really get ready to greet your guests, Cora. I'll see you later, pip-pip."

"Herbert's taking over that responsibility," I say. "I'm going to find me a nice shadow on the gallery here and hide inside it for as long as I can. I get good gossip that way."

The two of them start off down toward the tent and pretty soon everything looks ready. The white lights in the trees flicker on and resemble fuzzy white stars. The smoke from the barbecue grill hangs gauze thick and bumps up against those Christmas lights, casting the prettiest blue haze along the treetops. The torches that ward off the mosquitos are set aflame. The lanterns sparkle and dance.

As the cars begin to line up along a grassy knoll east of the driveway and folks get out of their cars and start walking toward the tent, I can hear Flossie overhead on the veranda, pacing and humming some tune. I only hope she has on clothes.

"Hey, Mayor Osgood," she says, leaning over the banister. "You *are* going to save me a dance, I hope."

The mayor turns red as a beet with his black self and just smiles. "I'll save you two." He has the nerve to hold up two fingers, knowing durn well the mere thought of dancing is enough to stop his ancient heart. He tips on over to the tent, buoyed by Flossie Jo's attention.

My guests wave at me when they see me up here on the gallery. Herbert directs them to the tent. "Good evening!" I yell down, waving. "I'll be over in a second. Go with Herbert and let him take your picture for our festival book. We're going to have a good time tonight."

A blue van with the Halley's Comets Little Leaguers parks behind two Cadillacs carrying Halley's five council members. A group of church members pull up, followed by members of Flossie Jo's beautification committee and a few of the cab-drivers in their Porter cabs.

The boys file out of the van like little robots, looking all stiff and proper. Little Bailey Rogers steps out of line to scope out the property and Ben, Bailey's father and this year's coach, reels him back in.

"Let those boys play," I say to Ben. "They can't hurt a thing. Let them be boys."

"How are you, Miss Hoskins?" Ben tugs on the bill of his baseball cap. "They can hurt much more than you know, ma'am."

"They can't hurt dirt and grass and trees. Go on, boys," I tell them. "You all play until you get tired. This land is many moons from sacred."

Ben nods to the boys and they break out across the yard, climbing the trees, darting in and out of the rows of sunflowers.

A heavyset one who stretches his uniform to the limits can't quite keep up with the others, although he's huffing and puffing, trying hard. One boy throws his new mitt down on the ground and stomps on it. The others gather nearby, seeing just how much he can loosen it. When that is done, he spies the bicycle on the side of the house. It's El's old ten-speed. The boy rushes over and rolls it out to the front yard. Bailey sees me looking at them. He grabs the boy's arm. "Can we play with this, ma'am?" he asks.

"Sure you can," I say.

"As long as you don't steal that bike the way you stole my clothes," Flossie says.

"Hi, Mrs. Penticott." Bailey looks up. His eyes pop like he just saw a haint.

"Don't you 'hi' me, you little swindler. I've got a good mind to come down there right now. Go get your father, please."

Bailey hands over the bike, backing up, tripping over his feet. He turns and runs to get his father. Ben comes back and stands under the gallery like he would serenade Flossie if she could keep quiet long enough.

"Ben," she says, "are you aware your son and two other hoodlums stole some personal items from Miss Thelma, Miss May Ruth, and myself the other day while we were swimming?"

Bailey smiles to himself.

"So that's why you didn't want to come," Ben says to Bailey.

"And he didn't just steal our clothes. You could say he and his friends walked away with our dignity and self-respect, too."

What she really wants to add is that she's sure they saw her ass, and though she's only mildly embarrassed by that, she's even more perturbed because they got her old dowdy dress and, to tell the truth, May Ruth's tits.

"Bailey." Ben yanks his baseball cap off and places his hands on his hips. "Bailey, what kind of devilment have you gotten yourself into now? I have told you good character has to apply off the field, too. You keep messing up and I'm tempted to take you off tomorrow's roster."

"Dad!" Bailey's face turns way past sour.

Feeling a little sorry for Bailey, I say, "Well, now, those boys didn't take anything of real value." And, to my understanding, that includes Flossie's *dignity and self-respect.*

"We'll deal with this tonight when we get home." Up to Flossie, Ben says, "You let me know how much everything costs. I'll be happy to pay for it, Flossie."

"Well, considering you've been wonderful in helping me battle those nasty little cicadas all summer, draping that cheesecloth over my flowers and everything, we'll call ourselves even."

Ben smiles and walks back over to the tent. Bailey and the other boys hurry along with the bike, pushing it out to the top of the driveway. They take turns riding it up and down the hill. The hyped-up dog wants to chase the bike, but he doesn't. He runs out a few paces and jerks himself back, barking his head off.

Out over the downtown, the sky looks like one of those ragged tie-dyed shirts, though in a pretty, respectable way. Red-edged clouds and the blues in the sky divide and separate yet meld into belonging. I catch a glimpse of the Ferris wheel in the fairgrounds behind the church. White lights wink at me through the trees. The roller coaster down there retreats in and out of the western horizon, weaving streaks like hair ribbons across the evening sky. Lost balloons float leisurely over the river.

Here the boys rip and run, oblivious to the world, to the caterers' hors d'oeuvres, to the crickets' songs, to all that chatter, and to dancers who are already swaying like nimble stalks to the horn player's deep, mournful notes.

Here nothing with breath stands still.

When it's time for dinner, we all gather under the tent. I make my rounds to the tables and sit with Thelma, who's still wearing that same drab dress, and with May Ruth, who already is well on her way to la-la land.

The band stops playing for a moment as Herbert stands in the center of the circle to say the benediction. He's wearing his Pinkster's King Charlie outfit, a bright red coat with gold trim, like that of a British brigadier. He walks around the remnants of slavery in the center and touches each one.

"We're here tonight 'cause it's always been tradition for Aunt Cora to have a get-together before the start of the Emancipation. And because of this get-together it's always been tradition that we take a moment to pause and reflect ahead of time on what freedom means. What do it mean? There used to be a time, before the Surrender, when black folks' lives was directed by nothing but bells and bugles, ram and signal horns. Our uncle Arthur, Aunt Cora's husband, used to say: 'Long toots told you when to wake and break water; short ones told you when to eat and sleep. When to hit them cotton fields, yoke them steers. To feed, to breed. To die.'

"When it was time to eat," he went on, "the young children, in particular, was lined up at a trough and fed some mess you wouldn't hardly slop together for hogs. I say all that to say this: As we partake in good portions tonight, let us not forget. Let us be thankful, but let us not forget all the children. Those with us and those gone on to Glory. Let us not forget the children. Or the hard times. Amen."

Thelma says "Amen" louder than she expected and it stuns her. She looks up quickly, then returns to her empty plate. Herbert goes to check on things in the house.

At the table behind us, there's talk of a boycott on All-Rite Liquors because every August the owners set up their barbecue tents with lemonade and sell those old ugly mammy and minstrel dolls, syphoning dollars from our vendors. And there's more whining about the interstate signs our congressman promised us and never delivered. Three intermittently placed green tourists' signs would tout our festival, our comet, and our canal. Guaranteed, he said, to boost our local economy. Course, we haven't seen those signs.

To break up the monotony, I nod in the direction of the table across the circle. "I heard Ben Rogers over there is considering moving back to town. You both remember Ben Rogers, don't you? Ben moved away when his wife died a few years back. Nobody heard word one from him since he left. He came back at the beginning of June. I hear now he might be moving back to Halley for good. Never did sell his house. Flossie says he forwarded his mail to someplace in Arkansas. It's my impression that he's kind of sweet on Flossie Jo. And that doesn't happen often. Men are drawn to her, like to water, at first sight, but run in the opposite direction soon as they take a sip. Ben seems to be more of the patient type."

As if summoned, Flossie enters the tent wearing denim shorts, a blousey white shirt whose hem knots over her belly button, and a rather betrayed look that she flashes my way without hesitation in between that smile she flashes for the guests. Her damp hair stretches back into a ponytail and she's not wearing a lick of makeup. It's a look of defiance, true enough, but Flossie Jo seems to wear almost anything well. Though she wouldn't hear it from me.

Flossie hugs and kisses people on her way to the table. After pulling out the chair furthest from me, she glares at the food on May Ruth's and Thelma's plates. She turns up her nose and sits down. Not that there's anything wrong with the food.

"Flossie Jo," I say. "That nice Ben Rogers over there wants you to save him a dance."

"Don't you start on me again about Ben Rogers, Cora."

"Cora says he's taken quite a shine to you, dear heart." May Ruth sounds almost gleeful and she toasts Flossie with her milk, the only liquid she consumes that doesn't originate in a distillery. "Do tell us more about him."

"You can see for yourself he's a handsome man," I say. "He's good with his hands, too. Bailey Rogers is his son."

"I definitely remember Bailey," May Ruth says.

Flossie folds her arms across her large, imposing bosom.

"Ben's a fine, fine man," I say. "Still says 'ma'am' and 'sir.' Look at how broad his shoulders are. And when he walks, you'll see, he walks tall and straight like he's got good arches in his feet. Course, his teeth are a little stacked, but not so much that it detracts from his beautiful smile. And he just smiles and smiles when he's around Miss Flossie. Look at how he's smiling now." He turns to wave at our table. May Ruth and I wave back at him. "He's been coming by this summer to help with chores. It's a small world. I have a friend in Ohio who taught both of his parents. They were sharp as tacks, she said. Which means he hails from good stock."

Flossie says, "Cora, he's nearly ten years younger than me. And regardless of the prior generation's stock, Ben's son is a pervert-in-the-making. And a little thief."

"Sins of the son have nothing to do with the father. Besides, nobody told the three of you to go out gallivanting stark naked, splashing around in that water out back. What do you expect from a nine-year-old who's out minding his own business"—Flossie sucks her teeth—"and comes across some spectacle he's never before witnessed in his young life? I'm sure people don't run around naked in Arkansas. He just got a little high-spirited, that's all, and stole your clothes." I scoop some potatoes onto my plate, then extend the bowl to Flossie, but she disregards me. "As far as the age is concerned, in the right lighting and with the right panty girdle on, you don't look a day over thirty-five. You're lucky; dark skin acts as a preservative, a natural buffer against the aging process. So who would know the difference?"

"The whole town, that's who," Flossie says.

"Not like you've cared about that before," Thelma says. We turn to look at her because until now she's been so quiet.

May Ruth takes a sip from her milk again. "You know, dear heart," she says to Flossie. "It sounds like this Ben fellow is quite a catch. I daresay, Flossie, you'd better use all of your God-given *assets* before they dry up and turn to dust in your knickers."

"You're a pervert, too, May Ruth," Flossie says.

"What? Get your mind out of the gutter."

"Thelma," I say. Her attention has returned to her plate. "Thelma, you remember Orinda, Ben's wife?"

"Of course I remember Orinda. She died of a heart attack, about four years ago. And so young. She was only thirty."

"That bad-ass Bailey won't give me a heart attack," Flossie says.

"It wasn't the boy's fault," Thelma says.

I say to Flossie, "She had some congenital defect that finally caught up with her, poor thing. I remember she wore lots of braids in her hair and those dashiki clothes. They say when she was carrying Bailey, she thought she was expecting a girl. She'd been a fan of that *Roots* program, and that was right about the time when everybody was naming their kids those African names. She said she was going to name her daughter Kizzy from the show. Lord, it's a good thing she had a boy."

"And a good thing Orinda wasn't as fond of the name Chicken George," May Ruth adds, snickering. "Speaking of Chicken George: Thelma, what should I take Pepper for his reading pleasure tomorrow?"

"I don't know what you should take him," Thelma says. She wipes her mouth with the back of her hand, smearing barbecue sauce across her cheek, and skewers a few peas onto her fork even though she doesn't eat them.

"According to Cicero, 'To add a library to one's house is to give that house a soul.' I suppose it fits for jail cells as well." May Ruth leans over to Thelma, placing her hand on Thelma's wrist. "You know, dear heart, Rosa Luxemburg, the great Jewish-feminist-socialist revolutionary, found a love of birds while in a German jail. They put her there for speaking out against the War. The first big one. I suppose Pepper's also a bit of a revolutionary, in a way. Not leaving jail as a matter of principle—"

"Please, May Ruth," Thelma says. "Don't you go making fun of him, too. It's enough that his own aunt despises his very being."

"What aunt?" Flossie says.

"The aunt who can't have a heart attack because she doesn't have a heart. The aunt who talks fine in front of my face but hates my son behind my back. You, that's who."

"You're insane," Flossie says.

"Not now," I say.

"Not everybody comes into their sanity at the same time," Thelma says. She blows her nose into her napkin. "Not everybody has the same revelations."

"Thelma, don't put me in the middle of this. Pepper's own father says Pepper needs to grow up and stop acting like a damn fool. That's what his own father says."

"You're already in the middle, Flossie Jo. Right smack dab in the middle. What he needs is for you to forgive him." Thelma realizes her voice just turned up a notch. She looks around at the table behind us. But it's too late. Because the music has stopped, people hear better than otherwise and stare. They pretend not to stare, but they do. "Pepper made me promise I wouldn't say anything, but some promises just can't be kept. Some promises you got to break in order to make the teller whole. Pepper says you haven't forgiven him, Flossie Jo. I told him that there was nothing to forgive. And if there was the slightest inkling of something, the slightest inkling, then you'd forgiven him already. I told him nobody's to blame. For El. But Pepper said no. He said, Aunt Flossie"— she lowers her voice—"Aunt Flossie wishes it was me that died up there. I said, Did she say that to your face? He didn't say anything further. He started to cry and there was this sound coming from my boy that I, his own mama, have never heard. Like something was slipping from him and he couldn't stop it, or worse, he didn't even know it was leaving. So what I want to know, Flossie, is this: Is there a need for you to forgive my son?"

"What the hell are you talking about, Thelma?"

"Not now," I say. Luckily, the music swells around them, muffling the sound. But that doesn't stop people from staring.

"Have you forgiven my boy? Have you?"

"Thelma, honey, I'm sorry Pepper is in jail," Flossie says. "I'm sorry he's screwing up his life. I'm really sorry. But he's here. He's got the chance to do so much more and he's not doing it. So I can only feel so much sorrow for a boy that has every chance in this world to straighten up and keeps dragging his feet."

Flossie looks off in the direction of the band and folds her arms. Thelma says, "My God, he's right. He's right, Aunt Cora."

"Pepper is yanking your chain," Flossie says quickly. "That's what he's doing. That's what he has always done. He yanks and you jump. Yanks harder and you jump higher and higher. He's always known what chord to pull with you, Thelma. Always."

"He needs you to forgive him, Flossie. That's his bond. He needs you to set him free. He needs you to forgive him, and for real this time."

"I don't have to sit through this crap." Flossie scoots away from her plate. Wax from the citronella candle splatters across the tabletop. She looks down at her watch and taps its face. "What is today? Let me think: Piss All Over Flossie Jo Penticott Day?"

"Lower your voice," I say to her.

"First that goddamned dog craps on me, then Cora here lambasts me. Now you, Thelma. May Ruth, it's your turn. Come on over and spit in my face."

This time even May Ruth has nothing to offer.

Flossie leaves the table and heads out toward the house.

Thelma leans over toward me. "I've got to go for a walk, Aunt Cora."

"Thelma, you know Flossie doesn't wish Pepper were dead. She may be many things, but she's not that coldhearted."

"A heart can't even be cold if it doesn't exist. I'm going down to the river to stick my feet in the water. I'll be back after a while."

After dinner several of the tables are dismantled and put away to make room for the circle dance. Flossie, looking completely recovered, stands next to Ben Rogers, holding his hand. I wind up in between May Ruth and Viola, both of whom have a history of being hell on my toes. Everybody, including the boys and the band members, gathers around. I look for Thelma, but she's nowhere in sight.

Once again, Herbert stands in the center.

"Back in the day, when people used to dance, they ain't had the benefit of no music or nothing. Truth is, they ain't had the benefit of no joy, neither. So they used what they had. They'd blow into a jug; beat on a skillet lid or a frying pan."

Herbert takes up a flute made of reed cane and blows it like a train whistle. The dance starts out slowly, without any music, only railroad chants and grunts. The breaths and chants are reminiscent of a train pulling from the station. We hold hands, and the circle expands. We hold hands tight, getting solid grips, making sure we don't dare break the chain. Again, I turn to look for Thelma. Herbert slowly bows his head and we move to the right, taking three short steps before dipping. Same thing to the left, three short steps, before dipping. Herbert is the caller. The men continue the chants. We women sing behind Herbert.

Herbert says, "My Lord, my Lord."

We say, "My Lord, my Lord."

He says, "One day, one day."

We say, "My Lord, my Lord."
"Hear my cry, Jesus."
"My Lord, my Lord."
"Free my soul, Jesus."
"My Lord, my Lord."
"Make me whole, Lord."
"My Lord, my Lord."
"Three-fifths no more."
"My Lord, my Lord."
"On the other side."
"My Lord, my Lord."

We keep singing it over and over. We're all dizzy and hot. We drop hands and clap hallelujah. Some continue stepping, but stepping in place, waving their hands.

May Ruth helps me to a seat.

Herbert is coming toward me about the same time one of the caterer boys is coming. The young man says, "A woman named Sweet Alma is on the phone, ma'am."

"You get Flossie Jo," I say to May Ruth. "You tell her her child wants to talk to her."

I grab Herbert's hand and we hurry inside.

Herbert wipes his hands on his coat jacket before he picks up the receiver. I sit down in the chair. He holds the receiver to his ear with both hands. "Sweet Baby? Hey, girl. You got some good news for your uncle?"

When May Ruth and Flossie get to the door, he cups the phone and beckons for them. May Ruth enters. Flossie stays outside under the gallery light. I don't stare at her long because her mood is still iffy.

My phone is old and the rest of us can hear bits and pieces of Sweet Alma coming across the line. Course, it almost sounds like she's standing down the hall, or maybe just outside on the gallery. I imagine her face. Sweet Alma's got the kind of face that tends to look strange on a black woman: dark brown skin like her mother's, but narrow features like her father's that angle more than normal. And then there are those deep-set, hazel-colored eyes that seemed mix-matched when set against the rest of her coloring, eyes that'll swallow you whole if you don't take care. I imagine Sweet Alma kicking off her shoes and propping her feet against the banister, head tossed back, her laughter mixing with that of the bullfrogs and the crickets.

Herbert says, "You don't say. You don't say."

May Ruth pinches at Herbert's sleeve. "What don't she say? What don't she say?"

Herbert says, "So you won't be able to make it after all, huh?"

"Oh, it's far too soon to say for certain now, dear heart," May Ruth says into the phone. "We've got a whole day before the opening parade. It's far too soon."

"To hell with it," Flossie says. "I don't give a shit whether she comes or not. Nobody's going to beg her black ass."

Herbert cups the phone. Flossie turns and goes back down the steps. She walks down the driveway to the tent to grab a beer, then over to the Little Leaguers, who have started tossing their baseball among them. She grabs that big boy's baseball cap and puts it on backward. Then she spits on her hands, commandeering the game by standing on a little mound in the center of the turn circle. They're forced to throw the ball to her. After she catches it, she tosses it like a pitcher, rearing back and kicking her leg, trying to let go of more than that baseball.

So now this phone call of Sweet Alma's has just one redeeming quality.

It's got her mother out there laughing on the pitcher's mound, wrapped up in the laughter of those little boys. This, for the time being at least, is as close as we can get to feeling like we're still standing on the eve of a celebration.

Herbert
AFTER MIDNIGHT

The party is over.

Ain't nothing worse than having your sleep come down on you halfway. I'm heading to the kitchen partly 'cause them spicy crepe whatcha-callits is having their way with my ulcer and some ice water right 'bout now sho' seem like the right thing for it. Other reason is sleeping with that woman of mine ain't doing neither one of us a bit of good, what with both of us tossing and turning like fish outta water. Her mostly. Try sleeping with Thelma when any one of our boys got some trouble on 'em and it ain't easy. But when it's Pepper's turn, which is more oft than not, her whole world falls to pieces.

Soon as I start down the steps, the light from the front porch nearly blind me. Up here, when night falls, the country-side spread out black and thick as my hand. Even the slightest hint of a glow tend to overwhelm the senses. At the bottom of the steps, I hear the snow sound from the television and I smell something burning. I hurry on back to the kitchen.

A few puffs of smoke linger 'bout the stove and high-up cabinets. Sis lies bent over the kitchen table with her head jammed 'gainst that telephone. I turn off the flame on the tall pot of ham bones and remove them from the eye. Sis done gone and let all the water cook out of the pot, and now all that good seasoned meat just sits there scorched and too tough for salvaging. Plain wasted, it is. And so is she. When she wake up, she won't have a clue as to the true cause of the zinging in her brain: the contents of the glass tipped over on her lap or that hard telephone jammed 'gainst her head. And the onliest thing that done saved her from learning a damn good lesson 'bout falling off with a lit cigarette is the singed butt that hang lazylike between her two fingers. The fan catch the last bit of ashes and blow them 'cross a couple of burnt concave depressions on the tabletop.

I click off the television. I take Sis's glass and place it in the sink. She can worry later 'bout the splatter marks it done left on her outfit. That and the green stains on her shirt from the collards thrown all 'round her. One batch of greens soak in a great big bucket of salt water. Two brown paper sacks of them stand upright on either side of her legs. One hold the throwaway stems and leaves that are brown-tinged and too wilted for the pot; the other hold greens that ain't yet been picked. She got a head of cabbage on the table to mix with the greens. There's measuring utensils flung 'cross the table. Bowls sitting cupped in one another. Knives turned every which way getting ready for mischief. Not a thing looks even close to readiness.

I open the window to let the burnt smell out and a cool briny mist rushes in along with a whiff of gunpowder. Even at this time of night, off in the direction of town, somebody's setting off fireworks and the gunpowder smell travels all over Halley on the light breeze. It's them snapdragons. I can tell from the way they going off. Reminds me of the times we got something brand-new and my boys would get ahold of the packing bubbles and wring them till all the popping was gone and nothing remained 'cept dead plastic.

I pull the chair back and set myself down next to Sis's bags and that bucket. I notice she got three whole bags under the table that I couldn't see while standing. Then I notice a letter addressed to Sweet Alma sticking out of Sis's back pocket. It's got a stamp and everything, but that don't mean nothing toward whether it'll be mailed.

Just out of something to do, I start separating the stems from the leaves and placing them in her bucket of salt water. I watch the clock on the wall.

Sometimes it's the hardest thing in the world, sitting and waiting for the air to clear.

Last year. One year ago today, truth be told.

We was sitting in that parking lot of that mini-mall, watching the sun go down. El and Pepper was in the backseat. I was sitting in the front next to the basket of fried chicken and coleslaw we'd just bought from the Kentucky Fried in the mini-mall. That good smell was getting wedged up in our noses, only we didn't have time to think long 'bout that good smell after we started hearing that song, "Take Me Out to the Ball Game," coming from the interstate.

The top was down on the car and we could hear the music getting louder and louder. El jumped up and started pointing toward them trucks rolling off the ramp. Rolling single-file, hissing and bouncing.

El sat on top of the seat to see better.

Wasn't no ordinary festival trucks El was gawking at. These was real spiffy, big ol' tractor trailers. White in color with bold red letters that read, PAUL'S CLASS A GROUNDSKEEPERS INC. Lightbulbs flashed like merry-go-round lights 'round the top cabins. That song, "Take Me Out to the Ball Game," played from the loudspeaker of the first one. That first one was little and squat, half the size of the three trucks that followed. Followed like they was being led by a little pied piper. Them three trucks hissed when the first one hissed, squealed when the first one squealed. Single-file, them trucks crossed the railroad tracks and hit Old Riley heading toward town and playing that song. "Take me out to the crowd."

El say, "Them the people coming to set up the baseball trivia exhibit."

"Uh-huh," I say, studying more on my chicken wing than on that boy.

El say, "If Sweet Alma ever brings herself out of the store, we can go watch them unload. Right, Uncle Herbert?"

I say, "I don't think Sweet Alma gone want to watch nothing on no baseball. She too busy baby-sitting Rena Davies's baby."

El say, "We can drop her off at home, Uncle Herbert. Sweet Alma ain't got to go."

Pepper leaned forward again, this time for a chicken leg. El loved to copy Pepper, but El didn't bother with that food. That boy's eyes was greedy more for them trucks and for baseball rather than for that good chicken.

When Sweet Alma came out, El waved for her to hurry on account of her taking her time talking to some young fellow.

"C'mon, Sweet Alma," El called for her. "You making us late. I'll be glad when you take your butt back home to Chicago." He sat back down for a second, then stood back up. "Say, mister, she slobbers when she sleeps. You don't want nothing to do with her."

Sweet Alma wasn't paying El no never mind. Neither was I, at first, to be truthful. But then it hit me, what he said, and I yanked him back down in his seat. We was laughing hard. "She do slobber quite a bit, don't she?" I say to him. And we laughed some more.

By the time Sweet Alma got in the car and we started down Old Riley, El had his lip stuck out far enough for him to walk on it. They got to fussing 'bout all that time she done took. Fussing and fussing all the way down Old Riley to the driveway, and Lord have mercy, we pull inside and that little pied piper truck sitting as big as it pleased in front of the house. El was leaning 'gainst the back of my chair, breathing down my neck. He sat up arrow-straight when he saw that truck.

"Paul's Class A Groundskeepers Inc.," he say, reading slowly.

That truck was still flashing and blinking. Though now that song had done stopped playing.

A little bald-headed white man was standing on the porch talking to Aunt Cora and Rena Davies. Rena Davies was a white girl who had stayed with Aunt Cora for a spell years ago on account of that husband of hers fighting her. Though she had long left her husband and Halley, she came back every year for the festival, and last year she had a brand-new baby on her hip.

Aunt Cora say, "Herbert, y'all, this here is Mr. Paul. He owns the company that laid the new baseball field."

Sweet Alma say, "Hey," like he wasn't really there and walked right past him to get Rena's baby. She reached into her brown paper bag and pulled out a teething ring for him.

"Please to meet you," I say to Mr. Paul. He swung his cigarette from one corner of his mouth to the other and grabbed hold of my hand hard, trying to wring it dry.

He say, "This good lady is nice enough to allow me to be an imposition for a few days."

Aunt Cora say, "I've got plenty of room now; it's no problem at all. You can share the third floor with Rena and Jamie."

Mr. Paul say, "I thought for certain I could make sleeping arrangements when I got to Halley. But everything at the hotel is booked. Must be some kind of festival. Reverend Fred sent me here to Mrs. Hoskins's place. He tells me this festival draws potentates from all over the world. We're only going to stay a couple of nights. I'm here to make sure everything runs smoothly on that new baseball field and to help set up the exhibit. I had to come personally since there was more delays on y'all's field than I've ever seen. Unseasonable rain; the drainage tubes not wanting to carry the water out correctly; the anchors for the bases not gripping right; the foul poles measuring off by too much. This never happened to Groundskeepers Inc. before, I assure you. We ain't never had a project plagued with so much bad luck. I got five workers with me and they're staying at other homes in town, too. But I think I got the best deal."

To look at Mr. Paul, he didn't seem the type to amount to much. He wasn't a no-count-looking man or nothing. But he definitely didn't seem the type to be driving such a fine truck or to be bossing them workers of his 'round. He was bald-headed, like I said, and not much taller than Pepper—though I s'pose he was taller than Pepper. He just didn't seem like it. I couldn't hardly make heads or tails of his words sometimes. Mostly on account of his Louisiana drawl that was high and sireny and kinda made him sound like a woman. That alone woulda made most men shy away from conversation. Not Mr. Paul, though, he just yapped and yapped till his words flip-flopped over one and the other, and the chatter reminded me of the ticking sound that old spinning jenny outside made. The sound of gathering thread and winding it here and there, in no particular fashion.

Mr. Paul scooted his cigarette to the corner of his mouth so he could talk to El and Pepper without the smoke wafting up into his eyes. He say, "Y'all boys play baseball."

El say, "Yes, sir."

Pepper didn't say nothing.

Mr. Paul say, "Well, of course you do. I must be a damn fool to ask. I'm gone teach you a few tricks that we don't include in this exhibit. I got me an appointment right now that's going to run late. But tomorrow I'll teach you two a few tricks of the trade."

The next afternoon, the boys was setting up the party tent.

Mr. Paul parked his truck and came walking up with his suit coat slung over his forearm. El and Pepper was in the front yard. El was hanging upside down from one of them trees in the middle of the yard. Hanging like a little monkey, which he liked to do. Pepper never cottoned to heights, so his feet was planted steady on the ground and he was tossing that baseball up in the air and catching it with his mitt, which he liked to do. Sweet Alma was sitting on the porch, coaching him—or trying, 'cause he wasn't really listening—and rocking little Jamie on account of Rena Davies stepping out for a while.

Mr. Paul slowed his pace to talk to them boys. He say, "You two come on over here for a minute. Whew, buddy, that's the nicest tent I've seen in a long time. We gone have a wingding of a party tonight."

Mr. Paul kept coming toward the porch. When he got there, he hung his suit coat on the banister and loosened the knot in his tie. He placed one foot two stair steps up and leaned on his knee.

Pepper and El walked over slowlike, with Pepper walking ahead of El like he was a bodyguard, even though El had a more imposing look than Pepper.

Mr. Paul say, "Now, I'm gone learn y'all the real, bona fide secrets of baseball. Like I said I was gone do. I'm a man of my word, sure enough. Y'all want to know the secrets of winning, don't you?" He winked at Pepper and motioned for him to throw the ball.

Right away, El say, "Yes, sir. We sure do. We've been waiting for it."

Pepper say, "We know about corking bats, scuffing balls. That ain't nothing new." He threw the ball into his glove hard, then tossed it over to Mr. Paul.

El tried to move 'round Pepper so he could see better. But Pepper held him at bay. Wasn't nothing to see. Mr. Paul had the ball in his hand but didn't do nothing with it. Didn't throw it up or hold it like a two-finger fastball, didn't shift it between hands or squeeze it to check the amount of life left.

I think we all expected him to do something with it since he had done asked for it.

Mr. Paul say, "I'm sure Alma won't mind if you gather 'round closer. I won't bite you. Gather 'round, boys."

But Pepper still kept his distance. Pepper say, "Man, what kind of tips you got?"

"First you got to promise." Mr. Paul rolled up his sleeves. "The both of you. Promise never, ever to reveal a word."

El extended his hand to shake Mr. Paul's. Pepper didn't. He just spit over his shoulder, which I s'pose was enough for Mr. Paul, who looked at the both of them and rubbed on his chin. To Pepper, he say, "Now, I know you too old for Little League, son. But these some good tips nonetheless. In case you ever get picked for a Major League farm team."

"A farm team. Ha," Pepper say. Pepper knowed his coach at school already done told him he'd never be elevated beyond third string, still you could tell he wanted like the dickens to buy into what Mr. Paul was saying. Sounded good to him just being considered in the same grouping as somebody with potential for a big-time farm team.

"Sure," Mr. Paul say again. "I can look at your arms and tell you got a good swing. Your hands say your fastball and change-up is solid."

"My foot speed ain't worth nothing," Pepper say.

"You do have a pair of donkey legs, don't you? But, you know, Ernie Lombardi was known for being slow, too. Lumbered around them bases like a bull. He did just fine, though. Batted over three hundred ten times in his career and even won a coveted Most Valuable Player award."

Pepper was smiling broad now. Couldn't see it on his face as much as you could see it in his eyes.

Mr. Paul say, "Let's say you playing a team in which the boys can run like the wind. Always stealing bases. Let's say you wanna slow them down. You know the best way to do it?

Second only to not letting the batter get a base hit in the first place."

Them boys shook their heads.

Mr. Paul looked over his shoulders like somebody was close by, listening. But wasn't nobody 'round 'cept them boys, Sweet Alma and that baby, and me sitting in the living room listening to it all through the opened window.

Mr. Paul say, "In between innings you can get a batboy or somebody to take a little hose and mist the clay part along the first-base line. That batboy'll look like he wetting down the sod. But he can let some of that water spray the first-base line. That runner'll feel like his cleats are trudging through quicksand."

Both boys was wide-eyed now. But that's how secrets tend to do you—make you open up wide and lower your guard.

"Now, here's another tip," Mr. Paul say. "Let's say you coming up 'gainst a team of strong hitters. They can knock the cork out of the ball. Before the big game, you take your balls and let them set in a steamy shower for as long as you can. One day. Two days."

"What'll that do?" Pepper say.

"The steam makes them balls heavier. They don't get the same type of connection with the bat, so when the batter hits it, it don't go that far."

I started to get up, but Sweet Alma beat me to it.

"Another thing you can do," Mr. Paul say, wiping at his forehead.

"There won't be any cheating," Sweet Alma say. She adjusted that baby on her hip. When she got closer to Mr. Paul, he looked up at her and started balancing the ball on the back of his hand, letting it roll up his forearm and back down to his palm. He tossed it back to Pepper.

"I didn't mean to cause no trouble," he say and he grabbed his suit coat.

El say, "Yeah, Sweet Alma, mind your own business."

Sweet Alma say to El, "You sound like you want your butt kicked. Is that what you want? And you think I can't do it because I have this baby. I can easily find a place to set him down. Keep messing with me." She say to Mr. Paul: "You haven't caused trouble. We just don't believe in cheating. A man can't get ahead by riding another man's back, that's what I've always been told."

"Last thing I'd mean to do is cause a disturbance," Mr. Paul say again. "I'm simply trying to give El and Pepper the upper hand."

The next morning, Rena was in the kitchen, nursing her baby. She had that towel throwed over her shoulder. Mr. Paul came in, hesitating at first.

"I don't mean to interrupt," he say.

"I'm nearly done," Rena say. She twisted so she could pull Jamie away and a trickle of milk spilled from his mouth. His cheeks just kept on sucking, unaware that the breast was gone.

Mr. Paul sat down next to Rena. I handed him a plate and he sat there dabbling at his food. Don't think he cared for it at all, but he dabbled to be polite, talking more than eating. "It's my experience," he say, in that squeaky voice, "that some young mothers these days don't work so hard on their young ones. Don't keep them smelling as good as yours. And, you know another thing I notice, that baby never cries."

Rena say, "Oh, he cries enough."

Mr. Paul say, "I listen at night for that boy to cry and he don't make a sound. And I'm a light sleeper, too. I have always been a light sleeper. Sometimes I wake up from the heat and walk 'round just to get comfortable. I listen for that baby boy, but I don't hear a thing." Mr. Paul stirred his fork 'round in his plate and burped loud and ignorant, like he was alone and he was the one that just finished eating, not that baby.

Rena say to me: "Mr. Paul was nice enough last night to listen in for Jamie when I came down here to the party and then later when I went dancing at the Blue Flame. Sweet Alma was going to watch him, but she went dancing with me. I haven't danced this much in years."

I turn 'round to look at her.

Mr. Paul say, "Oh, it wasn't no trouble. I don't mind at all. I must admit, though, I had my trepidations 'bout looking in on such a little fellow. But, by golly, he's a mannerable little guy. You'd never know he was up there."

I turned back to the stove.

Mr. Paul say to Rena in a low voice—not low enough so I couldn't hear it but low enough so that it was supposed to be a signal to me not to listen—he say, "Tell me something, Rena, ain't there a lot black folk down at that Blue Flame? You must not mind going down there and sticking out like a dollop of cream in all that black coffee. At least at the party last night there was white folks around here." He laughs to hisself. "So tell me how a woman like yourself, without a husband on her arm, come to be involved in this festival? Isn't this the E-MAN-cipation Festival for black folks?"

Rena didn't answer on account of being embarrassed. I didn't turn 'round. I kept scrubbing on the nasty grease spot on the stove under the back iron that flares up every now and then when the stove gets good and hot.

"That's not to say anything wrong with congregating with black folks. No, I don't want to leave that impression. Look at me, I sure am having a fine, fine time. I just may come back next year." He laughed again. "Well, good morning, miss."

I turned 'round. Sweet Alma was standing at the foot of the stairs.

She walked in yawning and grabbing little Jamie.

Rena say, "Be careful, he may spit up on you."

Sweet Alma lobbed him over her shoulder, petting his back real light. "He won't spit up on me. And if he does, it's okay."

She rocked him like he was a play toy and he seemed just as at home in her arms as he was in his mama's. She petted him some more and he let out a burp like a grown man like that Mr. Paul. She put him back in the crook of her arm and he just smiled at her as she smiled at him.

Mr. Paul say, "Look like you ready for a whole litter of babies. After you finish law school, that is. I hear you're going to be a big-shot lady lawyer."

"A lawyer will be good enough," Sweet Alma say, looking down at that baby.

"How many children you want?"

"If you must know," Sweet Alma say, "I don't want any." Little Jamie's finger wrapped 'round hers and she kissed it real light.

"You don't want no babies?" Mr. Paul say. He looked at me, turning back to Rena. "What you say? You young enough to have a whole passel of babies. And you don't want none? You'll change your mind when you get married."

"Who says I want to get married?"

"Oh, that's what you say now. What's that they say 'bout youth being wasted on the young? But you won't stay young for long. I bet you'll have a whole passel of little crumb snatchers. You mark my words. My old grandmother would look at you and say you got the kinda hips that's good for bearing babies. Got wide, strong hips."

"Pardon me." Sweet Alma stood with the baby in her arms. "Mr. Paul, you just open your mouth and all kinds of shit comes out, doesn't it?"

Rena say, "Sweet Alma!"

Mr. Paul say, "I beg your pardon, miss. I'm not meaning no harm. I just think it'll be a shame if you don't have no babies. That's all. Look at you with little Jamie. Look at how you hold him and how he look back at you. Sure would be—what you people like to say—a sin and a shame if you don't have some of your own."

. . .

When I think back on it, it seem near impossible to believe that little nothing ass of a man was in this house only three days and, in that little time, raised so much sand. Seem near impossible that one person, one single solitary person, could cause so much havoc.

Well, later that evening Aunt Cora and May Ruth was at the fairgrounds minding our Victuals table. Thelma was fixing on them no-taste finger sandwiches of hers under the tent, which we kept up an extra day. Sis was waiting on Thelma to finish so Sis could ride her and them sandwiches over to the fairgrounds.

I was sitting in the kitchen, tearing the greens from the stalks. I'd done made it through a couple of bags when, not long after that, Rena came running down the back steps into the kitchen.

"I'm going out," Rena say. "You don't have to worry 'bout li'l Jamie 'cause I've asked Sweet Alma to take care of him until he falls asleep. Then Mr. Paul will look in on him if it's necessary."

"Rena," I say. "You sure you feel comfortable leaving that baby with a stranger?"

"Mr. Paul has watched him for the last couple of nights and both have been just fine," she say, heading toward the door and lotioning her hands, leaving the smell. "I don't even consider Mr. Paul a stranger anymore. Not that he isn't a little strange. He's almost like a crazy uncle. And I've got loads of them."

"I'll make sure Sweet Alma go up there to check on Jamie, too. I'll make sure of that."

Rena didn't hear the half of it 'cause all the while she was headed down the hall, out the door.

I was down in the kitchen for a good long time, trying to help Sis with the rest of them collards. El and Pepper wandered in, after a while. Then Mr. Paul came. He made a few words of conversation before heading up the steps. Sweet Alma came in with that baby on her hip. She took him upstairs, then after a while she came back down and got on the telephone. She propped her feet up on the desk next to the typewriter and her transistor, which was playing low. She was laughing and talking.

I watched two shows on the television, full to the end. I pulled 'bout five more bags' worth of collards, dipping them in and out of so much water my fingertips didn't know whether to stay wrinkled or not. I peeped over into the hall and held up a handful of greens so Sweet Alma could get the hint to cut the yapping and help me. But she kept on yapping.

Finally I grabbed me a nice cold watermelon from the fridgerator. The house was as quiet as it wanted to be. Nothing stirring.

Then just as I slid the knife through the watermelon and started pulling it apart, I heard—me and Sweet Alma both heard—this loud crack. For a second I thought it was the watermelon cracking open. It was cold enough. And fresh, too. But the sound grabbed hold of the house and I think just shook it. Sounded like a heavy piece of dry oak breaking in two. Woulda sounded like the house settling if it wasn't so loud. Then we heard a thump.

"Pepper?" I say. "El?"

Sweet Alma pushed back from the phone desk to look in the kitchen at me. I shrugged 'cause I didn't have the slightest notion what the noise was. I figured since them boys ain't screaming, or running toward us, they must be okay. So I went back to my watermelon and them collards. Sweet Alma went back to her phone call. Neither one us paid that racket no never mind. Them boys was always running and falling all over themselves.

A few minutes later, El was standing on the bottom step of the back staircase. He was holding little Jamie 'round the waist so the baby was hanging like a sack of potatoes. Look like all the blood was draining from his little face. His arms was flung back.

El was shuffling, too, from one foot to the other, mouth open but not letting out a sound.

I say, "Boy, what's wrong with you, coming down here, holding that baby all crazy like that? You gone strangle him to death." I got up and grabbed the baby myself. "That ain't no way to hold a little fellow."

El didn't say nothing. It was like his mouth was wadded up. He just kept shuffling them big feet like he was some deaf mute or some dummy. Like he was confused. I walked over to him. Sweat was running in his eyes, but he didn't even have sense enough to blink it out.

I say, "El?"

He swallowed hard.

"El?" I say again, but louder.

With me calling his name so and that baby starting to stir, Sweet Alma say, "I got to go." She placed the receiver down, but it didn't fall right. She wheeled the phone chair into the kitchen, stopping at the table. Then she wheeled over to that boy. "El," she say. "What's wrong with you? Stop acting like a fool."

He say, "I think Mr. Paul is dead."

"El, stop playing," Sweet Alma say again.

He say, "I ain't playing. I think Mr. Paul dead."

I say, "You take care of these kids, Sweet Alma. I'm going upstairs."

As I broached the steps, I heard Sweet Alma say she was coming, too. And she tried to get El to come, but he wouldn't. He started to cry and say, "You can't make me go back up. Man, you can't make me." I could hear them pulling and tugging on each other, scuffling on the steps. That baby was crying, too.

"Pepper?" I yell for him. I started to hurry 'cause, naturally, at that point I was worried 'bout my boy.

Soon as I got to the third floor, I could see Pepper standing in the doorway with his arms folded. Pepper looked 'round at me, then looked back into the room.

I took one step in and that was when I saw Mr. Paul, laid out on the floor, holding his head with both hands. Head looked like it was beat pretty good according to that purple knot, which had done muscled up out of his scalp. He was moaning. I could barely hear it.

He say, "I'm gone kill that li'l nigger for hitting me. I'm gone kill him."

That white shirt of his had done turned red with blood. Sweet Alma followed so close behind me that I couldn't push her back fast enough. Sweet Alma had that baby in her arms, and when she saw Mr. Paul, she gasped real loud and held the baby tighter.

"I'm gone kill him," he say again.

"What the hell done happened here?" I say. I hurried to get Mr. Paul's pillows and covers off the bed to prop his head up. "What the hell done happened here?"

Pepper didn't offer up a word.

I kneeled down to look at Mr. Paul's head. I reached for his telephone, and when I reached 'cross the bed, I saw the bloody baseball bat that was on the floor beside the bed. I picked up the receiver to call the ambulance and I happened to kneel closer and that was when I saw Mr. Paul's fly. I put the receiver down. Even though Mr. Paul's shirt was buttoned right, his tie still straight 'round his neck, his shoes still shining, his fly was wide open and his shriveled-up self was hanging out the side.

"Sweet Alma," I say. She still had her hand 'gainst her mouth. "Sweet Alma, I want you to hear what I say now. You take that baby and go on downstairs, you hear me? Pep gone come down in a minute." I nudge her along. "You take that baby. Go on, now. Go on."

Sweet Alma saw that boy's blanket and wrapped him up even though that heat on that third floor was a natural man. She left for downstairs.

I was still kneeling over Mr. Paul when I asked Pepper what happened. He say in his ordinary way, "You don't wanna know."

"If I didn't wanna know, damn it to hell, I wouldn't be asking, now, would I? Talk to me, Pepper. Why this man bleeding? Why he exposed like this? Why he threatening to kill somebody?"

Pepper looked at me mean and say something on the order:

"I was tired of El, so I came up here to get me some rest. I brought me up a book to read and a sandwich, too, and I went into the alcove under the bookcase. It's cool down there and I could get me some rest. The baby started to cry and Mr. Paul went to Miss Rena's room to get him. Mr. Paul didn't see me 'cause I was tucked into the alcove. He went in that room, talking real nice to the baby. 'Now, now, junior. Now, now.' All nice and everything. He in there for a while, till the baby calms down. Then I see him walking pass again with the baby on his shoulder, taking him back to his room. I finished up my sandwich and started reading again. But by then El done found me. I told him I didn't feel like being found. He wouldn't listen. And he said he was gone sit out there in the hall with his bat till I came out to test the ball he done wet up, so we can see if Mr. Paul was telling the truth. I ignore El and he comes back over and say, 'Pepper, I hear something funny.' I go over there with him and I listen, too. I hear something funny, too. I hear grunting or laughing. El and me go over to Mr. Paul's door and Mr. Paul ain't paying no attention to us. He in there with that baby. Baby laying on his lap. So I pushed El back so he don't see what I see. I grab El's bat and I swing as hard as I can so I can get him to stop. I swing as hard as I can upside his head."

I lay my hand on Pepper's arm and told him to go on downstairs.

I waited till Pepper was clear out of sight before I reached down and pulled Mr. Paul up by his shoulders. Blood was everywhere. Despite all this, he was still awares, barely.

"I despise your kind," I say to him. I ratcheted his arm up real good and grabbed for his jacket, his wallet, and anything else I could get fast enough. I made him fix hisself up to respectable. "You take and take. You take from a little innocent who ain't even old enough to scream when things ain't right."

I lead him down the front steps so them chil'ren didn't have to see him no more.

"We can wait for the police right in your truck. I'm gone take my time callin', and hopefully you'll be dead by the time they get here. And if you think about 'killing' anybody, I'll handle you myself."

Mr. Paul didn't say nothing. He was studying too hard on his head.

I placed Mr. Paul in his cabin and left him there. I went back inside and called the sheriff. I tried to get Rena at the Blue Flame, but I just kept getting put on hold.

I waited on the porch till the sheriff came to cart him away.

When they got here, I explained what happened, as far as I know. They talked to Pepper and El for a good while to get things straight. We all talked on that porch, then we went up into that room. We talked some more.

When the police had done left, that truck was still sitting in the driveway, big as it pleased. I went back up to that third floor and I filled a bucket with water. I got down on my knees to scrub the blood up. Most of it came up fairly quick enough. The rest, it seemed, the onliest way to get rid of it, was to press it further into the grain. Just so you didn't have to see it no more. I stripped the bed of its sheets and covers; put everything in bags. I emptied drawers of underwear, disturbing everything of its nice neat rows and folds. I tore down night-clothes that hung in the closet along with three suits and white shirts. I bagged it all up. Didn't want anything left of him.

I would burn all of it when everybody went to sleep.

But for right then, I tied everything up good and tight and started downstairs. I got to the second floor and I heard Sweet Alma in the hall bathroom. Water was filling in the tub. She was crying and checking the baby over. He lay down on a towel spread out on the floor. When the water was ready, she lowered him into that water nice and slowlike. She busied herself soaping up a face rag real good while singing, "Hush, little baby. Hush, little baby." Wasn't no need for singing "hush" on account of him not saying nothing. She was the one doing all the crying. "Hush, little baby," she just kept singing, though, and it seemed like he was enjoying hisself well enough. He just kicked them little feet of his. When the rag got into a good lather, Sweet Alma laid it on the baby's head, his face, all over, washing him from head to toe. Dipping him in that water and soaping him up again. Dipping him and soaking him.

When I got back downstairs, I placed the bags by the door. And got on that telephone again. I took the phone back into the kitchen so I could sit down at the table in there. From where I was sitting, it was a straight shot to the opened front door. Pepper and El sat on the porch. El was standing on the top step leaning against the banister, wrapping hisself 'round the spindles. One of his paper-clip bridges linked the two rails and caught the porch light. Pepper paced back and forth in front of the door, watching me, watching over his shoulder at that truck.

"I guess you a hero, Pep!" I yell out to him while I'm on hold with the Blue Flame.

"I ain't no hero," Pepper say.

"Oh, yes you are," I say. "I don't think I been this proud of you ever in my life. Man, you the man of the hour."

El say, "Why did Mr. Paul do what he did, Pep?"

Pep say, "How the hell I'm s'pose to know."

"My son the hero," I say again, holding on the line.

El say, "You think he dead?"

"Nope. You saw them police talking to him, didn't you? You think they talk to the dead?"

"Oh, yeah," El say, like he was remembering. "You think he's coming back?"

Pepper say, "He ain't coming back." Pepper stopped at the door to look at me sitting at the kitchen table. "You don't have to worry 'bout that."

El swung hisself 'cross that banister, balancing on the edge. Them big fireflies skipped 'cross they heads and into the black beyond. "I sure hope he don't come back," El say. "I never want to see him again. Never."

"He ain't coming back," Pepper say. "You don't have to worry none 'bout that. He ain't coming back."

Sweet Alma came down with that baby boy in her arms. Pepper walked over to the door like he was pulled there, watching her walking and singing to that baby. Li'l Jamie's finger curled 'round hers. Sweet Alma had that boy going from the living room into the dining room into the kitchen. Pepper stood at the door, looking inside, watching her.

At the kitchen table, watermelon juice was running on my legs, dripping onto the floor. It hit me that I was still holding on when I heard Rena's voice on the other end. I didn't quite know what to say at first.

So all I managed to say was that Mr. Paul had to leave and she had to hurry and come back to her son.

When the timer on the stove rings, I nearly jump out of my skin.

Sis stirs but not enough to wake up. I wipe sweat from her forehead with the back of my hand. Then I take the apron from the wall hook and lay it crossways 'gainst her back.

Ain't no sense in trying to wake her right now. If that timer didn't do it, I sho' can't. Before long, she'll clean herself up and I'll come back later and clean the kitchen and nobody'll know the meat got scorched, or her cigarette run down to ashes. Soon everything will be righted again and looking presentable.

I close the window.

I check the knobs on the stove to make sure ain't nothing on. I check the spigots over the sink to make sure the water is turned off. I start back upstairs when I'm stopped by a swooshing sound. I look 'round till my eyes fall on that bucket beside Sis's legs. In her stirring, she musta kicked it, and now loose collards slop against its walls, rising and falling in the salt water.

Salt water always been known to draw out the worst in things.

To draw out all you can't see straight forward.

Things you know is there but can't put a finger on directly. Things you'd prefer to forget 'bout between them folds.

Then the next thing you know the water unsettles the earth and the grit betwixt them leaves, coaxing out every speckle and every bit of rock and dust and sand till it all floats up to the surface.

Sho' ain't much better for that than salt water. Not that I've seen.

Day Three

Florence Johnson Penticott
LATE SPRING

In the late spring, after the rains, the catalpa trees bloom.

White flowers with deep purple centers burst forth across the countryside and can be seen for miles, up and down the hills, along the banks of the river and Old Riley.

Cora says that Halley's first catalpas were planted along the river by a slave woman brought up in the 1840s on a lease. She served as one of the many water girls for the workers—enslaved black men and free Irishmen—carving out Halley's six miles of the Edison Trading Company Canal.

Legend has it that when the slave woman was down South, she created the most beautiful grove of catalpas. And on the day she was to leave, an overseer snatched her up before she could say good-bye to her children. All she had on her person was a handful of catalpa seed pods, which she'd stored away in a secret pocket in her dress.

To this day, I look out on all those beautiful trees and I can't help but wonder how wrenching it must have been to stand on free soil. Planting on it. Cultivating it. How wrenching, knowing that with her babies left behind, no soil could ever be truly free without them.

Flossie

SUNDAY, AUGUST 5, 1973

It was the time of morning when shadows were barely possible. That morning, I decided to leave Solomon. Though I would return to get my fourteen-year-old, at that moment, I was leaving Sweet Alma, too. I awoke with a strong taste for solitude, for quiet, for peace of mind.

For the longest time, I lay in bed, staring up at a darkened ceiling as if cracks and sweat circles could give me some semblance of direction. Below our bedroom, the night dispatcher's radio buzzed and crackled. After five months in Halley, I'd grown accustomed to the noise. Now, the sound sunk, like needles, into my temples. By that time on a Sunday morning, very few of Halley's residents needed cabs. The exception was the stragglers down at the Blue Flame. Every now and then I could hear Billy calling a driver for a fare, shuffling back and forth between the office and the adjacent bathroom every time a call interrupted him. (The sound of flushing can be traveling music when you're wading through self-pity and all kinds of crap, losing the battle to stay afloat.)

Solomon's side of the bed was undisturbed. There was a time when I wouldn't have been able to walk away from Solomon Penticott, despite all his little indiscretions. There was a time when, in leaving, I wouldn't have been able to take one last glance at our bed. In the darkness, I would have imagined us lying there: his body sprawled across the covers, his back wide and glistening; one arm dangling over the side, the other pressing me against him. The sight of us, the smell of him, would have stilled me. Instead of leaving, I would have found myself, years later, standing in his kitchen, stirring in his pots and rocking my own regrets.

I got up and quickly showered.

I threw on the first skirt and blouse I could find. I gathered my savings, which had bottomed out at about fifty-five dollars because I'd been dipping into it to stretch meals. Solomon kept his uncle Arthur's pistol in the back of the closet, shoved into a pair of work boots. When I found it, I placed it in my purse. I put on the gold watch he'd given me for our tenth anniversary. He had won it in a poker game.

I left the bedroom.

At the end of the hall, Sweet Alma lay on the pull-out bed in the living room. Stale gasoline air drifted up from the garage, billowing the sheets and nudging at a corner of wallpaper that sagged over her head. My daughter was tangled up in the bedsheet. One single white sheet wound securely about her legs, thighs, and midsection, which, itself, in a few months would begin to tighten around her. And all the world would know the little secret my fourteen-year-old had successfully hidden from me until just hours before.

For now she would be in good hands with her father, when he returned.

Downstairs, Billy was in his office. Black-dye sweat poured from his temples as he sat hunched over a paper basket of steamy fried chicken. Every now and then he looked up at the two stacked televisions by the door. One offered sound but no picture; the other a picture but no sound. The station was signing off for the morning.

Standing in the doorway to his office, I cleared my throat.

"Miss Penticott." He fumbled with the basket and then remembered a tall brown paper bag that was sitting next to it. I looked away so he could hide his liquor. "What you doing up this time of mornin', ma'am?"

"Billy, is there a car available? Out back maybe? I can't seem to find the spare. I want to borrow it for a minute. I'll be right back." I was sure he could tell I was lying.

"I let Wilson take the spare home with him," Billy said, licking his fingers. "Blue Flame just closed. I had him run over and get me some food before everything shut down. I told him to g'wan and take the car. I wasn't thinking there'd be no need for it this time of mornin'. Where you headed, Miss Penticott? It can't wait till Solomon get back? He due back from St. Louis tomorry."

I had no idea where I was headed.

As Billy's fan lifted the papers tacked to his wall, I stood there watching a group of flies dance around a Folgers coffee can of sugar water before spiraling in to their deaths. I felt light-headed.

I sat for a moment in the off-balanced leather swivel chair by the door.

Earlier that spring, one of Solomon's friends had convinced him to take up selling life insurance for Supreme Liberty Life, a black-owned insurance company. He would sell five-hundred-dollar industrial life policies, a nickel due every Saturday for the insured (preferably, one who hailed from a prolific family, for repeat business's sake). Insurance, Solomon's friend said, allowed you to make ends meet by turning in the minimum amount by the end of the week, and saving a bit for your own bills, then replacing that for the next week.

Maybe selling insurance wouldn't have been so bad if the timing hadn't been so bad. Solomon had had to take the state licensing exam twice. By the time he passed in late February, we were already two months behind on our mortgage payments. So the celebration was tempered by the reality that his first solo day out, he had to hit the ground running. There was no room for making mistakes or listening to sad stories about why people couldn't afford to buy. People had to buy.

Well, unfortunately, nobody thought much about dying. Or maybe they were too busy trying to figure out living that they didn't have time to consider how their "family would get by in the event of their untimely demise." Solomon heard all the excuses. There were those who unabashedly didn't give a damn whether their kin would have to plop them in some potter's field and then fend for themselves; and others who always deferred to next Friday, payday, which no matter how early on Friday evening Solomon arrived, already had passed; and still others who waved him off, claiming to have been duped one too many times by white *assurance* agents, mostly those selling burial insurance, who'd taken their money and left them with policies worth little more than the paper they were printed on.

Each day, Solomon started earlier and earlier and stayed out later, but we simply ran out of time.

That March the bank began foreclosure on our house, a tiny Georgian that we'd lived in for just over a year. When the man came to the door to deliver the news, Solomon cursed him and went out to the backyard, leaned into his hands, and cried.

On the day we left our home, his insurance license and papers littered the alley with the other garbage. He pulled the car he had borrowed around to the front of the house and hitched a trailer with our things.

I walked through the house one last time under the guise of making certain we had remembered everything. The walls needed painting, badly. There were other repairs that we hadn't been able to afford. Bushes needed to be replanted, flowers rebedded. Beyond that, there were things I'd wanted to change when we'd first moved in that I had learned to live with. The sallow gray carpeting in the foyer, for example, had been the first thing on my list to go. Now, though still worn, it was outstaying us.

I suppose Billy got tired of waiting on my answer.

"Hold on, hold on, Miss Flossie." Billy dabbed at his mouth and his neck with a worn silk handkerchief. "Wait here; maybe I can call somebody to run you where you need to go."

When Billy left, I walked over to his desk and searched out that brown paper sack that he'd hidden in a side drawer. I stuffed it into my purse and I sneaked out of the garage.

Outside, a thick fog hung over the river. Old Riley offered little more than a stretch of darkness with just-awakening hues. In the opposite direction, the lights shone in Greater Faith's sanctuary. Everything else was dark. All of the businesses were closed, shades pulled, curtains drawn, on the first and second floors.

I began to walk the three blocks toward the church. My footsteps surrounded me. But as I got closer to Greater Faith, I could hear moaning coming from the sanctuary. I walked up the steps and entered the first set of doors. The moaning was low at times, barely audible. It sounded like a child crying. Looking through the glass partitions in the second set of doors, I saw a woman at the end of the center aisle, at the altar. She was folded in half in prayer. I could only see her back. She wore a pink-and-white polka-dot dress with a broad white belt. White shoes. I almost felt like joining her up there in prayer. Only I wasn't sure what there was left to pray about. Finally, when the woman stood, I got a quick glimpse of her blond hair, her face. She was a white woman. That pissed me off at first. I wondered, What in the world does a white woman have to moan about? Then, as quickly as she stood, she stretched out on that altar, lying as though in sacrifice. Her moaning stopped.

I left the woman and walked around to the back of the church. I sat under a large tree. Sweet alyssum and daffodils encircled me and the smell lulled and rocked. In the foreground the back of the church stood nearly as stately as the front. The only part of the church that was stirring at that time of the morning was its heart, the basement where women filed back and forth past two windows. Pretty soon the smell of bacon and sausage was as distinct as the sounds of clanking pots and the women's voices.

It wasn't until I decided to pull out Billy's brown paper sack, wipe the opening with the hem of my skirt, and take a long hard swallow that Thelma appeared from the back door of the church.

Carrying a small bucket and a tray of glasses, she descended the stairs mumbling to herself, "Lord, I try to please that little woman. I try. I try."

I leaned around the tree so that she could see me.

"Flossie Jo?" she said, loudly at first. Quickly she lowered her voice. "You waiting on somebody?" The canal gurgled and fanned water over the limestone. The sound of laughter floated out of the basement window. "You hear that? I know those old biddies are in there having a time at my expense. That little woman, I swear before an honest God, just likes to make fun of me." As she sat, she lowered the bucket to the ground and sudsy water sloshed over the sides. She placed the tray on her lap. The glasses clinked like at a party.

"Do you know she wants me to wash all ten of these glasses again because one of them still got a little crust of milk at the bottom? Yes, indeedy. Made me bring every one of them out here to suds them up real good. Then she's got this steaming hot vat inside. I have to wear this rag on my head so my curls don't fall when I bend over the vat. It's got so much bleach in it, my hands peel like crazy. I asked her, 'How come I have to wash all the glasses a second time? Why can't I just wash this one glass?' Nobody told her to hold them up to the big light over the dining table, anyway. Nine times out of ten, if you do that, of course you're going to see a little speck of something. These glasses are the tallest in the kitchen. It's mighty difficult to reach all the way to the bottom. Do you know she got right in my face and said, 'These glasses are unacceptable, Thelma, honey. We must make them acceptable.'"

"Thelma," I said, "may I ask whom the *she* is you're referring to?" Thelma studied a second glass, holding it out in front of her.

"Aunt Cora, that's who. Who does she think she is? I fully know that she had a hand in raising me. But my mama is dead and I got children of my own who try to boss me far enough. Who says I got to be bossed any further? That Cora Hoskins is more particular than any white woman I've ever known in my life. Everything has to be just so. Napkins placed so the corners match right. Food spread on the plate so it doesn't look slopped. I told her, 'We ain't serving dignitaries. These just church folk.' And that's when she all but lost her mind. Said, 'We don't have to be serving dignitaries. We're serving human beings, not hogs, and that's enough for me.' The way that little woman jumped on me, you'd've thought I'd asked her to line parishioners up along a trough and force them to eat that way. Now everybody thinks I'm nasty just because I made a mistake and left a little dab of milk in a glass. When I was little everybody used to joke and say I was lazy. People I didn't even know would look at me and assume I was lazy or thought I considered myself too good for cleaning. Can you tell me what about me looks lazy?"

"Not a thing that I can see," I said.

After a short while, she dabbed at her face with her apron. She grabbed my wrist to look at my watch. "Girl, the baptismal service is held down by the river. Besides, you're too early. You got enough time to go back home and sleep for a good hour." She bent down to listen to the ticking. "I don't think this time is right."

I had begun to feel a sudden disengagement between my body and my head. And the way Thelma went on hadn't helped much, especially after my earlier indulgence. "I need some air, is all."

"You okay, Flossie? You don't look so good. I'm not used to seeing you looking half-assed, if you don't mind me saying. Now me, I often look half-assed. But I got all these kids and that old lady who worry me to death. Then there's Herbert. . . . I realize part of my problem today is that I'm wearing yellow. In fact, we both are, but it looks far better on you. Think about it: In the few months you've been here, you've never seen me in yellow. I don't normally wear it because Aunt Cora says it makes me look too sickly. Like I've been sucking persimmons or something. Now, blue, blue is my lucky color. It gives me good, sharp contrast."

"I'm just damned tired, honey. That's all. Damn, damn tired. I've decided to run away. From your brother and Miss Sweet Alma."

"Can't say I haven't felt that way a time or two. Yes, indeedy. It blows over after a while, though. Normally, for me, it blows over by the time I get down to our front fence and I realize the few steps behind me is far shorter than the long road ahead without my boys. Children need their mother. Yes, indeedy. I know that firsthand." She looked down at my purse and saw Billy's bag. I hadn't shoved the bottle in deeply enough. She looked up toward the door, then pointed to the bottle. "You mind, girl?"

"I don't mind if you don't mind going back in there with it on your breath."

"I don't normally take a nip, but I could sure use something this morning. When Pepper was a baby, though, his crying was always about to drive me to the crazy house. To get

him to quiet down, I used to slide a little whiskey on his gums.
I would take a little for myself, too, truth be told. He and I
would sleep just as sound. The house could be falling down
and we wouldn't hear a thing."

Thelma took one of the glasses from the tray, blew in it to
clear away any undesirables, and poured the thin yellow liquid until it reached halfway up the side. "I wouldn't have
taken you for the kind that drinks this stuff," she said, taking
a sip. Her face twisted and she tilted her head to shake her ear
as though water had entered. By the third try, it seemed to go
down easier.

"When I was growing up," I said, looking over to her, "we
were taught to keep our business behind closed doors." I
paused. I paused only because it struck me that I had never
planned to say what I was about to say in this way. I had
wanted my daughter to tell me she was expecting her first
child. I had wanted us to cry tears of joy together. I had
planned to throw a party. And, in the middle of the evening, I
would get everybody to settle down to attention by tapping
some slinky crystal glass. I would call Sweet Alma and her
husband to my side and after much fanfare say, "I have an
announcement. I am about to become a grandmother." Then
I would deliver the news and we would all kiss and hug and
celebrate. Solomon's role in this fantasy had never quite man-
ifested itself.

I had wanted my daughter to have a nice picket fence to
lean on.

I turned to Thelma. "Your niece is going to have a baby.
She's fourteen years old and she's going to have a baby.
Unmarried, barely educated, barely alive . . ."

"Oh, Lord in heaven, " Thelma said. She gulped the rest of
her glass and handed me one, filling both. "I had Herbert Jr.
when I was eighteen. Thought I would die. That boy weighed
over ten pounds, all of it in his head. Shaped just like a watermelon, it felt like. And those blocky shoulders. He must have

sensed my discomfort, because he was nice enough to break his collarbone while coming out. That gave me some relief. It mended fine, but Lord, without it I would have been left wide open as a football field. And Aunt Cora used to tell me babies came from hollow logs. Now, that was the biggest lie I've ever heard." She patted my hand. "When'd you find out about Sweet Alma?"

"Last night, she was expecting me to be home extra late because I told her I would be cooking over at Sister Lila's house. The kitchen in our apartment is too small to manage all that food. I told her not to wait up for me. I got home much earlier than I planned, about ten o'clock. And Sweet Alma was nowhere to be found. I called over to your place and Herbert said he hadn't seen her. I went down to the garage. No Sweet Alma. I walked back to the park. Then I decided to come home and wait for her. It's eleven o'clock, midnight, one o'clock, and finally I hear keys jingling outside the door. My Sweet Alma slinks in like she's fooling somebody. She's got her tennis shoes tied together and thrown over her shoulders; her clothes hang off her all funny and she's nearly falling out of that blouse she's wearing. I walked right over to her and asked her what she'd been doing. The where was no longer important. And then I look down at her belly and for some reason it's looking strange to me. Normally, Sweet Alma has the flattest stomach around. And now I see this little pouch that on anybody else would be unremarkable. I run to the window to look out. I see Delaware Matthews standing outside, talking to one of the drivers. I run back over to her and I grab her shoulders and pin her against the wall. 'Where have you been and what have you been doing and with whom?' I ask her. Miss Sweet Alma has the nerve to drop her eyes and say, 'Nothing,' like a damn two-year-old. I pull her blouse up and she says, 'Mama, I can explain. I think I'm going to have a baby like Gayl.' Gayl was her friend from home. Gayl was sent down South last summer. She returned pushing a baby carriage around our neighborhood. Last night Sweet Alma slunk and started to cry. I asked her if she was raped and she shook her head. I screamed, Thelma. I screamed until all of it shot through the top of my head. I said, 'Sweet Alma, you stupid. Stupid. Stupid little fool.' She started running down that hall. I chased her like some wild animal had gotten inside of me. I grabbed her neck and slammed her into the wall. All your nice little pictures fell around us. I can still feel my hands tingling from thumping her over and over against the wood. I've never touched her like that in my life. You have to believe me, Thelma. I have never touched my child like that, but in that moment, I thought I could kill her. I could have choked the life out of her to spare her from walking down this road. She's not even allowed to wear rouge and eye shadow, but she's about to have a baby. It's over for her now, Thelma. Once you become a mother at her age, it's so hard ever to be anything else. So goddamned hard. I talked and I talked to her. I begged her not to let anything like this happen. I talked and I talked. Let's see, what kind of mother can I be? I'm just now seeing her stomach. She's nearly five months pregnant, how could her own mother have no idea?"

Thelma placed her arm around me. "You weren't looking for it, Flossie. That's all. It's hard enough to see those things we *are* looking for, let alone the ones we aren't. Then sometimes things can be right in our faces and we can miss those, too. You don't know what to look out for when so much other stuff is coming your way. I know that brother of mine isn't acting right. I know that. I haven't said that I know. But I do. You almost want to squinch your eyes up real tight and not see any of it and hope it'll all go away. Sweet Alma name the father?"

"I just assumed it's that Delaware. He was with her last night. We've been here nearly five months. Any fool can figure this out. Even this fool. And to think, Delaware has been helping out so with my committee. I bet he was simply trying to get closer to Sweet Alma."

Thelma tapped the rim of her glass. I poured more of the wine inside my glass and hers. I swallowed and now it burned going down.

"Delaware?" Thelma pinched her cheeks. "Come to think about it, you know, there were rumors last year that there was this young woman he was spending a lot of time with. She was closer to his age, about nineteen or twenty years old. One minute her belly started to rise and the next it was on the way back down again, if you know what I mean?"

An early Sunday-school class had begun. Inside, we could hear little melodic voices reciting Scriptures.

"Did you know that when Sweet Alma was three years old she could read?"

"No, I didn't know that," Thelma said. "I can't say the same thing for her cousins. Each of them start out dumb as tree stumps. Luckily they get better as time progresses."

"I remember her sounding the letters out, her little pursed lips struggling to manage the words. And how we celebrated after each sentence. How proud she felt. How proud I was."

"Delaware?" Thelma said again.

I kept filling my glass until I fell asleep. Because my system wasn't accustomed to liquor and I hadn't truly slept that night, it didn't take much to send me on my way. I dreamed I was back at my elementary school in Chicago where I'd been a school social worker for the past twelve years. I dreamed some girl was standing at my door knocking and I could see her through the opaque glass, but I couldn't open the door no matter how I pulled and pulled.

Thelma woke me up. The glasses had fallen off her lap. Some were broken, others had rolled down the grass. "Oh, my God," she said. "If I look half as bad as you, I'm going to die. What time is it?"

I looked down at my watch, but I had no idea what it showed. She looked down at it, grabbing her head. She slipped out of her apron.

"Look at me. Herbert's due to come get me soon. He can't see me like this. Aunt Cora certainly can't see me like this. Those old biddies would have a time. I've got to go home and change clothes. I've got to get the boys in order. I've got to make myself presentable again." She turned away from me and toward the canal wall, which was now laden with dew and nearly reflective. Seeing a faint yellow figure in the limestone, she leaned toward it. "Oh, my God. There's a bus that should be arriving soon. I can take it home and come back here with Herbert. Herbert normally picks me up so I can go back home and get the boys ready. I'll just beat him to it. That's what I'll do." She took off running toward a gravel pathway that followed the side of the church, branched out under the wrought-iron arch, and opened out onto Old Riley and the bus stop.

My head was spinning as I watched her lope across the fairgrounds. I fell asleep again, and the second time I awoke it was to singing. To a baritone that I recognized right away as belonging to none other than Delaware Matthews even though it sounded like it was under water. "O Freedom. Freedom." My watch said six o'clock and I thought Delaware was in the sanctuary rehearsing. I knew the musicians were with him. But I thought surely there wouldn't be anyone else at that time of morning.

I dragged myself over to the back door of the church. I traveled through a labyrinth of halls until I arrived at the doors of the sanctuary.

Thelma was coming out of the bathroom, hanging on to the door. She was walking bent over and could barely stand without holding on to something.

"Didn't you just get on that bus?" I asked her. "What are you doing here?"

"I got on more than an hour ago, I think. When we crossed the bridge, I started feeling funny. I told the driver I had to throw up, so he let me off down by the river. And don't you know that man left me? He pulled right off and left me. I tried to chase after him, but he wouldn't stop. So I had to walk all the way back here. Yes, indeedy. I didn't think I was going to make it. I considered hitchhiking, but the streets are deserted. And look at me. I look a mess. Who would pick me up? My legs kept feeling like jelly. I don't know how I made it here. I was too embarrassed to stop by the cab place. Lord, the shame that would have caused. After this morning, those women already think I'm nasty because of those glasses. Imagine what they'd think if they got wind of me now. It's a good thing we can sneak out of the side door. Come on, Flossie, help me walk."

While Thelma talked, I watched Delaware singing, stretching his arms out. I swear I only saw Delaware. I'm told there was a full choir behind him. The pastor stood nearby on the pulpit. The congregation faced him. But my head was in a fog and I only saw Delaware. I saw him singing without a care in this world, as freely as a little bird. I thought, Why should he have a care? He wasn't going to have to change one diaper. Stay up late one night worrying about colic or a high fever. He wouldn't have to bandage one knee.

I walked over to the door.

Thelma whispered loudly, "Flossie, where are you going? Flossie? Flossie?"

I pushed opened the door and was as stunned as everybody else when it shattered, but I kept going down the center aisle.

I remember scrambling through my purse, feeling that bag of voodoo wine. I remember reaching for the gun and hearing, "Oh Lord, Sister Flossie. No, Sister Flossie. No, baby."

I remember turning toward the Mothers Board and trying to figure out when they came in. Then I looked around and the church was full. The loft was full, as was the choir, the pulpit. It was like in a dream when all of sudden a scenario changes and the dreamer simply adapts.

"In God's name," Delaware said. "What in God's name have I done to you?"

"Nothing in God's name, if I recall correctly. It's what you've done behind his back. I'm going to count to three, and if you haven't shown your face, then I'll just aim where I think is best. And after I hit you square in your ass, I'll tell everybody what you did."

"What, tell everybody?" Delaware said.

"I'll tell everybody. Tell God. The church. The minister. I'll tell everybody what you did."

The next thing I knew, the sun was going down. I lay stretched across the backseat of Herbert's car, staring out of the open window. The wind was so weak it barely rustled the tops of the trees.

When I tried to shift, black vinyl stuck to my thighs. Splashes of that liquor left stiff circles on my blouse, and the smell, as well as the car speeding up, slowing down, following the contours of Old Riley, did little to settle my stomach.

Thelma sat in the front next to Herbert. Her one arm was bent backward across the seat, holding a wet cloth against my forehead. Another cloth was affixed to her own forehead.

"Girl, this is a mess," she said when our eyes made contact. The car had turned up an incline and I was raising up trying to see. "You may as well turn back over and remain passed out for as long as you can. This day is done. No sense waking up to this mess."

"Now, Sis," Herbert said, "don't you listen to Thelma. Everything's gone be just fine."

When the car stopped, Herbert blew the horn. Thelma said, "Okay, you get the door and I'll carry her up the stairs."

"You can't carry Sis. How will it look for me to be walking empty-handed alongside my wife and she's the one carrying the heavy load? That ain't right."

"Herbert Jr.'s as heavy as she is," Thelma said. "And I carry him all the way to his room when he falls off under the porch."

"You ain't in no condition to be walking nowhere, let alone trying to carry somebody. Thought you still had that swimming in your own head from walking back to the church earlier this morning?"

"I'll take care of myself," I said, snatching the towel from Thelma and lifting up like I'd just crawled out of a gutter. They both looked over their shoulders. I looked out the window. "Where are we? Where are you taking me?"

"You're at Aunt Cora's house," Thelma said. "You've been here once or twice before, haven't you? Aunt Cora's made arrangements with Sheriff Lawton. She's a member of the county board and has run unopposed for the last twenty years. They love her down there and they trust her. So they listened when she told him she'd look after you over the holiday. Afterward the judge could decide whether he sees fit to go forward with charges. Didn't make any sense for you to have to stay locked up, Aunt Cora said, especially since nobody was hurt. And the pistol didn't have bullets."

"They must have found the wrong gun," I said, "because Solomon's gun always has bullets."

Herbert turned around. By then I was fidgeting with my shoes. The goal was to place each on the proper foot. "Now, Sis, I'm gone say this one time," he said. "Halley's Landing is a small, small town. Law works a little different sometimes in a small town. Way I see it, you can get yourself in a whole heap of trouble if you don't hush up that talk about bullets. Or you can listen and we can get beyond this thing." He scrunched around in his seat some more so I could see his face squarely.

"The pistol I fished out of that return didn't have a bullet in it, you understand me? And you ain't got to worry none about Delaware pressing no kind of charges. He owes me more than a few favors. And I explained to him that you've been under a lot of hardship lately and never intended to harm him. They may hit you with a disorderly or disturbing the peace. Something like that. But that's a whole lot different than attempted murder or outright murder. When things done calmed down, we can get your pistol back to you."

Thelma nodded, folding her cloth and repositioning it across her forehead.

I turned toward the house. It was a large white building with a dark green gabled roof and dark green shutters. The bottom portion was made of stone, and the second and third floors, clapboard. A first- and second-floor veranda wrapped around the front of the house. Tea roses wound around the banisters and, in some places, climbed the limestone. Dusk made the house lean forward as though in a curtsey.

A white woman was sitting on the porch.

Herbert said, "We gone leave you with May Ruth."

"May who?" I said.

"Now, don't you go tearing up your face. That's May Ruth. She good peoples. Come in every year for the festival. She don't stay too long, but she been coming 'round for some years now. She just like family. She don't bother nothing."

Thelma reached behind me to straighten my hair. Somehow she must have thought this would make me presentable. Then she licked her finger and started toward my face.

"Thelma, if you attempt to wipe spit across any part of my body, I will do you severe harm."

"But you got crust in your eyes and in the corners of your mouth."

"I don't care. Besides, look at yourself." She quietly withdrew.

I opened the door of the car, and when I tried to get out, my legs rolled from under me. Herbert ran around to pick me up. He carried me to a chair on the porch.

May Ruth held the back of the chair. "So this is Mrs. John Dillinger, I presume?" she said, smiling.

"What the hell does she mean by that?" I said to Herbert.

He didn't have time to answer. Thelma stumbled, catching herself on the bottom step. Herbert hurried over to her. He took a deep breath. "I told you to take it easy, Thelma. You still walking scatter-legged, baby. You got to take your time. I got strict orders to tote you back to the church, where you gone stay put for a while—if I have to tie you down."

"Whose orders?" Thelma sounded groggy.

"Aunt Cora's, that's who. Now, I told you, she wants you to come on down and help her with the dishes. Sis in good hands with May Ruth."

Herbert took Thelma's arm and she followed, sulking. "I'll see you in the morning, girl," she said over her shoulder. "I'm tired of doing dishes. I'm going to shrivel up and float away. Everybody always sees fit to run my life." She tried to pull her arm from Herbert. But he wouldn't let go. "I'll see *her* in the morning," she said to him.

"You two'll be off now," May Ruth said. "Mrs. Penticott will be all right with me. A sherry for both of us will get us off to a fine start."

Midway to the car, Herbert stopped as though he'd forgotten something. He leaned Thelma against a front post in case there was more swimming in her head. He walked back up the porch steps. I sat with my chin cupped in my hands.

"Sis, I just want to say that after all this has settled, don't you go feeling sorry yourself. You hear? You had the nerve to stand up in God's house and pull a gun out on a man before the largest congregation of the year. You summon up that same spirit now. Better people than you have made bigger fools of themselves. Don't you go thinking you'll be the topic of everybody's conversation long after sundown."

"Thanks, that's encouraging."

Herbert's pants puddled around his feet as he turned to walk away. He yanked on his pants and then on his wife's arm, peeling her from the post. They got in the car and pulled off down the drive.

"You know, dear heart," May Ruth said. "I've never really thought that much of Delaware. What a tight little knot he is, eh? He needed a touch of humbling, if I have anything to say about it. And I guess that's what he got a good dose of this morning."

I turned away from her, rolling my eyes.

"I hear you've run away from home, dear heart. Fancy that. Thelma tells everything. Not that it's her fault, really. She doesn't mean to. You know? I ran away once. Since then I have not looked back. That was roughly ten years ago. I was at the University of Illinois, not far from here, getting ready to begin the fall semester. I teach French Literature. Leroux, Balzac, Stendahl, those blokes. I was married to a rather boring professor of philosophy. His name was, and perhaps still is if blood continues to course through his veins, John Morgan Wainwright. What a dreadful bore he was. He belonged to one of those bloody genius fraternities, but he wasn't terribly clever. From the start, he wanted me to join the Ladies Aid Society and play auction bridge; or attend teas and brunches with state senators and the board of governors for the university. Can't you look at me and tell I abhor stuffiness? As well as those salty little nuts and gumdrops that accompany auction bridge. One night after a most god-awful dinner party, during which the conversation skidded from allegories of caves to talk about self-actualization and the elusiveness of freedom in a capitalistic society, I decided I couldn't stand another moment imprisoned in that house. By the time John Morgan slid into bed and covered his head, my decision was cemented. I went downstairs to put on a pot of boiling water while I wrote him a letter. Afterward I left. I drove about thirty miles before I stopped in Jaspar County. That ride was the most liberating of my life—I felt like flying in a wide-open airplane. I was planning on going to Chicago, but I must have taken a couple of very wrong turns, and somehow I ended up going south instead of north and landed here in Halley's Landing. It was during the 1961 festival. I reside out east now, but I haven't missed a festival since. In fact, I travel to festivals all over the world. Verona, Holland, Mount Fuji, Munich, Salzburg. Nothing compares to the Freedom Festival here in Halley. I, however, recently did find a new one in the Upper Peninsula that runs a close second. The natives there celebrate Thanksgiving with a Turkey Testicle Festival, if you can believe that turkeys have testicles. Well, just the male ones, obviously. The residents fry the testicles in deep batter and they're quite a delicacy. Do you fancy testicles—rather, traveling—dear heart?"

I didn't say anything.

"Perhaps that's a silly question, when one considers you're traveling at this very moment, aren't you?"

May Ruth stood and walked to the banister. At the foot of the property, down by the road, I could barely see a couple of children playing along the river and gulls lighting on a sandbar along a southern tip. Fireworks zoomed overhead, making the sky electric.

"I hear this is your first festival," May Ruth puttered onward. "Tomorrow the butterfly girls will march through the town serenading the homeowners. It's the most beautiful sound you'll ever hear. They sing a cappella and they have the most heavenly voices. Absolutely extraordinary. I remember the year Sweet Alma was a butterfly. Thelma and I helped make her wings. Lopsided as the wings were, your Sweet Alma still was the prettiest butterfly I've ever seen."

May Ruth walked over to the main door.

"Okay, now, I will burble on endlessly if someone doesn't put a stop to it. There is a fine breeze coming up from the south. Won't last too long. So you sit here and let it stir around you for a while, as they say. You'll start to feel like yourself again before long, dear heart. I promise you that. And never you mind your daughter. She most assuredly has wings. I'll go upstairs and open the windows to your room for some fresh air. The rooms are stifling hot and sticky this time of year. In the meantime, if the bugs get too troublesome for you, just press on some of that baking soda. That'll keep all the little critters at bay. And if they bite, we've got some jimsonweed and elm leaf. Cora says elm leaf makes the swelling go down."

Finally, May Ruth passed through the fixed blue line of the porch light, entering the house. The door clapped against the frame. I was so grateful for the solitude, I turned to watch her walk up the stairs. I could see her through the window. It dawned on me that May Ruth was the woman I saw earlier that morning. Even though I had only seen her for a second, I was certain she was the woman praying in the sanctuary.

12

Flossie

A wire-link fence followed the slope of the yard, separating Cora's property from that to the west. Rose hips and azaleas climbed through the metal links, but in dwindling numbers because they now were being strangled by brush and bramble. Only a few stark pink petals remained, reminding everybody that all along that fence their vines once dominated the area, before the soil conceded, allowing the weeds to take over. Yet you could still imagine the flowers, so prolific along that fence that when you looked over there, instead of a lattice of harsh metal, you saw life.

May Ruth's absence left me to my own thoughts, which probably wasn't good. At least her chattering was a distraction. I was beginning to feel a part of me retreating deep inside some black hole, where nothing existed except self-pity and blame and wanting. I wanted to cry, but I couldn't muster the energy. Same with screaming, though I'd done quite a bit of that with Sweet Alma. It wasn't that I couldn't move; there simply wasn't much reason to. It wasn't that I no longer knew where I was, I just didn't want to be anywhere particular. I craved stillness. I wanted the wind to stop. I wanted time to stop and turn backward. Juvenile, I know, but that's how I felt. The peace I had longed for earlier that day, that I had set out for, seemed more distant now than ever. I longed for my own room, where I could shut the doors, draw all the curtains, and, even if only for a short time, lock out Solomon, Sweet Alma, God. Lock out the last year, or the fourteen before that, or as many as I chose. I wanted order restored and I was at a lost as to how even to begin.

May Ruth returned to the screened door. She offered me a glass, and when I didn't reach for it, she placed it on a round table. The glass sat next to a service of lemonade that already was attracting flies.

"Oh, dear, I forgot to draw your bath," she said. "You're going to simply adore the room I've chosen for you. It's right above our heads and overlooks the yard and the river, which you seem to have taken a liking to." A cannon sounds. I jump. May Ruth places her hand on my shoulder. "Don't be alarmed," she said. "All that bloody bombing is the truly treacherous way the town of Halley scares its gulls. About a couple of years ago, one Viola Miller, next door, proposed decorating a portion of the canal by luring a handful of seagulls from Bell Harbor. She lured them with sorghum and expected a few to roost on ledges of ivy near the park. What she got was hordes of birds. Virtually a stampede. And two years hence, they continue to come. Only now they're lured by the hatching moths, nesting in the infield. I keep telling people that it's not their fault that they come. Every year, I explain how inhumane it is to sound those bloody cannons, but nobody listens. They're only concerned about how the birds flap about the fairgrounds, leaving white splat marks all over the amusement rides, the bandstand, the bleachers, and the trees; and the holes they peck in the tents. It's all a dreadful mess. Anyway, dear heart, give me five minutes and take the stairs to the first landing, turn left, and walk straight ahead. I know you'll be most comfortable in your room."

She left for a while only to return. "Are you all right, dear heart?" May Ruth asked, stepping back out onto the porch.

I didn't answer and she pulled her chair beside me. Twice she reached over to hold my hand, to rub my knee for comfort. She hummed and tapped her glass.

When Herbert's car was coming up the drive, May Ruth left her chair to meet the car.

"She won't utter a word," I could hear her saying to Cora through her lowered window. Herbert got out of the car to help Cora get out. Then he removed two heavily foiled trays and a brown paper bag from the trunk. May Ruth took a tray from Herbert. "Perhaps she's had some kind of temporary breakdown or something."

"Black folks ain't got no time for no breakdowns, May Ruth. That's what I keep trying to tell Thelma."

At this Thelma, who lay sprawled across the backseat, raised up. Her hair was smushed against her face. Wiping her eyes, she got out of the car and ran up the porch stairs. She kneeled to look into my eyes. Hers widened.

"Flossie Jo! Flossie Jo!"

"Pipe down, Thelma," Herbert said, rushing up behind her. "She ain't gone deaf." To me he said, "Sis? You doing okay this evening? We got all this good food for our big party tomorrow. Aunt Cora throws a party every year, a few days before the goings-on."

Thelma stood and turned to May Ruth, who now was standing on the bottom step. "What've you done to her, May Ruth? I leave her here with you, under your watch, and look what you've done to her."

"I haven't done a thing, Thelma. Cora, honestly, I haven't."

The four of them formed a short arc in front of me. Cora, May Ruth, and Herbert stood. Thelma sat down beside me, legs crossed, alternating between measuring my temperature with the back of her hand and comparing it with that of her own forehead, and scowling up at May Ruth, who said again, "Thelma, I have done nothing wrong. I assure you."

"Sweet Alma's fine, honey," Thelma said to me. "She's going to spend the night with us. She's with the boys right now. She was a little hang-backish at first because of this morning, but Herbert went and got her, talked to her, and she joined the crowd just fine." Thelma paused, patting herself down, searching her pockets. "You know what? Your collards have been nominated for a prize in the vegetables category. Sure have. I accepted the nomination on your behalf." Thelma's voice rose an octave. "Nobody mumbled one word about what happened this morning at the church. Not in my presence, at least. If that's what's got you all clammed up. If that's what you're wondering. Is that what you're wondering about, Flossie? Those busybodies aren't gossiping or nothing, like you might think they are. In fact, after Esther and Benjamin Knowles had their annual fight in the middle of the baseball field, everybody went on with their own business. Didn't they, Herbert?"

Herbert didn't answer. I could hear him fidgeting with the change in his pockets. He pulled out a handkerchief and wiped his forehead.

Down on Old Riley, two cars peeled past, drag racing. Their engines roared as they zipped in front of the house and kept going down the street. We each listened for them to take the bend about a quarter of a mile down, wondering if they'd go sailing into the river. But they made it just fine.

When that was over, Thelma crooked her mouth sideways to Cora. "You think we should contact the nervous hospital?" she asked.

"Shush now, Thelma," Cora said. "There won't be a need for any such foolishness. This child just needs to rest, is all. She's had quite a day. Herbert, you carry her upstairs. Thelma, you get her undressed and help her into a nice tepid bath. Everything's going to be just fine."

· · ·

Herbert lowered me onto a sleigh bed and turned on a ceiling fan. Gently he placed his hand on my shoulder and left it there long enough that I thought I would cry. But I didn't. I just sat there until he left the room.

In keeping with the rest of the house, the bedroom was rather large. A dresser with a mirror was next to the bed. Across the room, on the wall facing the bed, was a fireplace, an armoire, and, adjacent to them, a sofa, a coffee table, on top of which were two ashtrays and a hooded hair dryer, and a waist-high bookcase, holding three rows of books. And on the wall opposite the door were windows and a French door leading out to the veranda. With all of this, the room still felt wide open.

Thelma entered and began removing my clothes, lifting my feet and taking one shoe off after the other, then placing them in a corner by the dresser.

"You know," she said—she caught a glimpse of herself in the mirror and stopped to fluff her hair; to pinch and slap her cheeks—"sometimes I don't feel much like talking either. No, Lord. Sometimes I, too, just want to stare off into the Great Beyond and give my mind a chance to idle for a while—Herbert says it idles well enough on its own without me concentrating much on it. I don't listen to him, though. I truly believe that if I can get just two minutes of quiet, then when I wake up I can solve every one of my problems. With just two minutes, I could figure out how to make it so my panty hose won't sag in the crotch; my fried chicken won't come out soggy; the boys' feet won't grow so fast and they'd learn to play clean games so I won't have to be toting laundry all the days of my life. But, no, indeedy. Herbert and those boys never give me enough time to chase my thoughts. Seems like when I can snatch me a moment for a breakdown, somebody comes along and snatches it right back." Her voice got high-pitched again. "You should have seen Sweet Alma in her little sailor outfit. She looked just fine. You couldn't tell at all that she's expecting. Nobody was the wiser." She glanced down at my skirt, then picked up the hem and placed it back, throwing both hands up to her mouth. "Did you know your skirt is on inside out? Well, I'll be darned. Your skirt is plumb backward, Flossie Jo. Surely, you didn't know or you would have changed it, right? Have you had it on that way all day? Poor thing, have you been walking around with it that way all day? Well, you just wait right here and rest your mind until I freshen up your bath. I'll be back in a second to finish taking off your clothes. You just try to relax until I come back."

Thelma left the room and the white sheer curtains leading out to the balcony ballooned. Pipes clanked and squeaked as water poured from the faucet.

I finished undressing myself and walked over to the bathroom door. Thelma smiled. "I just knew you weren't ready for the nervous hospital. I just knew it." She pulled my hair back, looping a rubber band around it. I stepped in the tub and she handed me a large sponge and a bar of soap. I began to wash my back, then my arms, slowing at my wedding band, which I removed and placed in the soap dish. Thelma took the sponge over to the face basin to rinse it, and as I always do in a bath, I slid down so that the water flowed over my shoulders, covered my neck. I lay back so that soon even my face was submerged, my head bobbed backward, and the fluorescent ceiling light blurred.

In the time it took me to go under, Thelma must have been distracted by the rinsing, because she looked over and decided that I was trying to drown myself. She began to scream, "Help! Oh, Lord, Help!" Naturally, this nearly scared the life out of me. I lost my bearings and water gushed into my mouth and nose.

Cora came running in. She stopped as soon as she saw Thelma dragging me out of the water. I lay slung over the side of the tub like a thick wet towel. Thelma, sitting on the edge, locked my arm in hers and refused to let go.

"It ain't worth trying to kill yourself because your daughter is going to have a baby," she said. Her eyes welled with tears.

"I wasn't trying to kill myself," I said, coughing into a towel. I begin to laugh, which could only be explained as all-out hysteria. I couldn't stop. "And tell the world my business, Thelma, why don't you?"

Once again Thelma threw her hands to her mouth. "I'm so sorry, Flossie."

Cora said, "Thelma, please leave Flossie and me alone for a second."

"But I can't leave her. Not in her condition. Look at her, she needs me—"

"We'll be fine," Cora said. "You can return in a moment. And if she needs you before I'm done, I promise to call you at the first sign."

Thelma's eyes raced between Cora and me until simple deductive reasoning suggested it was in all of our best interests for her to leave. She brushed by Cora, mumbling to herself, pulling the door toward her slowly and keeping an eye on me until it was completely closed. All the while, Cora stood right by the edge of the vanity, coming no further into the bathroom than was necessary to qualify for being inside. She stared into the face basin.

"Ma'am," I said, catching my breath, "it's so kind of you to take me in. I'll stay the night, Miss Cora. But in the morning I'll have to get back to my family. I'll straighten everything out with the sheriff. I'll pay you for your trouble. It won't be right away, because we're going through some financial hardship right now. I'll pay you, however. My word is solid."

"Suit yourself," she said. "Whatever you decide to do, none of it should precede a good night's rest."

She paused, turning toward the door. We could hear Thelma talking to May Ruth and Herbert, who must have come up when Thelma screamed.

"All day long she walked around with that skirt on backward," Thelma said. Her voice was just loud enough for us to hear. "Herbert, I didn't want to scare her, but you remember what old folk used to say about how unlucky it is to leave the house with your clothes on backward?"

"What?" May Ruth asked.

Herbert answered: "I have no earthly idea, May Ruth."

"It's unlucky," Thelma said, exasperated, "because the universe doesn't know whether you're coming or going and can get confused and send you in a wrong direction." A moment of silence. Then Herbert said, "I'm going to check on the boys. You coming with me?"

"No, I've got to keep my eye on Flossie tonight."

"I'm turning in, too," May Ruth said. "I'm suddenly quite fatigued."

Thelma went on, oblivious, "I believe you're supposed to spit on the hem to point yourself and fate back toward the proper course. But Flossie doesn't take too kindly to spit."

Cora grimaced and turned back to the face basin. "As far as Sweet Alma is concerned, she's not the first young woman to come up pregnant; won't be the last. And you must know that you won't be the last mother to find it so unpleasing that you're willing to do anything on this earth to make it right. This town, these people have seen their share of disappointments. In the scheme of things, this is just another example of life taking one of its sharp turns."

"Remind me," I said, "to tell the world next time before I tell Thelma something."

"Now, now, it's not Thelma's fault. She means well enough. It's just that things tend to slip from her without her being the least bit aware," Cora said, snickering. "Besides, you think after this morning you're still harboring a secret?"

I stared down into the water. "The whole thing is just so unfair," I said, shaking my head. "It's so unfair."

"Flossie Jo, I don't know you very well, but I'm willing to give you the benefit of the doubt."

"For what?"

"That you got some sense in that head of yours. You look like you've got some sense. So you tell me this: Who in this world told you anything in this life was going to be fair?" Cora walked over toward me. Neither her step nor her gaze wavered when she pulled her glasses up to her eyes. "Who sold you that bill of goods, child? I will tell you, officially on this date, that if you wake up every morning expecting fairness, then even before your feet hit the floor, you will be sorely disappointed. Fairness exists mostly by accident; quite often only by some act of a benevolent God. There are people who are in far worse predicaments than yourself, Miss Flossie Jo Penticott. You are owed nothing. Least of all, something that rarely exists. That child will be fine. Hard to see it right now. But she will come through this. So true for her mother. Nothing that God can't help you work out." Cora smoothed her dress, then turned to walk back toward the door. I sat up straight in the water, pulling my knees to my chest. "I've seen you shouting and cutting up in that choir; I know you know to call on the Master. I know you know there's nothing he can't fashion a way out of."

"Miss Cora," I said. She stopped and turned back toward me. But I couldn't look at her. I stared at the silver plate around the faucet, at my reflection, which bent so much that my face was distorted, overly oblong. "God doesn't hear me or see me anymore, Miss Cora. I had suspected as much, but now I'm certain of it. I've stepped too far out of favor. And I don't know how to get back. Sometimes I feel like the road back has been washed out and there's nothing I can do about it. Nothing I can do to make it right again. Sometimes I feel like I can hardly summon a prayer. Sometimes I can't remember simple verses."

"Hush that silly talk, Flossie Jo. You're no further from God than you've ever been. He doesn't move from us—it's always the reverse that's true. And even then, he still doesn't move from us. Your talk is utter nonsense, honey."

"I want to tell you something. I have a secret."

"I told you, you don't have a secret, child. I know about Sweet Alma."

"No, ma'am. Not Sweet Alma. *I* have a secret. Last night I thought about having my daughter abort that baby. All last night, that's what I thought about. You know how such a thought came so easily? A couple of months ago that's exactly what I did myself. When I learned I was pregnant. Solomon and I haven't been doing too well, and I decided there was no way I was going to bring another child of his into this world. God knows how many others there are. So I took a day trip back to Chicago. I went to an office building on Wells Street. This cute little woman, about your size in fact, used what looked to me like a tumbler spoon. I call it her magic wand. She waved it and everything went away. But last night I kept thinking the only difference is this: It's much easier early on to pretend that the thing growing inside you is nothing more than a tiny glob of nothing. But five months? I know somebody would be willing to do it. Maybe even my little woman with her magic wand. But I remember Sweet Alma at four months. She was this little butterfly baby flitting around in my belly. Between four and five months, she wasn't a little butterfly anymore. There was no mistaking who or what she was. As much as I want to tie Sweet Alma down to that table and give her a second chance, I can't make her get rid of that baby. Not now. I may have been able to do it a couple of months ago. But having gone first myself, and having watched the blood rush out of me, I can't make her do it. I feel as though I've sacrificed both children."

Cora sat down on the edge of the tub, handing me a towel to wipe my face. She leaned against the wall. "Flossie Jo, this life is so full of lessons, child."

"I know you want to help, Miss Cora, but you can't make me feel better—"

"Oh, I won't even begin to try to make you feel better, honey." She opened her eyes to mere slits against the glare. "I don't have any salves—or solutions, for that matter—up these old sleeves of mine. I'm just stating the facts as I see them. After all you've just said, I still believe we're as close to God as we want to be. He leaves that decision up to us. Nobody gets through this life without some hardship. You're old enough to recognize that by now. In the meantime you've got to pull yourself up and start moving again. No time for feeling sorry for yourself or Sweet Alma or anybody else. There are other pressing issues that you'll have to concern yourself with, Sweet Alma's and your future being chief among them. You can't see it now, but everything's going to be all right."

Cora got up and walked over to the door, peeking into the bedroom.

"It looks like you've got company tonight," she said. "Your sister-in-law is hard asleep at the foot of your bed, curled into her usual ball. Doesn't take that child two seconds to find slumber. I don't know how those babies of hers made it through the night before they could start fending for themselves. The short time she lived with Arthur and me, she would come right into our bedroom and lay at the foot of our bed on the floor, nearly every night. Arthur always had a time waking her up, trying to get her to go back to her room. Arthur had these great big old arms, and he was strong, too. Course, Thelma's never weighed nothing. But he would pluck her up real gentlelike and carry her to her room. And Miss Thelma would just come right back here, as though she had a boomerang on her person. Arthur and I didn't know much about children, since the good Lord never saw fit to give us our own. But we had a quick course with Thelma."

"We'll be fine," I said.

"You aren't telling me one thing I don't already know. Now, please get out of that tub before you leave a ring. And get yourself some rest if you can."

She was about to leave the bathroom when I said, "Miss Cora, I have one more question. What's Ruth's story?"

"May Ruth? What do you mean, 'What's her story'?"

"I saw her—at least I believe it was her—at the church this morning praying at the altar. I suppose that's what she was doing. She was moaning and whimpering like something was tearing her apart. Whites, you know, they're much more reserved, more formal, when it comes to God."

"Everybody's got a story, Flossie Jo."

"White people don't know the half of it. Reminds me of Frank Sinatra singing 'Ol' Man River.' What does a rich white man know about 'I gets tired; I gets weary'?"

"When I was growing up, there used to be this great big ol' black woman on Greater Faith's Mothers Board. Her name was Miss Eula Mae. As black and ashy as slate rock. She would get the Holy Ghost and twist around like a big ol' tornado. She was something fierce. The entire pew would rumble and shake. The wood sounded like it would crack in two. Sometimes that woman would get up and walk the aisles, waving her arms. 'You don't know like I know, what he's done for me,' she'd say, tears coming from her eyes. 'You don't know like I know, children.' My girlfriends and I would bust our sides laughing at her. But secretly I used to wonder what in the world made her act out like that. I never learned her story, as you say. But as the years flowed, don't you know that I stopped wondering? As I got older and faced my own trials and tribulations, and saw myself being pulled out of fires so to speak, it was easy to understand why she did what she did. As for May Ruth, you can't look at the surface and think you know people by what your eyes are telling you. White folks do it to us all the time and they're wrong. And we're wrong when we do it to them. Suffice it to say that some folks' stories will break your heart in two and make you glad that your burdens—and yes, even *your* burdens—are yours and not theirs. Some people twist and turn; others stretch out before God. Two in one hand, half dozen in the other. Now, you put some clothes on, you hear? And don't get in the habit of showing all your business like that. World would be a finer place if people remembered what shame was. Ass wasn't meant to be an open book."

Cora smiled and left the room. I got out of the tub and pulled the stopper. A breeze came in through the bathroom window and I sat there, right on the edge of the tub, watching as the water swirled down the drain.

As I stood, I was surprised to see a lone moth on the other side of the window glass. It pinged against the glass so many times that the window rattled lightly against the sash.

It's true that moths aren't so much lured by the light as they are driven mad by it. The light baits them, then pulls like some drug they can't get enough of, so they keep coming toward it, banging their little heads against that thing—any thing—that separates them from the glow and the warmth.

As a small token of kindness, I walked over to the switch on the wall and turned off the light.

13

Flossie

The next morning, I was sitting on the porch. The sun hid behind groupings of clouds, indiscriminately leaving sections of the yard in soft-edged shadows while placing other sections in bright light. White sheets dried on a line a few yards from the driveway. Breakfast had ended and I'd left Cora in the kitchen with her crossword puzzle; Thelma was finishing the dishes. The smell of bleach drowned out all other scents on the first floor, possibly throughout the entire three floors of the house.

Down on the river, a parade of canoes and gondola-like boats formed a line out along the southern bank. I was watching a slow procession when Thelma burst through the front door.

"Flossie," she said, sounding out of breath. "I've got something to tell you. You're going to just bust your sides when you hear the irony of it." She laughed a fake laugh and wiped her hands on her apron before sitting next to me. "Aunt Cora said I should just come out with it." She got up again, walking over to the banister. She stuck her finger into a hanging pot of petunias to check to see if the plant needed watering. When she pulled back moist clumps of mud, she decided the soil was fine. Absentmindedly, she wiped the dirt on the seat of her white shorts. "Oh, shoot," she said. "I'm so mad at myself. It took me three washes to get these clean again. I treated Walter to an ice cream back in the spring after he got an A on an arithmetic test. He multiplies and divides like nobody's business. Herbert jokes that he gets it from me on account of all the multiplying I've done down through the years. You know how Herbert talks, rounding off words all the time. I don't know who Walter gets the dividing from. Anyway, I was wearing these shorts when I took him to the parlor and I lost count of how much he was eating—his appetite, he gets from Herbert. We got halfway home and he threw up ice cream and syrup all over these shorts. And now look at this stain. I just can't seem to keep white white. Just like a child. I don't know why I don't wear black every day."

"We know why you don't wear yellow."

"Bet I'd manage to keep black white."

"Thelma, honey, what is it you want to tell me? Will you please say it before we grow old and I grow senile?"

"Do you promise"—once again she sat next to me, this time leaning forward and biting her nails—"you won't get mad?"

"I promise."

"Now, I have to have your word, Flossie, because you can't say you promise not to get mad, then get mad, because it's not Christian."

"I promise." I removed her muddy finger from her mouth. She spat over her shoulder.

"As it turns out," she said, standing again and backing up to the railing, where tea roses draped her hair, "Delaware can't be the father of Sweet Alma's baby after all. Isn't that the craziest thing you've ever heard?"

"How can you be certain?"

"I talked to Sweet Alma this morning. I called over to check on her and the boys. I asked her, offhandedly, what she and Delaware were going to do about her situation. And she asked me why would he be doing something about her situation. I said because he's the father. And she said he wasn't the father. And I said, 'What?' And she said it was some boy back up North in the city. And I said, 'Are you sure?' And she said, 'Of course I'm sure, I've only done it one time.' So I asked her why Delaware was with her Saturday night and she said he's been trying to convince her to tell you. He's been praying for her. Isn't that the nicest thing you've ever heard?"

"Praying? Are you really that damn gullible, Thelma?"

"I most certainly am not nearly. Sweet Alma has spent enough summers here for me to know her well enough. And you know her better than I do. We both know she's not the loose type. I believe her and you'll have to, too. Besides, she told me the father's name. It was in confidence, so I can't tell you, Flossie. I gave her my word, so I won't tell you. I can only give you the initials. Something like L.D."

"Oh, hell. Larry Davidson."

She nodded, but said, "I can't confirm anything."

"Larry was the same little bastard who was rumored to have fathered Gayl's child. His dick's probably been in every crevice in the neighborhood. And those silly little girls have been passing him around as easily as cherry-flavored lip gloss."

"My lips are sealed."

"So I made a fool out of myself and nearly shot the wrong boy?"

"You could put it that way," she said, almost nonchalantly. "If you want, I'll go with you when you apologize."

"When I apologize?"

"Oh, yes, Flossie." Thelma sat down again. "We—you have to make this right. Things will be all out of whack if you don't. Not to mention, Delaware going the rest of his life not knowing why you said what you said and did what you did. Yes, indeedy. You have to make this right. Or I'm going to be the talk of this little town forever and ever. You know how people can brand you. And people will think I've short-circuited and that I'm unfit to be a mother or any old regular upstanding citizen in the community."

As a blessed distraction, Herbert's Chevette pulled into the drive. Sweet Alma sat in the front seat hemmed in by three of the boys. The others were squished, and sitting on each other's laps in the backseat.

Thelma leapt to her feet. She waved as she hung over the banister, shielding her eyes. Turning back to me, she said, "Okay, now, she's here. Sweet Alma's here. You're done with all the fighting and everything, right, Flossie? I mean, I promised her that there wouldn't be any more fighting. We can put this behind us now, okay?"

"I'm done," I said. "But everything behind us will be sitting right out front in about three or four good months."

Thelma jumped down the steps, taking them two at a time.

Behind me, I could hear Cora coming down the hall. "I'm gone, May Ruth!" she yelled upstairs. An elongated groan wound down from a distant second-floor window. "Take a tablespoon of that castor oil I put on your nightstand. You'll live." To herself, she said, "Then again, if I'm mistaken, you're well on your way to being preserved for all of eternity."

Cora stepped onto the porch, pinning a small pink hat to her hair. She came over and stood beside me, smoothing her pink print dress.

"I've been meaning to ask you all morning, Flossie Jo: you like flowers?"

"They're fine," I said, watching the boys file out of the car.

"If you get around to it today, before you leave, I want you to go over to that weed patch over there along the fence. If you can muster the strength, I want you to turn the ground over for me. You don't have to dig down that deep. Just break it up enough to get your hands through it. The soil on my property is some of the richest around. Even dreams flourish here, my Arthur used to say." She looped her purse over her arm and looked out over the river. "Back when those slaves were brought up here to build the canal, a handful got the idea that one day they would escape and come back to this property. So they began to stockpile the limestone they unearthed. The plan was to return later to build themselves a life. Course, it would take years and years, but after the Surrender, a few of them did come back. White folks didn't understand why anybody would want hilly land like this. Clay soil in many patches made farming difficult, if not impossible. Early on, dysentery and cholera ran rampant from the canal. The river itself often overflowed its banks and turned fields of sorghum and corn into a sodden, muddy mess, where birds died by the dozen and mosquitos propagated by the millions. To the naked eye, this land offered nothing. But now look at it. Look at ol' Halley's Landing. Lord, it's something to behold." Cora started down the porch. "Get Herbert and the older boys to help you. In the fall, I'll plant some bulbs. Come next year, something pretty ought to be growing over there. Yes, ma'am, come next spring. I still keep Arthur's hoes and clippers and all the rest under the back gallery. Just remember to put his things back the way you found them."

As she started down the steps, May Ruth moaned again and cried out, "Jesus Christ. Heavens to Betsy. My head!" Even with that accent of hers, she sounded like any old dignified alley wino.

"Take a sip of that castor oil, I said," Cora yelled. "You'll live."

When Cora passed Herbert's car, she bent down to smile at Sweet Alma, who hadn't left the front seat. Cora got inside her blue Cadillac convertible pointing down the drive. The boys, who were exploring in the yard, waved her down the hill.

Martin and Pepper accidentally got entangled in one of the bedsheets. Arthur, one of the older boys, ran over to help them and soon the sheet was floating over into thickets, the boys yanking on it, trying to free it.

Herbert and Thelma didn't see them, though, because they were wrapped up in Sweet Alma. Thelma opened the door for her, but Sweet Alma shook her head violently and grabbed the door, pulling it shut, locking it.

She refused to look up toward the porch at me. She refused to look over at Herbert, who was leaning into the lowered window on the driver's side, or at Thelma, who stood on the passenger side, nervously curling the edges of her apron, smiling up at me. Though Herbert and Thelma were talking to her, Sweet Alma didn't acknowledge them. At least not that I could tell. She just continued to stare over into Viola Miller's yard or at the boys fooling with that sheet.

The way Sweet Alma was carrying on, I wondered how Herbert had convinced her to get into the car in the first place.

After a while, Thelma opened the back door and sat inside. She leaned against the back of Sweet Alma's seat with her arms folded on the headrest.

I was about to go down to get her myself when Thelma got out and opened Sweet Alma's door again. Herbert was still coaxing from the driver's side window.

When Sweet Alma got out of the car, Thelma held her hand as she led her to the porch. It was as though Sweet Alma's feet would lock after every five steps. Thelma seemed to be pulling a jittery mule. She cajoled, she nudged and prodded. Because neither wanted me to know exactly how much energy was being extolled, their secret little tug-of-war had them both turning red, Thelma more than my child.

Sweet Alma's hair was combed straight back and she wore a loose-fitting blouse. A pair of white terry-cloth shorts crept up the inside of her thighs. She tried to pull inconspicuously at the fabric. She was no longer crying, but it was easy to see she had been. The red tip of her nose preceded her. Her lips and eyes were swollen.

Thelma whispered something to Sweet Alma and then lifted her apron to dab at her own eyes. She looped her arm back through Sweet Alma's.

When they got on the porch, I was still sitting and she stood before me with her head bowed. She started to cry. Her nose ran and she looked like a little girl, much younger than fourteen.

"Mama, I'm going to finish high school and go to college. None of that will change." She knelt and placed her head in my lap. "You just wait and see. I promise."

Thelma hugged herself, sniveling and craving resolution. She motioned for me to put my arms around Sweet Alma, to stroke her hair. But Thelma had birthed all boys and she would never know how it felt to have a daughter in such a predicament. No matter how many girls they impregnated, God forbid. She couldn't know how it felt to watch a child, your child, on the brink of shouldering one of the heaviest of burdens. Boys can always walk away and deny and pretend nothing ever happened.

Sitting there, my mind created a litany of things I should have, could have, done for my daughter so that this moment would never have happened. How stupid I was to think she was intact. I'd spent so many late afternoons with other people's children that I had forgotten about my own. Worst of all, I arrogantly believed that my child was destined for greatness. She was one of the good children. She was enviably smart; equally beautiful. *We had mapped out her future and she understood the plan; knew how to navigate the minefields and would never fall into the trap.*

From the moment Sweet Alma was born, I looked into her face and tried to see me in her. Some feature—her facial structure, a crook of her little nose, the slant of her eyes—something that linked her directly to me. That afternoon I saw me clearly. In her face, I saw my own cravings, my failings, my longings. Beyond mere surface features, these, too, had become a part of her that even I hadn't recognized.

Thelma grew tired of me sitting there as my child sobbed into my lap. She walked over and put her arms around the both of us, drawing us to her and, in the process, attempting to return us to each other.

14

Dorthula "Thelma" Penticott Gray
DECEMBER 1973

A couple of weeks before Sweet Alma's baby was due, Flossie and I were sitting in a church rectory outside of Chicago. Four wooden chairs had been pulled to the center of the room, arranged so that one pair faced the other and Flossie and I were sitting side by side, saying nothing. Flossie's face was squinched up, looking pained, sort of like when she's in church right before she gets happy. Though getting happy wasn't what we were there for, even though we were dressed like Sunday morning. Only it was a Wednesday evening and the church was pretty empty.

The only sound came from the radiator over in the far corner by the window. Bacon frying in a skillet, is what the radiator sound reminded me of. And the room was hot enough to feel like frying, too. After we'd been waiting for a few minutes, I leaned over to Flossie to ask if we should take off our coats. But she didn't say anything. Didn't move to take off her hat or her gloves, either. And because she didn't, I didn't bother.

The snow still was coming down. Coming down as hard as it had been during the three-hour drive to the church. Flossie took her time, giving careful concentration to every sign, to the flow of traffic, which speeded up the closer we got to the city, despite the snow and the ice. The way Flossie was driv-

1 6 4

ing, though; the way she was intensely focusing on the road had nothing to do with the weather. No, indeedy. Nothing at all.

My feet started to feel slippery from a puddle. Snow had melted off my boots and I was standing still with my feet slipping out from under me. It was the same beneath Flossie, too, but she wasn't wasting worry on slipping.

Flossie and I weren't saying a word because nothing else could be said. Flossie had made up her mind. My eyes stung from all the crying. Flossie hadn't cried. At least not where I could see. Flossie sat statue-still, not caring about the frying sound or the wet floor or the falling snow. I could hardly sit still. I got up and walked the room from top to bottom. More like stomped around the room, to tell the truth. Not hard enough to disturb anybody, but pressing hard enough to work spite from my craw. Spite doesn't do one bit of good, especially in God's house. I knew that, which explained why I was trying to work it out.

We heard footsteps that weren't my own. I hurried back to my seat. Flossie sat up straighter.

The man, a Mr. Chesler, came in, wearing a starched three-button suit and shined shoes that, like mine, had white snow circles. Before he sat, he leaned forward to shake my hand and Flossie's hand.

Mr. Chesler was dark-skinned like Herbert. And his strong Southern accent reminded me of my Herbert, too. Come to think of it, a lot about him reminded me of Herbert, although Mr. Chesler wasn't as thick and stalwart as Herbert and probably didn't eat nearly as much; and neither was Mr. Chesler's head bald or quite as boxy. Mr. Chesler's head was more normal-sized and his hair cut low, like in the military. Mr. Chesler was much more muscular than Herbert, too, and he walked straighter and he sat up taller. Unlike my Herbert, whose head starts to melt clean into his shoulders in the evening when he reclines in front of the television. And Mr.

Chesler had a nice, kind smile. Although Herbert's smile is nice and kind, too. So what reminded me most of Herbert, I suppose, was the way Mr. Chesler listened when Flossie talked. Mr. Chesler said his piece, too, but like Herbert he had this extraordinary way of looking deep into your eyes and honing in on you, blocking out the world and hearing every word you were saying and even those that you weren't.

"Pastor Miller says you can help us—my wife and myself," he said to Flossie. "I am so pleased you made the drive up. As I said to Pastor Miller, we would have come down there, but Pastor said you wanted to come up here. Your friend, Miss Laverty, said she's known you for years. Says you both were in college together, studied social work together, and graduated at the same time. She thinks a whole heap of you, miss. Well, Pastor Miller has informed us of your circumstances and he said you'd be willing to consider my wife and me as a potential solution to your problem. We're both hoping this meeting today will help you with your decision. It is my sincere hope that we can—"

"Mr. Chesler," Flossie said. "I thought I'd made it perfectly clear with the reverend that this meeting—although it didn't have to go for very long—would not proceed at all without your wife. Has she taken ill?"

"Why, no, ma'am. No. She's here. We thought it was best for me to come out first."

"Go get your wife, Mr. Chesler."

I waited for Mr. Chesler to leave the room, then I turned her around to look at me. "Flossie, honey, we don't have to do this. It's not too late. We can leave right now. We can jump right back in that car and be home in the same three hours it took to drive us here. Hell, these people can find somebody else." I threw my hands over my mouth and crossed myself for cussing, which I don't normally do. And for cussing in God's house, which I never do. "They don't know us. And even though we're sitting here in this church and leaving would be somewhat deceitful, seeing that they, too, have come a long way, God won't mind."

"I told you that Sweet Alma and I have agreed on this, Thelma. I knew I shouldn't have brought you along. And don't give me that sad, hurt face. You knew we weren't driving up here to sightsee. Sweet Alma wants this so she can have a future. She sees all of her friends playing around, footloose, and she wants the same thing."

"Flossie, she's a child. What does she know? She's scared and we're all scared. That baby of hers needs her mama, not some substitute. I know, Flossie. I know firsthand. Without a mama, how is that baby ever truly going to know up from down; know what color is and beauty and happiness?"

"Sweet Alma needs to have a future, and that's what's important here. Besides, we've agreed."

"Then unagree," I said. "Give me the baby. I told you I'll take it. I got ten, what'll I know different with one more? Give it to me. You and I can leave this place right now. And we can go back to the house and finish off what's left of the meat loaf I made last night. Sweet Alma is just tired, is all, Flossie. You know what these last few weeks are like. Add to that being fourteen years old. She hasn't seen her friends in months. She hasn't been to school or to church or even to the grocery store. You were about to set fire to all of hell last week when I got Herbert to take her for a little drive. Just a drive. And, of course, it was the worst drive we could have gone on because she saw all those kids ice-skating along the pond. She saw the carolers and the Christmas lights and she was ready to trade places with any one of them. No matter their circumstances. Of course, she'll agree to this now. She just wants to be free of it because all she can see is what she's missed. And you want to be free of it, honey. When was the last time you looked at her and in her eyes? I mean really looked at her. You don't look at her, Flossie. I've noticed that. You haven't looked at her in a while. You hardly know who she is anymore. All you see is her belly, and how it doesn't fit right on her. But she's more than that, Flossie. She's much more than that. What's going to happen years from now, years and years from now, when she gets this sharp feeling in her gut for her baby and she wants to run to it but can't? What about then? She'll have all those marks across her belly but nothing else as evidence that her child exists. What will you do then?"

The door opened.

I pulled my hat back down on my head and wiped my eyes with the back of my gloves. I turned my light-headed self back around. Flossie didn't hardly blink.

Mrs. Chesler was short and thin, delicate-looking with a narrow angular face. Her hair was parted down the middle, with two wispy braids crisscrossing the top of her head. Before Mr. Chesler sat, he held the chair out for her, motioning for her to be seated. Then he began again, holding her hand.

"This is Diane, my wife," he said. "We've been married for ten years. Pastor Miller has told you that we're upstanding people. I've got solid employment. I manage a grocery store back home. We've got a nice little house in a good neighborhood that we've lived in for nearly five years. I hope to have it paid off before long. We don't believe in holding a lot of debt or living beyond our means. I know the pastor has told you that we attend our church regularly and we tithe accordingly. I'm on the usher's board and Diane teaches a Sunday-school class."

Mrs. Chesler scooted her chair forward closer to Flossie and Mr. Chesler stopped speaking for a moment. Mrs. Chesler rested her hand on Flossie's knee. At first I was certain Flossie would tactfully pull away. But after a few seconds she didn't, and soon it was as though the two of them were alone in the room.

"Mrs. Penticott, what sold us on our house was the backyard. It's got a nice jungle gym swing set that hardly gets any wear. The paint is still brilliant. There are hardly any rust spots. I believe any little boy or girl would love to climb it and swing on it. I can't speak for John, but that's what sold me on the house. It's a shame to not be able to share it. If you're concerned as to whether ours is a good home, a solid home, then I invite you to come for a visit. If you choose us to raise your grandbaby, you will always be able to visit. You have my word." Mrs. Chesler stood. She said, "C'mon now, honey, we don't want to take up any more time."

Mr. Chesler said, "We await your decision, through Miss Laverty and the pastor. And may God bless you. And guide you."

Up until the day El was born, Flossie still had that fool notion in her head that she could give him away. Up until the minute she wrapped that baby any which way in his blue blanket and was walking out to the car with him and that Patricia Laverty woman, did Flossie still think she could give that beautiful little boy away. Herbert had offered to drive Flossie up to Chicago to meet the Cheslers and hand over the baby. That would be instead of sending the baby with a stranger, he said. That way the woman could still come down with her papers, then she could trail them back to the city.

That morning, I stood at the window in Sweet Alma's hospital room. Sweet Alma was asleep. I was watching her and looking out the window. I waited until I saw Flossie and that Patricia Laverty heading toward the cars. Flossie, who was carrying that baby, got into the car with Herbert. That woman was carrying her briefcase full of signed and resigned papers. She got into her car. My legs felt weak when they drove off.

Herbert said Flossie sat in the backseat, holding the baby the entire time. Herbert was looking at them through the rearview mirror. Flossie had the coldest expression on her face. As cold as when she took that baby from the nursery and wrapped him in those blankets. Herbert said El would stir and Flossie just kept trying to ignore him, as much as she could. He'd whine a little bit—he wasn't a crier like my Pepper was—but he'd give off just a little polite, gentlemanly murmur or gurgle, here and there. And Flossie didn't do a thing on his behalf at first. Herbert said he could hardly look at the road for looking at Flossie and the baby in the rearview mirror.

Herbert said when they got to the interstate, he sunk down in his seat and threw his arm up over the back of the front passenger seat. "I think that boy looks just like Sweet Alma," he said to Flossie Jo. "I sure do. I was looking at him last night in the nursery. Looks just like her. You think so, too? I saw you in that nursery last night. I didn't want to disturb your singing to him, the way you was. How does that song go?"

Herbert said he started to hum something.

"He looks like me," Flossie said, looking through the front window, staring a hole in it. "And he looks a bit like Sweet Alma now. Though Sweet Alma's so young her face hasn't had time to set properly. Who knows how she'll end up looking."

"Got them funny toes like Sweet Alma's, too," Herbert said. "That fourth toe curves in just like hers. I wonder if he gone have her foot-speed, though. I bet that boy will have it. Would be a shame to have feet as big as I can tell he's gone have and not have his mama's foot-speed. And I bet he gone be somebody, too, when he grows up. Yep, he'll be somebody fine. A doctor or a lawyer. Somebody tall. Whoever he'll belong to will make somebody out of him." Herbert started to whistle that song Flossie was singing to El the night before. "Yep, whoever he'll belong to will make somebody out of him."

"Go to hell, Herbert," Flossie said.

"Don't cuss me, Sis."

"Don't try to tell me what's best for my girl."

"I shouldn't have to tell you," he said. "You should already know. Ain't nobody in this family ever gave up a child. Ain't a mouth we can't feed. Not one."

Herbert said they drove for about a good half hour without speaking then. Snow falling, light at times, hard at others. He drove slowly, but, once again, not solely because of the weather. Flossie just kept staring out that window with empty eyes—staring, Herbert said, like she was trying to reconstruct her life. As well as that boy's. Make it work out, rearrange things. Like she could imagine him growing right before her very eyes. She knew that cute little bundle wouldn't last long. There would be that first step, then toy cars and baseball and, eventually, dirty magazines and girlfriends. Herbert said simple staring never looked so busy until you saw her eyes. He said once in a while she'd shake her head a little, or her mouth would form inaudible words, like she was talking to herself, but not regular mumbling like I do all the time, but holding a full discussion. All the while, she kept staring at the falling snow.

Then Herbert said, right about the Lawndale turnoff onto the I-57, Flossie began to cry. She said to little El, "Damn you, child. I prayed and prayed you'd come here stillborn. Even when I saw you coming out, I prayed and prayed that somehow you wouldn't be allowed to take a first breath. But look at you. You're just as pretty as a little girl. Just look at you." Herbert said she wrestled the baby out of his blanket, holding him close to her chest. "Stop this car," she said.

Herbert said, "What you say, Flossie?" Even though he heard her plainly.

"I said, stop the goddamned car, man."

When Herbert could, he pulled over onto the shoulder. So did that woman behind them.

Herbert said Flossie Jo began to shake and burst into tears like on Sunday morning. Yes, indeedy. Flossie grabbed that baby up and fixed on those mud-brown eyes and placed his cheek next to hers and hugged him so tight. Herbert said she was breathing him in. And at that point you can't turn around or change your mind or doubt how you feel or wonder about tomorrow, even if there's nothing but wonder ahead. You dive in all the way.

Herbert got out to talk to that Patricia Laverty. She was talking fool nonsense about how papers had been signed. Herbert simply said, "Unsign 'em." He didn't waste worry on her long. When he got back to our car, Flossie was still crying. El didn't cry, though. Not one little bit. Herbert said he expected the baby to be fearful because of the way Flossie was crying. El lay still like he'd been in this world before. Surely didn't act like a newcomer. He knew every bit of what was happening. The outpouring couldn't stay hemmed up like that for long. He wasn't afraid of it at all. Just a few hours old and he seemed to be quite knowing. Those little eyes consoled. Yes, indeedy.

And it seemed in just those few days, the longest weekend I've ever known, we needed more consoling than ever before. Flossie still couldn't leave well enough alone. She wanted so bad for Sweet Alma to start over and she didn't believe that could happen in Halley or anywhere else. There would always be busybodies around. As for Halley, everybody knew, even though nobody had the nerve to say anything to us. Everybody knew about Sweet Alma. You could hear it in their voices when they asked about her at church or at some social. I could hardly walk through town for people standing around waiting for something to slip out of me. Some little nugget that they could run with.

Flossie wanted Sweet Alma to start over.

We were standing on the front porch. Flossie was holding El. Sweet Alma was holding an old ragged teddy bear she'd had since she was a baby. She was sitting next to her three suitcases on the top porch step. Pepper was standing between me and Flossie, not caring about the noise the other boys were making inside the house. I was holding on to Pepper's hand.

Soon as Sweet Alma saw Solomon's car, she jumped up, clapping. "Whew, look at my daddy's new car! It's too fine. Look at it." Sweet Alma kissed me, then she kissed Flossie, throwing her arms around her and that baby. She said, "Love you, Mama."

Flossie said, "I love you, too. Now, watch your milk, you hear? It should dry up within a week or so. And remember, nobody has to know a thing. Not one word."

Sweet Alma was already down by the car, struggling with one of her cases. She couldn't even wait for Solomon to get out of the car to help her. Pulling the suitcase, she tripped over her feet and tumbled to the ground, face-down, arms splayed. Flossie moved forward to catch her, as if she could catch Sweet Alma in time, from where she was standing—up there on that porch with a little baby in her arms.

Everything about moving to St. Louis thrilled Sweet Alma. It was her heaven; it had been Solomon's for a just a few months. But he, too, made it sound like heaven. For Sweet Alma, it offered her the freedom she'd longed for during the last four months of being cooped up in that old house with that baby cooped up inside of her.

The night before, as Sweet Alma packed, she talked about starting high school. She and I had spent nearly every after-noon reading and studying so she wouldn't fall behind. I got her all the books that she would have needed for her fresh-man year at Halley High School. And then she also read the books Cora had around the house, picking and choosing from all kinds of fancy ones.

Packing her books, she said, "You know, Aunt Thelma, you should take some classes at the community college."

"I just might do that," I said. "I just might follow up on that one."

"Aunt Thelma," she said, "Daddy told me that people in St. Louis celebrate Emancipation on June nineteenth. They call it Juneteenth. August eighth means nothing to them." She stopped long enough to pull on her blouse and rub at the slight milk dribbles. "Daddy says the reason people in St. Louis celebrate differently is because slaves all over the country heard about freedom at different times. Wasn't like they could all turn on the six o'clock evening news." She laughed to herself. "They say a soldier traveled by mule to deliver the news, and depending on when you heard it, that's when freedom came. For some it was January first; in Philadelphia it was February first."

"Some even wanted to celebrate on February twelfth, Lincoln's birthday," I said.

"People in Texas celebrate Juneteenth, too."

"Well, you think you can get used to June nineteenth? Seems far too early for me. Just wouldn't feel right with the temperatures being so mild."

"I'll twist my arm," she said. "Besides, I won't be back this August, but Mama says I can come back next year. So things will be back to normal then."

When it was time for her to leave, Sweet Alma jumped inside the car, waving. She didn't seem to realize that Solomon was walking up to the porch.

Flossie didn't even say good morning to him. She said, "If her milk doesn't dry up, she's got to see a doctor, you hear?"

My brother nodded, kissed me, then reached for the baby. He smiled. "Damn, he looks just like his grandmother." That was a peace offering. A small token. But Flossie didn't grab hold. I wanted to smile back at him, only I couldn't find the strength. My face was completely dead.

Solomon bent down to Pepper. "Hey, man, how's my nephew?"

Pepper sang out, "Fine," which he wasn't. None of us was.

I kept watching Solomon as he went inside with the baby, walked down the hall to the kitchen, back to Aunt Cora and Herbert. Pepper was watching, too, eyes moving between Flossie and Solomon and that baby.

"It's an optical illusion," Flossie said, walking down the porch steps.

"What?"

"Watching your brother with his daughter, with his grandson. It's all an optical illusion. Looking at him, makes you think he's capable of loving one wife, one family, one existence at a time. He's not. Don't be fooled."

I covered Pepper's ears.

"Don't be so scornful, Flossie," I said. "Not many men would take his child so easily. And without one word of comment. Not many men would do that. That alone should raise him some in your estimation. That should count for something."

"Maybe, maybe not." Flossie kept going to the car to talk to Sweet Alma. When she got there, Flossie pointed to a patch of dead trees, telling Sweet Alma what her plans were for the spring. Her garden of sunflowers, rows and rows of them, would replace the trees. Sweet Alma squinted, not completely seeing what her mother saw, which was easy enough to understand. It was hard to look at those dead trees and see the promise the land held. It was hard even for me to see, especially from where I was standing.

Solomon returned with Aunt Cora and Herbert. Flossie was walking back to the porch, so he handed El to her. Solomon kissed me again, mussed Pepper's hair, and started off toward the car. Herbert followed. "You can come down whenever you want," Solomon said. "That goes for all of you.

Maybe for Easter Sunday. Just say the word. I'll come up and get you."

Flossie nodded, holding the baby close to her, pulling Pepper against her hip.

"We don't get second chances much in this life," Aunt Cora said. "You and Solomon are giving that little girl a precious gift. Hard as it is."

I placed my arm around Flossie's waist, as always bracing myself more than Florence Johnson Penticott. "She'll be just fine," I said. "Hard as it is."

"It's only four years," Flossie said. "In four years she would have left me anyway for college."

Four years could very well have been a lifetime. Four lifetimes.

Solomon opened the trunk and slammed it to make certain everything fit right. He turned to us and tipped his hat before getting into the car. Sweet Alma waved briefly and yelled, "I love you all!" For the first time since she sat in the car, she stopped waving. She sat up straight and completely still, facing forward as though settling in for the long drive ahead.

Waving at the moving car, Flossie yelled out, "Call me tonight! You hear? When you get there. Sweetie. Don't forget. Before you settle in. Call me."

15

Flossie

After the Adamsdale intersection, Old Riley splits into a V.

I veer north to pick up Route 83 and follow the wall of the canal for a couple of miles to the Latham property. Near the turnoff, the road changes several times from asphalt to gravel. I turn at the PRIVATE PROPERTY, NO TRESPASSING sign.

About a half mile in, a yellow police horse that normally blocks the way has been pushed off the road into the weeds and cattails. I pull inside the property and bump along under a canopy of trees to where the road dead-ends. Sucker trees have overtaken the drive, which used to wrap around an ornate concrete fountain. The brick house still stands, but leans mostly, ever since the fire on the second floor caved in the eastern wall. Nobody ever found out who started the fire. The police suspected a group of young hunters from The Famous Johnny Weston Hunt Club, the property next door.

I pull up into the carport behind Solomon's brand-new black Continental. I grab my picnic basket from the seat next to me and I start walking up a brick path toward the back-yard.

The path curves under a trellis of dead vines and opens out onto a patch of wildflowers, cordoned off by a short limestone wall.

Solomon sits on the wall with his back to me. He faces the pool house and, beyond that, the hunt club's sunflower-and-millet field. The sunflowers are bright orange and red and stand nearly six feet tall.

A blanket spreads out across the grass.

"You come alone, Sweet Flossie?" He doesn't turn around. His white shirt is open and the tails fly back. His beige suit coat and tie lay folded next to him on the wall.

"Every year you ask me that same fool question."

"Does that mean you've come alone, Sweet Flossie?"

"You think I'd bring an audience."

"Hell, an audience might learn something."

Standing, he takes my basket and places it on the blanket. He extends both hands, grabbing mine and pulling me toward him. "You sure look good, Miss Flossie. Like the meat on a Sunday plate."

Once a year, I allow myself to feel at home in his arms. I lay my head against his chest, breathing in a light minty cologne. I feel my heartbeat quickening, becoming one with his.

I turn around and lift my hair. He kisses the back of my neck, full and hard, and begins to unbutton my dress. He touches me and my eyelids pull down like curtain shades being lowered, blocking out the world. Halfway down my back, he says, "Hold on a second, I've got something to show you."

"Hold on? You've never said 'hold on.' Maybe *during*, but never before."

Solomon walks back over to his suit coat, pulling an envelope from his breast pocket. He reaches behind the wall for a box. He walks out to the center of the grass, gets down on both knees, and unties the string on the box.

"This is an envelope," he says, being smart. "But what I have in this box is a single-line delta wing, all assembled and ready to fly." He pulls a red kite from the box. A spool of string tumbles behind as the kite shimmies awake and begins to mount the breeze, growing smaller as it climbs. Birds fly near, painting the sky in dark clusters.

He takes my hand and leads me to the blanket. He sits. I watch him for a second before sitting next to him. The veins in his arms expand. Suddenly I feel like I'm the one up there floating on the other end of that string. But that doesn't take much effort. I lay next to him. The wind pushes at my dress. The grass tickles my ears. And the entire moment makes my tongue stick to the roof of my mouth like I'm tasting cotton candy.

"Is this some kind of kinky sex toy I don't know about?"

"Not to my knowledge, but we can consider it."

"Okay, why the kite, Solomon? How come you're not ripping my clothes off me and having your way?"

"In due time. In due time." He waves the envelope in front of me.

"What the hell is that?"

"This, my dear, is a property deed. You, Sweet Flossie, are looking at the new owner of what was formerly known as the Latham property. I bought it last spring and I didn't want to tell you then. I wanted to save it for a surprise."

"I thought Latham wasn't selling to *coloreds.*"

"Well, sometimes in life, when you're standing at the right place at the right time, good fortune shines on even a colored man. I got a call back in the spring from Billy. Billy just happened to be out driving a cab one night. He was driving as a favor for somebody. He got a call from the hotel from this young white boy. Said he wanted to be driven out to the Latham property. Billy and Boy Wonder got to talking and the boy said he wanted to sell it bad. He said he wanted to sell it but there were covenants on that land that might or might not hold up in court. And the boy didn't want to worry about court. He said he just had to find the right buyer. And who would want land in the middle of nowhere, which also was part of the buffer zone for the hunt club? He said his granddaddy had just died and bequeathed the property to him. Well, Billy told him that he knew of a fellow that might want to buy it. Billy didn't tell the boy I was black. Billy told him that he would make a few phone calls. Billy said the boy wanted to get rid of the property so bad, he thought the boy was saving up to buy him a good piece of ass or something. You know how Billy is."

"Crude as hell," I say, sitting up further.

"Whatever the boy needed the money for, far as I was concerned, was his business. He could burn it up bill after bill, for all I cared. After I talked to Billy, I got in touch with this white driver of mine. I told Steve I needed a favor. It would mean two weeks of extra pay for him. It would also mean a new suit. In all the years Steve has worked for me, he has never worked his ass into a suit. But that's how white boys are. All you have to do is clean them up and they pass muster faster than anything. Well, we drove on up to meet with this boy and his attorney. I told Steve what to say and what not to. We went over it time and again to make sure he had things right. Steve said he wanted to purchase the land on behalf of the Penticott Cab Company Trust in St. Louis, Missouri. That boy was asking one hundred thousand for all fifteen acres. That's what we offered. No quibbling, no discussion. Boy Wonder didn't give a damn about looking into who owned the trust. Nobody said anything about covenants or deed restrictions. I don't think the boy really cared. He wasn't caught up in all that color shit. Nice red-blooded yuppie American boy. In the end, the big green won out. And everybody was happy."

Solomon stood, tying the kite's string to a branch. He pulled me up with him.

"Now, I know what you're thinking. Don't you go hassling me about spending so much money on land that may as well be salted over. I haven't blown anybody's inheritance. If something happens to me, Sweet Alma gets ten times that much. She will be taken care of mightily. This land is worth every dime paid for it. I know you've heard this before, but I had to have this property. I just had to have it, baby. When I was younger, I used to stand right in that carport area and watch my daddy rub on Mr. Latham's car. I would watch him scrubbing it, buffing it, like it was his own. He couldn't have done a better job if it had been his own car. And Mr. Latham would bring his ass out and jump in the backseat without commenting once on the shine. Not once. Then when my father died, Mr. Latham thought he was doing something by giving my mother a job in his kitchen. He'd come in there every now and then to make small talk, always coming around to his question: 'Tell me again, what made a fine Irish woman like you marry a nigger? You know, I just don't understand it.' I remember the night my mother said there was a big party, so she had to work late. So Mama sent me over to Aunt Cora's. I remember the phone rang and Uncle Arthur went to get her. But I was so sleepy, I couldn't keep my eyes open. The next morning I went into her room, she was crying on Aunt Cora's shoulder. She said Mr. Latham had raped her. I was about nine or ten years old. I'll never forget my mama crying. I'll never forget the shame in her eyes when she realized I had heard her. That morning I marched right down the hall to Aunt Cora's and Uncle Arthur's room and got his gun from under his bed. I didn't know whether it was loaded or not. That wasn't important. Uncle Arthur was on the front porch. I had the gun in my hand. He said, 'Boy, where you think you're going with that pistol?'

" 'I'm going to kill him,' I said.

" 'Boy, you'd do much better to get that fool-ass idea out of your head. It won't serve anybody a bit of good. How you think your mama will feel if you kill him and then you have to go away from her? She wouldn't have nobody then, would she?'

" 'No, sir.' I was crying and crying.

" 'You don't have to hang your head, boy. People get what they deserve. You remember that. That gun will be yours one day. And when it's yours, there won't be a thing I'll be able to do to stop you. But before then, you don't have to worry about Mr. Latham. Somebody will take care of him. When he least expects it. Somebody will come along and shoot him down like the damn dog he is, and that person himself won't even know why. The shooter will leave his house one morning with a gun and an itchy trigger finger. And when he comes across ol' Latham, he'll shoot him dead and leave him to fester in his shoes. And that'll be for you and for your mama.'

"I still hated Mr. Latham. I had so much hate in my heart for him that sometimes I would just shake and my stomach would cramp. My mama had to go around with her belly stuck out because somebody had stolen from her. I would dream about him sitting at that party getting drunker and drunker and waiting until everybody left. I would see him chasing my mother through this big ol' fine house and catching her. I would hear her screaming for my daddy to save her. In my dreams, I always shot Mr. Latham. But the bastard never had the decency to fall. I hated him for that, too. For not dying even in my dreams. But then months passed, and Mama saw her little reedy girl's face. And when she fell in love with her, I couldn't help but fall in love. Mama asked me to name her."

"I don't know where Dorthula Jane came from," I say.

"Thelma hates me to this day for that name. It sounded pretty to me at the time. Thelma was eight years old when Mama died. I was already driving for Porter Cabs. She wanted to see where her father lived. I drove her by the house and then she wanted to know if he was rich. I said, 'Hell, no. He ain't rich at all. He ain't worth a dime.' "

Solomon lifts me and swings me around, kissing me. I laugh like a schoolgirl.

"Sweet Flossie Jo. Sweet, Sweet Flossie, I can't tell you what it feels like to own this property. You don't know what it feels like for me to own the place where my parents both had something stolen from them. I own it. Flat out. No liens, no mortgages. I can't do a goddamned thing with this property, with those crackers next door. But it's mine. Some people would wonder why I wanted it so bad. The way I see it, this property got blood on it. The way I see it, they can rest right easy knowing there's a little chunk of land that nobody's gone ever be treated like dirt on. Just a little plot of land where the soil's been turned over. That's the way I see it. You know something else? I used to bring Sweet Alma up here to fly kites. She used to run right through there. Right along there making that kite dance and swoop. 'Look, Daddy,' she'd say. 'Daddy, look at me.' Then when she was too grown for it, I brought El and Pepper and the other boys up here. I didn't tell any of them about all the history. They didn't need to be saddled with all that. I always told them one day this would be their land. I promised them that. That's why the members of the Penticott Cab Trust are Herbert Jr., Solomon, Arthur, Charles, Michael, Peter, John Otis, Walter, Martin Luther, and Robert Gray, along with Sweet Alma and Ellsworth Penticott."

"A couple of years ago, we found shell casings over here," I say. "I used to warn El not to ride his bike over here in the fall. He loved this property. He simply loved being out in the air, period, anywhere. But I told him I would kick his butt if he came up here in the fall because of the hunt club."

Solomon smiles and his eyes well up. "I wish he could be here right now. I wish he could see what I have for him."

Solomon turns away from me. I wrap my arms around his waist, leaning against his back. I hold him tightly and the sunflowers next door bounce and sway, blurring in my side glance.

I told El not to be fooled by the beauty of those sunflower fields. I told him they're supposed to look pretty in the summer. In the fall, they die and that's when they really have their power. That's how those mourning doves get here, by the hundreds. They're lured by the desiccated quills and the seeds.

Then the next thing you know, you're seeing all those men in their red jackets trouncing through toppled flowers. You're hearing their dogs barking and their gunshots, then watching birds tumbling like opalescent-gray and brown-winged seraphim out of the sky.

Those birds and those bullets don't recognize property lines or know a thing about boundaries.

That's what I always told El.

16

Flossie

Solomon is asleep, lying on his stomach.

One arm spreads across the blanket, the other presses me close to him. The tail of the kite traces the sky above us. A woodpecker knocks on the cedar part of the house, but that quickly is muted when the propane cannons toward town go off. After about five blasts, the cannons quiet and the only sound that remains is the breeze coming through the sunflowers, whistling high-pitched as though some seal has been broken.

I think about Sweet Alma when she was five years old. There was a spate of months when she would come into our bedroom in the middle of the night and stand at the door.

Back then Solomon and I were happy. I would sleep folded in his arms, and some nights, just out of instinct, I would look toward the threshold and see our daughter's silhouette. "Come on in, honey," I'd whisper, "there's room for you." Each night, she found her way through the darkness, climbing over Solomon and wedging herself between us. She said she was coming to make sure we were there.

I tried to reassure her that we weren't going anywhere. There would never be a day when she would wake up and we'd be gone. But she didn't believe me. For weeks she continued to come in the middle of the night, staying long enough to make sure the huddled mound just feet from her was her parents, before turning back to her room.

El, on the other hand, only came to my door once. That was the night Mr. Paul left.

That night, Pepper and Sweet Alma knocked on my door in the middle of the night. I was half asleep. All night I had been falling in and out, lying there in the dark, thinking about Mr. Paul. Thinking about all that confusion and upset.

Pepper and Sweet Alma entered the room. They said they couldn't find El.

I turned on the light, throwing the covers off me. I started out of my room when I happened to turn for my robe and I saw El's big feet. He was curled up at the foot of the bed on the floor.

Sweet Alma knelt and rubbed his shoulder. He awoke heavily.

"Sweetheart," I said, "why are you in here, sleeping on this hard floor?"

He looked up at the three of us, squinted a few times, and fell back off.

My curtains were open, and though Mr. Paul was gone, glints of light bounced off his little white truck still in our driveway.

17

ℱlossie

When I finally make it back to the house, May Ruth and
Cora are sitting in their chairs, napping on the porch. As soon
as I open the car door, I hear May Ruth snoring. Whether
Cora is asleep is questionable, since May Ruth's snore is
enough for the both of them to hide behind. Seeing me, Viola
Miller's dog runs over to the fence and starts to yelping. The
birds chomping at the feeder scatter.

May Ruth eases awake as I walk down the porch toward
them. Cora does not.

"Cora?" I say. Their bare feet are soaking in Thelma's shallow tubs of water. Thelma's foot buckets line the porch, along
with pedicure paraphernalia, scissors, wash towels, tubes of
cream, aloe, a book on sterilizing instruments.

May Ruth's glasses are sideways. She rights them so she
can see me. "Dear heart, did you have a good afternoon?"

"Tolerable," I say.

Cora's arms hang limp off the sides of the chair. Her head
is flung straight back and her mouth is wide open. Her upper
plate has shifted down- and outward and balances on her
bottom lip the same way her clipboard balances on the edge
of her lap.

"Cora?" I say.

She looks stiff and pale. I rub her hand and slowly bend down to place my head against her chest.

"I ain't dead yet," Cora mumbles, locking her teeth back into place. Her eyes remain closed as she slowly reaches up to rub her forehead.

"I didn't think you were," I say. "I was just noticing all those fine hairs under your chin and wondering when was the last time you plucked them."

"I may not be dead, but it surely can't feel much different from this. I suspect I'm as drunk as a whiskey fly in a still. Earlier I asked May Ruth to bring me a churn of buttermilk and she brought it to me in that Thermos jug of hers."

"In this heat, buttermilk spoils quickly sitting outside," May Ruth says. "I told you it would keep better that way."

"The doctor says you're not supposed to have buttermilk," I say. "It makes your glands and your feet swell."

"They only swell when you're here watching them, Flossie Jo. Otherwise they're fine." She rubs her eyes with the tips of her fingers, then turns to May Ruth and slowly opens her eyes. "I'd probably have been better off taking my chances with curdled milk, rather than trusting you to rinse that jug out better. I knew it was tasting funny. First time in all my days my milk ever gave me a headache and an ulcer simultaneously."

May Ruth stands and stretches but doesn't remove her feet from the tub. She looks down at them, just now noticing her loose white pants are rolled up and knotted around her calves and she's still standing in standing water. She reaches inside her pocket for her breath spray. "Dear heart, can I help you go inside to freshen up before dinner?" she asks Cora, smiling and wiggling her toes.

"No. Thanks to you, I won't be standing until Christmas, at the soonest."

"Flossie," May Ruth says, "would you be a dear and drive me to June's place this evening? I'm going to take her some dinner. Herbert is tired and I don't do well driving at night."

Cora says, "I still don't know what Pepper sees in that little hard black girl. Got herself knocked up on purpose, is my contention."

"Oh, now that makes a hell of a lot of sense," I say. "Pepper is such a prize. Young women are lining up for him to sire their children. And I told you about that black mess, Cora."

"That's just an expression. And it's not June's color, it's her ugly disposition. Face never bears a smile or any semblance of kindness."

"You're hopeless, Cora. And, May Ruth, I'll be happy to drive you. I only need to shower first."

"Have you spoiled in the heat, too?" May Ruth laughs.

I don't answer. I walk away, toward the door.

Cora says, "Say, Flossie Jo, did you know your dress is buttoned all crazy? And it looks to me—but don't take my word for it since I'm still in a partial coma—but it looks to me like you're not wearing any underwear, considering how your breasts are jiggling and your dress is sticking to your hindside. Now, don't go trying to pull yourself together for my benefit. Nothing to be ashamed of. You must have gotten dressed in the dark this morning, is all. You sure left early enough."

"Speaking of leaving early," May Ruth says, "Solomon called this morning. Herbert said he would have given you the message but you were gone before anyone woke up, dear heart."

"Avoiding her sister-in-law, is the reason," Cora says. "Thelma's been looking for you all day, Flossie. She's been over at that jail most of the day, though, trying to talk Pepper out of believing you hate him. He's over there walking a new groove into the concrete. That and shaving himself. Thelma says he asked her to bring him a razor, and not only did he shave his face, but he also shaved his head clean and then his eyebrows. She's wondering when you're going to see your nephew, if you haven't within the last hour. Not that it's any of my business when you see him. Thelma's arranged for one of the pastors to go over and bless the jail, to cast out demons and such. She's so tuckered from it all that she's taking a quick nap before dinner. Though I'm sure she wouldn't mind it if you woke her to let her know when you're going to see Pepper. Heaven knows what else he's shaved. Did I mention she was looking for you all day? Even went to the post office, and that's when we learned you took the day off. Didn't tell anybody here you were taking the day off. And you didn't spend it with us, that's for sure."

"Oh, that's right, dear heart. So what did you do with your day?" May Ruth says.

"I had errands."

Cora says to me, "Did May Ruth tell you Solomon called?"

"I just said that, Cora. Aren't you listening, dear heart?"

"Called early this morning. He said he wanted you to meet him to sign some papers. Now they've been divorced for nearly twelve years come November and she's still signing papers. Either he's got a stack like nobody's business or you two are doing more than signing papers. Solomon must think people are senile. The whole thing reminds me of that bird that flies two thousand miles from central Mexico to Canada once a year to breed. May Ruth, what'd you call that bird?"

"A hummingbird is one."

"Oh, yeah. That sounds about right. And, Flossie, what'd you call that little bug that's been out in the garden all summer? The locust bugs you hate so with the big red pop eyes?"

"The cicada."

"Yeah, that sounds about right, too. I hear those bugs spend much of their time underground, hanging on to tree roots. But every thirteen to seventeen years, they surface to have sex. Only thing is, soon after the male mates, he sheds his skin and passes right on out of this world. How fitting is that? Just up and dies. Then the female dies after she's laid her eggs. They must be sneaking around behind his new wife's back, if you ask me."

May Ruth says, "You know, dear hearts, the Puya plant blooms just once a century. It lays dormant for a while and then all of a sudden grows twenty feet tall and flowers, producing its offspring, millions of winged seeds. Shortly afterward it dies, too."

I open the screened door. "I will not dignify any of this with a response. You two obviously are talking out of your heads."

Cora folds her hands in her lap, closes her eyes, and starts rocking in her chair. "Oh, I wouldn't deny it one bit. Not one bit. But here's one more thing for you to chew on while I'm drunk enough to say it: Solomon has his good points, Flossie Jo. Like his sister says, there aren't many men who'd stand up to his responsibilities the way he did when Sweet Alma needed him. My point is, he did what he was supposed to do. Nothing more."

May Ruth takes Cora's hand. "Now, now, dear heart, don't you go stirring at the bottom of the bowl."

"I love Solomon to death," Cora continues, "and I know that boy would do anything in this world for me, but he has a side to him that I don't particularly care for. He thinks he can do whatever he wants with his manhood and it doesn't cost anybody anything, least of all him. And everybody seems to let him stick it wherever he pleases. You know I have never said anything about you and Solomon before. I haven't said anything about you not having anybody steady for twelve years, either. Twelve whole years. Unless there's something I don't know. Unless you're growing men in those sunflowers and that's the reason you spend so much durn time down there and that's why they wiggle so. Like I said, I try to stay out of your business."

I suck my teeth.

"Well, I try. But for now my inhibitions are nil and I'm speaking my piece while I have a good scapegoat: that booze, the comet. As far as Solomon goes, you should know better, Flossie Jo. You, as an ex-wife, should know better. He doesn't need any special treatment because he was doing what a father is supposed to do. He's supposed to love his child. He's supposed to put his life on hold for her. You don't owe him a thing. Now, that Ben Rogers fellow is a good man. And he's nice and widowed. And he could probably stand a little special treatment of his own."

I move to go inside.

"Flossie Jo?"

"What now!"

"By the way, I've told you time and time again that I won't depart this life without ample notice. By now God owes me the courtesy of giving me at least a moment's warning before He calls. I'll use part of that time to finish my crossword puzzle and the rest to notify you."

"Don't bother, old lady, I'll find out soon enough."

"You see that, May Ruth? Normally the tongue's a blunt instrument, but Flossie Jo wields hers like a knife. I sure am grateful the good Lord has allowed me to live so many years and not have too much of the feebleness on *my* brain."

I cross the threshold and head upstairs when I glance the phone table. I walk over to it and sit down. The new wallpaper behind the chair buckles where the walls meet. I smooth the paper, over and over, before dialing Sweet Alma's number. Over the last year, I've dialed this number countless times. It rings now and I hang up before she answers. I dial again and let it ring and ring until her answering machine clicks on.

I don't leave a message. But at least I get to listen to her voice.

18

Flossie

What's left of a Coors beer ad peels from a billboard behind June's apartment building.

The vines grow thick as rope up the cracked stucco and the area smells septic from so much standing muck and garbage.

My pickup wades through water from an open fire hydrant in front of the building. A slat of wood stuck in the hydrant's mouth diverts frothy gushes upward so children can stand in the downpour.

Those who aren't getting wet are playing on the lawn. They're supervised by a couple of young women in shorts and tube tops who sit outside in corroded aluminum beach chairs. The two also keep an eye on another group of kids in the playground. The women watch them through a jagged swath in the weeds.

The basket of paper plates, glasses, food, and plastic ware that has been sitting on May Ruth's lap continues to rattle when the truck has stopped. May Ruth pulls her hair up into a clip. She opens the door and I notice she's got one of Thelma's foot buckets.

"Why do you have that?"

"You know how rough feet become in the final months of pregnancy," she says. "I thought you might find it in your heart to help June with a pedicure, considering she and I haven't officially been introduced and considering we have all the tools at our fingertips."

"May Ruth, you can leave this mess right here in this truck because I am not about to be bothered with June's or anybody else's crusty ass feet."

When we get to the door, May Ruth knocks. I stand behind her, holding the basket of food and nothing more.

"Who is it?" June yells. "This door sticks when it gets hot, hold on." Finally the door uncorks, releasing hot, rancid air and dust particles. She sees May Ruth and says, "I don't want any. And I'd leave this neighborhood before it get dark, if I was you."

"Hi, June," I say, leaning toward the opening.

"Miss Penticott? I haven't seen you since Robert got fired from the post office. What y'all doing down here, slumming?"

"Herbert asked us to bring you dinner," I say. "We don't have to come in. This is May Ruth Albee. We're dropping the food off and you can go back to your evening."

June steps back into meager lighting and waddles over to a sofa with a white sheet flung over it. May Ruth enters. I grab for her arm, but she intentionally pulls away.

"I'm Pepper's aunt, too," May Ruth says cheerily. "You may call me Auntie May Ruth."

June gives May Ruth a look. But May Ruth doesn't care and is just as open to the idea as before.

"Mr. Herbert's been coming by every two minutes checking on me and bringing ice. His wife ain't come by, though. Haven't seen Miss Thelma yet, but I hear she's been visiting her son. I told Mr. Herbert I 'preciate him coming so much but he should stay home tonight. It takes the wind outta me to keep getting up for this door. And when he comes I have to keep this robe on and I can't stay in this thing for very long."

"Oh, there's no reason to, dear heart," May Ruth urges. "Take it off. We're all family, aren't we?" May Ruth helps her out of the robe, folds it, and places it on the back of a chair.

The chair, along with a sofa, cocktail table, and a television, are the only furniture in the living room. June's army discharge certificate sits in a plaque atop the television. "And don't worry about Thelma, she'll be along soon."

"I know she don't like me," June says.

"Nonsense," May Ruth says. "How could she not like you, dear heart? I can't find one schmilling of a thing not to like."

Hmph, I say to myself.

As June squats to sit, her tight T-shirt raises and her panties fall, showing pubic hair. Her bulbous stomach seems like its about to burst. And, only because of May Ruth, I notice that her toenails are so long they've begun to curl and yellow. Three fans blow on the sofa from different directions at high speed. A large pail of ice sits beside the cocktail table next to a stack of face towels. Even with the fans, the room suffocates. "I don't normally walk around naked like this," June says, "but I'm gone pass out in this heat if I don't have this baby soon."

I sit next to her on the sofa. May Ruth takes her shoes off and starts to unload the basket onto the cocktail table. *Wheel of Fortune* is on the television. The sound is down low, so we only hear murmurings when the applause or laugh track comes on.

I raise my dress so that my thighs can get some air, and I figure that by the time we finish dinner we'll all have passed out.

"Pepper was born in July," May Ruth says. "Thelma says it was one of the hottest Julys on record. All she could do was sit in a bathtub of cold water. Herbert kept running about to get her ice. The boys pitched in by alternately dumping cubes into the water." May Ruth takes a face towel and dips it in the bucket. She wrings it out and places it on June's forehead. "I believe her water broke right in that tub. She says old folks used to say that if a baby is born in heat, he's destined for riches and gold."

I don't ask why because May Ruth looks so pleased with herself as she passes the plates around. The room is quiet for a second. We watch the wheel on television spin.

"I saw Pepper today," May Ruth says, filling in the blanks. "However, he was asleep when I stopped by. I left him a couple of books. Jean-Paul Sartre, for his musing on existentialism—because confinement is the perfect place for this—and Albert Camus, for a healthy dose of the metaphysical."

"Robert is a fool," June says. She balances her plate on her stomach, mopping her mouth with a slice of white bread while simultaneously tearing into a barbecued chicken leg. "I am not going to that jail again. I don't mean no harm, but if your nephew thinks I'm gone baby him like his mother does, he got another thought coming. I ain't about to be raising nobody but this baby." She turns to May Ruth. "Miss Penticott got Robert a job down at the post office. Do you know why he really quit, Miss Penticott?"

"He didn't quit," I say. "He stopped coming and Mr. Otha fired him."

"Well, he stopped coming because he said he couldn't stand the way you stared at him."

"Me? I didn't stare at that boy."

"He said you would look at him funny and he couldn't stand it. He said you were boring a hole in him and he couldn't stand it. I told him, Pepper, you a damned fool. And he told me I didn't understand nothing. So I said fine. I understand one thing, you better find another job. Do you know why he was gone for them three days before he got arrested? I told him to get out and don't come back until he found a job. Period. Robert ain't worked in four months. To his credit, he started out looking after he lost his last job, but then he said he got *discouraged* and needed to take a break. It's hard for a brother to find employment, he said. I said, Brother, you better get a job. I can be a whole lot more sympathetic to the plight of the black man when he bringing home a check."

"You tell him, sister," May Ruth blurts out. She waves her hand.

"I'd leave for work and he'd be sitting in front of this television. I'd come home and he'd still be sitting right in the same spot, looking at this *Fortune* show or *Jeopardy!* He's proud of himself because he figures out the puzzles with so few letters that he's got enough time to draw sketches of the contestants. And he reads all the time and knows useless stuff like the circumference of the earth is near-about twenty-five thousand miles; and the reason spiders don't stick to their own webs is because only they know the parts that ain't sticky; pigs don't sweat, he say, instead they pant like dogs. Now, who the hell needs to know shit like that when the baby needs diapers and ointments and lotions?" Her voice cracks. "I don't mean no harm."

"None taken," May Ruth and I say in unison.

"Robert's got book sense, but he ain't got no mother wit." June wipes her nose with her forearm, then pauses to sniff under her pits, lifting one arm at a time. "Then, out of the blue, he started hanging around those nothing-ass niggers down at the Blue Flame, drinking and cussing. I told him this baby is on its way and I expect him to be able to help provide for it. That's when I told him to get out and don't come back. That first night was Friday night and I slept just as sound. I spread out 'cross the whole bed. I mean I slept till I got tired. I slept so hard because I can't half sleep with Robert here. He fights in his sleep. When he do sleep, he turning and twisting, wrestling with hisself. Then some nights he wake up coughing and coughing like something choking him. He sleeps with a glass a water 'side the bed all the time because he say his air gets cut off sometimes. So when he didn't come back, I tell you, I slept my head off. Then on Sunday night, he struts in here late, breaking up my rest. I asked him if he found a job. He said, 'Hell no.' See, I could tell somebody done puffed some bad air into his spine and his ass is out of joint. He comes and gets in my face. I sit up in the bed. I tell him to go on and leave me alone. He starts to pointing in my face saying that the next time I want him to leave *his* house, I'm gone have to pick him up and throw him out. He gets closer and I can smell the weed on his breath and Robert acts a fool when he gets himself a little marijuana in his system. I stand up. He gets closer, saying he the king and this his domain. So I ball my fist up. He bumps into me a little bit. He probably didn't mean it. But I haul off and lay into him. At first I'm just hitting at the air, but then I start whamming his head. Before we know it, we're hearing sirens and the police is banging on the door, carting the king off to jail."

Next door or a few doors down, someone is yelling, though I can't decipher what exactly is being said. This doesn't bother June, but May Ruth and I look toward the window, wondering if at any second some poor man or woman is going to come flying through it.

June pulls on her T-shirt. "This baby kicks me all the time. I think he's trying to move me out of the way."

May Ruth says, "I have a splendid idea. I don't know why we didn't think of it earlier. Why don't you come stay at the house with us, June? There's plenty of room. And you'll have around-the-clock service."

I look at May Ruth like she's crazy.

"Like I've told Mr. Herbert, I ain't moving. I 'preciate the offer. But this here's my home and I get to walk around as I please. I don't want to put you all out any more than I already have."

"You know it's really no bother a'tall," May Ruth says.

"Besides, I want to be here if Robert decides to come home and act like he got some sense. If he don't, no matter. My mama raised me just fine without my nothing-ass father, and I will do the same with my baby."

By the time I stand up to leave, the ice pail is full of water and condensation drips from the sides. The sun is setting.

"I'm going to replenish your ice supply," May Ruth says. "Is there anything we can do for you?"

"No. I'm fine. I just want to get some rest. I've only been able to sleep a couple of hours at time. And all of it sitting up on this couch."

"Well, we're going to leave and let you get your rest. We'll be back tomorrow."

May Ruth opens the door and the air is damp and sticky. The water from the hydrant has been turned off and the two young women who were out earlier are now joined by four or five young men, who dance around them with large boom boxes.

Different songs compete for space.

"You're lucky she refused your invitation," I say as we get into the pickup. "Cora's liable to evict both of us."

"Cora's a pussycat, dear heart. Surely you know that by now."

As we turn out of the apartment complex, we stop in front of the Quik-Mart at a red light. Two young men stand spread-eagle against a police car. One officer is frisking them, another patrols the marsh behind the mart with a flashlight, looping around the bushes.

When the traffic light changes, I turn north, going in the opposite direction.

"You know, dear heart, I do envy June."

"Only a crazy person could envy June's position," I say. "Pregnant, unmarried, her baby's father on a self-imposed lockdown."

"She's a very, very lucky girl," May Ruth says again. "I remember what it was like to be pregnant. I loved the feeling. I remember it after all these years."

"But you envy June? Are we talking about the same June, May Ruth?" I say. "Or are you referring to another?"

She's quiet for a second. Then she tilts her head and pushes her glasses up on her nose. "I'm afraid I've got another lump, dear heart. Actually, there are more than one," she says. This tangent throws me for a loop. I look behind me and pull over onto the shoulder, turning on my hazard lights.

"May Ruth, honey. I'm so sorry."

She takes my hand and places the tips of my fingers just below her clavicle. She traces what feels like a row of tiny balls. "I call it my pearl necklace. When I first felt them, I thought of a young girl's string of pearls that had been laid across my chest. But the pearls are not of equal distance apart and they're not the same size. My oncologist says they're petite but doozies. There's nothing left to be removed. Oh, it's okay, dear heart. I've resigned myself to it quite splendidly. You know I won't abide self-pity. Not anymore."

"Have you gotten another opinion?"

"I've gotten several. They all say the same thing. It's metastasized this time. I'm really fine with it, you know? But this is just between us girls, dear heart. I haven't told the others. I'll tell them before I leave."

"So why are you telling me first?"

"I had to tell somebody. You know how awful I am with keeping secrets. Whom else was I to tell? Cora? Cora would be out of her mind with worry. And, well, we all know Thelma can't keep a secret. She and Herbert have their own worries with Pepper. Besides, I didn't want to add to their woes."

"So it's okay to add to mine?"

"You're so resilient, dear heart. For now you must promise to forget all that I've told you. We must promise to go on as though I have not said a word."

I lean forward, folding my arms against the steering wheel.

"It's okay, really. Don't be such a soppy sentimentalist. It's so unbecoming to you, dear heart. Besides, fear marks so many portions of our lives that I'm not going to let it in here.

This is my territory. My bloody domain. And I will be the queen. Pepper and I share this fiefdom philosophy."

"Long live the king and queen," I say, smiling to her.

She rolls her Thermos around in her hand. "Flossie, dear heart, let's go to Springfield."

"Let's go where?"

"Oh, give us a ride, won't you, love? Let's go to Springfield. It's not even an hour away. If we hasten, we can get there before the sun goes down."

"I'm not hastening anywhere but home, May Ruth. I'm tired as a dog. I'm exhausted from that sauna of an apartment. From constantly hearing about Pepper. From fucking Solomon. And now from your news."

"What an absolutely brilliant idea this is," she says, ignoring me. "I don't know why I didn't think of it earlier. I haven't been to that marvelous little town in ages. I used to live there, you know? Yes, take me to Springfield."

"You must be out of your mind if you think I'm going to drive—"

"Oh, please, dear heart. Who knows when I'll get back again. If ever." She looks forlornly at me over her glasses.

"I must be out of my mind for feeling sorry for you."

"You know, clearly, I shall milk this for all it's worth. Oh, look, dear heart." She fluffs her hair, then points to the purple cow at All-Rite Liquors, about a quarter mile away. "Speaking of milk, would you be a dear and allow me to make a quick pit stop? I'm on empty."

"You certainly are."

"By the way, you'll have to loan me a few pennies, dear heart. I do believe I've left all my pocket money back at the house. And do remember to tell me everything about Solomon. I had no earthly idea. I thought you'd been celibate for years. Such a discussion in itself will make the ride most worthwhile."

Up ahead, beyond the bend, the sunflowers from the western portion of the Famous Johnny Weston Hunt Club sway and ripple like water. To our left, smoke hovers over the town. As I get closer to the turn-off onto Old Riley, I see the reflectors on a sheriff's patrol car that's sitting in the grass, shielded a bit by a grouping of flowers. I look at my gauge and slow down. The cinder blocks in the back clunk around as I brake harder than I planned. May Ruth and I ease forward, bracing against the seat.

At the stop sign, I remember to allow the car to roll back on its wheels before I make the turn toward All-Rite, and then off to the interstate.

19

Flossie

May Ruth fills her Thermos cup for the second time and turns off the radio, abandoning her search for a station.

"Speaking of Pepper," she says, even though we weren't, "earlier when I mentioned I saw him, I neglected to mention that his father was there, too. When I arrived, Herbert was standing outside the door, watching the boy sleep. We waited a few minutes, hoping he'd awake, and when he didn't, Herbert and I walked out together. He said it wasn't necessary for me to tell anybody, particularly his wife, that he was there. I zipped my lips and told him they were sealed. But he knows I can't keep a secret. Heaven knows why he trusts me a'tall."

A semi blows by, along with the smell of manure. The pickup shakes. May Ruth steadies her Thermos cup.

"Are you comfortable, Flossie?" She looks out the window, then back over to me. "Dear heart, we have hit a stretch, haven't we? We'll be riding for a while, isn't that correct?"

"The sign back there just said thirty-five miles to Springfield."

"Very well, then. I shall tell you a story. No, I shall tell you a secret."

"I don't want to hear any more secrets. We'll be headed to Timbuktu or some shit afterward."

"Awful time of year for Timbuktu, dear heart. It's the rainy season. But listen, I want you to know how I met Cora and started coming to these festivals. I must admit, dear heart, I wasn't completely honest with you years ago. Do you remember? It's not all my fault really—my dishonesty. We British are rather partial to half-truths, keeping up appearances, you know. We are a funny breed in that regard. Do you remember what I told you about John Morgan?"

"John who?" I say. Up ahead, I see the red lights from trucks that are lined up for a way station. When we pass, I see the hog trailer that passed us earlier.

"John Morgan," she says, "my husband. I told you, years ago, that I left because he bored the hell out of me. You don't remember, do you?"

"May Ruth, I can't remember a damn thing you told me yesterday, let alone years ago. And you had a husband?"

"Why do you say it like that? Is that so bloody difficult to believe?"

"No, I suppose not. I never knew anything about a man in your life, so I thought you were a lesbian or something. Doesn't bother me."

May Ruth spits her liquor. "A lesbian? Oh dear, that's funny. Me? A lesbian?"

"Well, you never talk about a man in your life. But those birds. Oh, we get plenty on them along with your travels: the damn cormorant in the Galapagos Islands; the quetzal in Costa Rica, and on and on. Ad infinitum. But men? Nothing."

"Neither do you talk about the men in your life, to be sure. Maybe I was thinking the same thing about you."

"And students, you talk about your students. But never your men. And you're lying, you ain't never thought I was a lesbian."

She smiles and twists the lid on her Thermos, closing it and placing it in her tote. She snaps the tote shut. "Because I never talk about the *men* in my life, I shall tell you now about my

John Morgan. I shall also tell you about my lovely daughter, Cynthia."

John Morgan Wainwright and I met in Paris in the summer of 1948. We met at a quaint brasserie in the Montparnasse district, where all the philosophers, artists, and deep thinkers assembled back then to ruminate about the war, Hitler, reconstruction, and the lot.

It's such a cliché when you really think about it: meeting in a café along the River Seine. But it's true. We were sitting a couple of tables from each other when I first saw him. I was in Paris on holiday with a friend. She and I both worked for a couple of well-to-do families in London. That's how we paid for our schooling. I was a governess, she was a live-in tutor, and those little urchins drove us absolutely mad. We both desperately were in need of a holiday.

I was waiting at the café for my friend, who had been delayed, so I sat there watching John Morgan.

He was heavenly in a scattered sort of way. He had important documents strewn about his table, books stacked on the chair beside him, pencils jutting out of his hair. He was bent over the lot, exasperated and flummoxed one minute, enjoying it the next. Coffee flowed out of his ears, he drank so much. His hair was a wonderful thick black mop that fell into his eyes over and over and he kept brushing it away.

I was twenty years old and quite a looker back then myself, you know. Fiery red hair, a quite handsome figure. The one time he looked up, he saw me watching him. I quickly averted my eyes. I was certain that by the time I looked back over to him, he would have returned to his papers. However, he was still looking at me and with this pixieish smile.

When he walked over to my table waving a sheaf of copybook paper, I thought I would bloody die. There I was, this poor girl who'd grown up on a chicken farm outside of Paddington, more accustomed to slogging through chicken shit and lately sopping snotty noses than sitting in quaint coffee houses with intellectuals.

Long-nosed, he said, "Five pounds if you can tell me how Nuremburg Meatloafing was so successful." He was an American and referring to the Nazi propaganda rallies of the 1920s and '30s, the art of stadia—getting people to follow the absurd.

Presumptuous as he was, he sat without being invited. "How do you get so many people to hate?" he asked me. I sat up straight. I kept searching the door, hoping my friend would come bursting through like the Royal army to save me. "People work and work and can't make purchases," he went on, "and they need someone to blame for their own inability to buy things; for their general unhappiness. Most people believe it's as simple as that. But is it really, you think? Well, answer up. The cat has your tongue, has it? Can't you speak?"

"Yes. But I defy you to be quiet long enough to listen. It would be rude of me to interrupt, now, wouldn't it?"

He waved his hand before me, as though allowing me to pass.

"You have some nerve. You have your own little hate war going on with the Negro, haven't you? Sometimes I believe people hate so strongly simply because they love so strongly. The opposite has to exist, and sometimes if the right chords are struck simultaneously, masses of people may sing the same tune. As awful as it is. I do believe it is as simple as that."

Or something like that, I must have said. My knees were quivering, that much I do remember.

Slowly, all of his things were moved to my table. He would posit this and posit that, ramble on and on, and go back to his table to get a book for further explanations and proof and positing. Trying to reason with the unreasonable. Like wrestling a fire-breathing dragon.

We talked way into the evening. I learned he'd just finished his doctorate in the States and was on holiday in Europe. He had already accepted a position as an assistant professor at one of the universities back home. When the café closed, we went down the block to the flat where he was staying and made love. What a lovely hussy I was back then. I'd never done that before, honestly. But in those few hours, I felt like I knew him. Or at least I wanted to make love, and that was reason enough for doing it. Quite simple, that was. Wonderfully deductive.

John Morgan and I sent correspondences back and forth for months and we were married not a full year after we met. Shortly after our marriage, we had a daughter, Cynthia. We adored that child. We adored each other. Our lives were so perfect, so well put together. He got a job at Haverford College in Pennsylvania and then another at the University of Illinois.

Cynthia grew into the perfect little lady. She played the piano. She read voraciously. On Sundays we attended brunches and teas. And she loved dressing real spiffily. She and I were lovely companions since John Morgan worked so much—attending conferences and the sort.

Some afternoons my daughter and I would lie out in the garden. We had all kinds of beautiful flowers out there. There were lovely butterfly bushes and catmint that the butterflies fancied. There were cone and cardinal flowers and trumpet honeysuckle vines, a favorite for the hummingbirds. Cynthia and I would lie out back staring up at the sky for ages.

Once, when she was about five years old, she pulled a bunch of dandelions.

She said, "Mother, what do you call these flowers?"

"They're dandelions," I said, placing one in her hair and the other in mine. "Do you fancy them?"

She didn't answer. Instead she held another up to her ear.

"What's the matter?" I said.

She said, "I'm listening."

"For what?"

"I'm listening for the roar."

"The roar?"

"Do dandelions roar, Mother?"

I answered, "No," without thinking. But it's possible that they do, I believe now. Perhaps everything in nature roars at one time or another.

When Cynthia was twelve and a half, she got a fever. Oh, we thought it was a simple fever that would go away after a few days. But it didn't and her condition started to rapidly deteriorate. We took her to the campus hospital, where she slipped into a coma. There were more tubes flowing in and out of her than I had ever seen in my life, dear heart, a tightrope suspension of tubes and cords and nonsense. Doctors swarmed about. Still we were certain she was going to be fine. Why wouldn't she be? Our lives were perfect.

Cynthia was in the intensive-care unit, but I remember there was a black lady who'd come and go every day from one of the other rooms on the floor. I inquired about her because every time she'd end her visit, her child would wail and we could hear the poor thing's cries echoing all the way down the hall. It was the most excruciating sound I had every heard in my life. But the mother couldn't turn around to go back because she had other children at home. There was no father and she had to tend to them as well. I remember the sound of that child wailing as she'd walk past the ICU windows and how the child would continue long after the mother was down the hall; long after the lift had closed and carted her away. Long, long after.

But I could hardly concern myself with that, now, could I? My own child lay lifeless in her own awful state. Day in and day out, John Morgan and I would take turns praying. We would take turns reading and looking for the most minute evidence that she was coming back to us. Her hand or eye would twitch. Her legs would kick. All the while that black lady would make her daily pilgrimage. Tired, filled with sorrow and grief. I never said one word to her. I have no idea her name or from where she came, but I knew our children connected us. We both shared this desperation to help our babies and this sense of powerlessness in that there was little we could do to change the outcome of their conditions.

A week after we arrived, I was reading to Cynthia one night and she started to breathe heavily. As though she were struggling. She'd never recovered from the coma, you see. But she started to gasp and wheeze. Doctors made every attempt to save her. But I knew she was slipping away from us. I knew she was slipping away from me. As wonderfully as she'd come into this world, she passed on. She was twelve years old. After the doctors unhooked their devices, I carried her over to a chair by the window, held her on my lap and rocked her. I sang to her. John Morgan was so bereft that he couldn't stand any of it. He sobbed and sobbed at her feet.

It's funny, you know. You think about all the little things children do in everyday life that drive you absolutely mad. However, you never realize how easy they are to lift when it's the last time. The last thing you think about is how much weight there is. That's the absolute last thing that's important then.

Cynthia had been gone about a month when I decided to leave John Morgan.

I was out of my mind with grief. Nothing fit anymore. My sense of normalcy was gone. I was numb. And that feeling wouldn't go away. I tried not to assess blame, but it's almost an eventuality, really. I blamed John Morgan. For what exactly, I'm not sure. I blamed myself. I blamed God. I cursed the bloody walls in that house and all of heaven and hell. I wanted to know why. And no one could tell me. So I left, in search of the why. And if no answer was immediately forthcoming, I was determined to find a way to ease the pain.

After a few days of hitchhiking and sleeping wherever, I happened upon Halley. It was the latter part of July and the air was frenetic with people getting ready for the festival. I walked all the way into the downtown. I was dirty and most unkempt and didn't care one ounce. Oh, I was a sight, really.

When I got to the fairgrounds, I crossed the baseball field and started up the hill in the woods. I followed the path to the top, where I saw a sign that said this was the highest section of the canal wall. I walked over to the wall and looked thirty feet down into the rushing water.

I sat on the ledge, sobbing, getting ready to hurl myself into the canal's deepest depths, when Cora happened by. She had been planting flowers on the other side of the church's courtyard when she saw me enter.

She said, "Young lady, I was wondering where you were going. I wouldn't sit up on that wall if I were you. You see the sign over there? These rocks get mighty slick this time of year. It's the humidity. Course, it's the dew, too. Dew clings to everything, even in the middle of day."

"Perhaps that's what I'm hoping for," I said. "Perhaps I'm looking forward to it being rather slick. Perhaps I want to jump in."

"Oh, so that's your intention, is it? Course, I've never known anybody who wanted to fall in." Placing her gardening tools on the grass, she walked over to me and began to peer down into the water. She really didn't seem to notice me a'tall. My eyes were on fire. I thought they would burst out of my head. My face was equally inflamed. And the odor was quite foul. But Cora looked right down into the water as though I were completely tolerable. She said, "What would you want to go and do that for? Jump in, I mean. Can't you find something better to do with your day?"

"This might very well be the high point of my day."

"You swim? Well, I don't suppose you have to answer that since that's not your intention. To swim, that is. What I believe you need is some rest. Now, just flip your legs back on over to this side of the world. God ain't ready for you just yet or he wouldn't have sent me along to fight with you. You just come with me and get some good rest, if you're so inclined. I just lost my husband a few months ago and I got this great big house that can stand some company."

You think that you haven't anything left in you. That you've been hollowed out and nothing remains and someone comes into your life and helps you rebuild. Piece by piece. Cora and I talked for ages. We talked and talked. There were days when I had nothing to say and Cora was fine with that, too. But slowly, very slowly, there was a resurrecting of the spirit.

After about a month, I contacted John Morgan and told him to come get me. He was out of his mind with worry. We found it very hard to resume our lives. Nothing fit right anymore. Not without our daughter. His face, my face, the house, were constant reminders of our loss. Not of our future. So, after a year, we decided to part. It was quite amicable, really. No hard feelings a'tall. He teaches now at Berkeley. He's got a family, a lovely wife and three daughters. And we talk every two or three years. Oddly, he, too, has discovered a love of birds. He didn't seem to care much for them before Cynthia's death. Isn't that strange?

I will always love him, I suppose.

You know, there's a time in the early morning when you're allowed—even for a few seconds—to escape from your troubles. It normally occurs when you're not quite asleep and not quite awake and the breeze from wide-open windows combines with the billowy comfort of the bed linens to surround you with a calm that is hypnotic. And you actually feel normal. But that lasts for seconds and that's as close you ever get to normal again.

I'm preaching to the choir, I suppose.

Years ago, when we first met and you were fretting over Sweet Alma's pregnancy, I wanted to tell you that I would have given anything to be in your place. What I would have given to be filled with anger and resentment, my heart shut so tight that I wouldn't have known what could possibly unlock it again.

What I would give to be in your shoes right now, dear heart, in such a quarrel with my child, my beautiful daughter.

I would be the happiest woman on this bloody earth. The absolute happiest.

May Ruth clicks on the radio, immediately settling in on a station. I breathe in and feel as though I've been holding my breath. My head throbs. My muscles ache. I want to cry for her, but I know she wouldn't want me to. She's made it clear she doesn't want to be pitied. I also know she's planned this ride, this discussion, and ordinarily I'd be angry about her manipulative tactics. But it's hard to be mad at May Ruth even under ordinary circumstances. And these clearly are not ordinary.

When it's time to exit the interstate, the sun has nearly set. May Ruth directs me through a commercial district to a road that winds through the woods. The campus is still fairly quiet because of summer. After a couple of turns, we're sitting in front of the brick house that is now a fraternity house. I stop the truck and get out. She leans out the window. Floodlights illuminate the facade of the building. A few young men with beers hang around the porch. Two are in the front yard, throwing a Frisbee between each other, with a big dog racing back and forth.

We get out of the pickup. I lean against the car next to May Ruth. She threads her fingers through mine. The boys stop what they're doing in the yard and turn our way. After a few seconds, one walks over.

"Ms. Albee-Wainwright?" he asks.

"Yes, dear heart, I am."

"I'm Mark, remember me?" he says, pointing to himself. "We met last summer? You helped us plant the poppies."

"I do remember. Good to see you, Mark. I trust you've been well?"

"I have," he says. "I'm a senior this year. I guess I won't see you next year."

"Oh, that's a shame. We'll have to remember to exchange our particulars. Do tell me how the primroses and the poppies are faring out back."

"They're doing fine. In full bloom. I'll take you back there."

I interrupt, "May Ruth, I thought you said you haven't been here in ages."

"That was unforgivable of me, now, wasn't it, dear heart? I hardly think, however, that if I had mentioned I drive over every year to check on the boys and the primroses, you would have come. Am I correct?" She takes my arm and the young man's. "Mark, this is my dear friend Florence J. Penticott. She's quite partial to sunflowers, which may or may not blend well with our current decor. We'll just have to see, now, won't we? And we'll have to introduce her to the rest of the boys and to the staff. Mrs. Penticott will be the one coming next August to tend the garden and quite possibly from now on. I very well may have another engagement."

20

Thelma
AFTER TEN O'CLOCK

I'm staring out this kitchen window when I hear the telephone ringing.

"Somebody gone answer that phone?" Herbert says, running down the front steps. By the time he gets to the phone
table, the ringing has stopped. "Thelma, didn't you hear the
phone? It's loud enough to wake the dead. Aunt Cora's
upstairs sleeping and I was hoping somebody'd get to it
before it woke her up. Thelma? Thelma?"

"I didn't hear it, Herbert," I say, still staring out the window. But I hear it now that it's stopped.

Now I hear everything clearly. The gurgling in the sink's
drain. The screened door slamming as Herbert goes out to the
porch. Talk from this television. I didn't even realize that the
television was on. But now, through the reflection in the window, I see old President Reagan coming across the White
House lawn, moving like a ghost in and out of our trees, talking about something. He's followed by a clip of Prime Minister Margaret Thatcher. I turn up the sound. They're talking
about the sanctions Britain, India, Australia, Canada, and
some others—I missed the rest—are imposing on South Africa.
Last week, when all those countries were just talking about
the sanctions, Herbert said sanctions weren't anything more

than a front; at best, a slap on the wrist against apartheid. But, I said, give them some credit, Herbert. Old Reagan and our Congress aren't even willing to do that. Herbert said the worst part is that unless the sanctions go on for a long, long time, they won't hardly affect the South African government and the businessmen; but they'll beat the hell out of the South African people. That's the way Herbert feels. Aunt Cora said it doesn't matter. She said that if you polled the people, they'd probably say go on ahead with the sanctions anyway. She said the argument that the sanctions would do more harm to the people they're trying to help is the same one slave masters used in explaining why slaves shouldn't be freed. They said the slaves wouldn't be able to fend for themselves without their masters and they would be in a terrible predicament. Aunt Cora said better to experience some discomfort, or even death, on the way to freedom, than be stuck in the *comforts* of slavery. That's how those South Africans must be feeling, she said. They can weather the unemployment and high prices the sanctions will bring. All of it is part of the journey. I tend to agree with Aunt Cora, though I won't say that to my Herbert.

As I think about it, I didn't hear the phone ringing because I was wondering what May Ruth and Flossie Jo were doing at June's place. I was just thinking: They could be having a time joking about me or my son.

Herbert comes into the kitchen and sits down next to his five-pound burlap bag of peanuts. He drags the garbage can over, grabs a couple of fistfuls of nuts, and places them on the table. He starts shelling them.

"Herbert, what do you suppose May Ruth, Flossie Jo, and June are talking about? You suppose they're talking about me or Pepper? June and I aren't exactly the best of friends."

He shakes the shells around in the garbage can. "Nope."

"How could you be so sure? You know, Flossie thinks I'm responsible for Pepper's—what'd she call it?—'failure to thrive.' That's what she said. Talking that social-work talk. And you know June doesn't like me. Not that I've done a thing to her. I just tell her that she should be a little more understanding of Pepper, a little more supportive. . . ."

Herbert says, "Nope. Maybe they talking 'bout that radioactive cloud from Chernobyl, or maybe they trying to find out whether O-rings or booster rockets or some such caused those poor astronauts to perish. Something worthwhile like that."

I watch him shelling those peanuts, tossing them into his mouth. Smacking his lips. He reaches back to turn off the television. I take a handful of nuts for myself.

"You think he'll find himself, Herbert?" I ask him. "You think Pepper'll ever forgive himself? I got ten sons and all the hardship always lands on the one at the bottom of the pile. He's the only one whose luck isn't worth a dime. I keep trying to figure out how I can help that boy."

"Pepper got to help hisself," Herbert says. He spits, mostly air, over his shoulder and rubs on his belly. "And he'll find hisself or forgive hisself if he want to be found or forgave. That's number one. Number two is, I done told you about lying to yourself, Thelma. Them other boys ain't doing much better. They just look better on the outside, maybe. But they just as messed up as Pepper. I asked each of them to come this year. Sweet Alma, too. And you see any one of them here? That's for starters. The way I see it, you can blame yourself all you want. I ain't about to own up to any of this mess. They all got equal portions. Our boys did. We gave them all equal portions."

"Maybe they needed more than equal portions, Herbert."

"Let's take some for instances. Let's take our Solomon. He a big-time lawyer. Got a fancy car and a big, big house in upstate New York. Got every material thing you can put a dollar figure on. But his mind is one-track. He got a good wife that he never sees. Can't spend no time 'cause he got responsibilities that are bigger than the both of them. With all that house, ain't no enjoyment anywhere within them walls. I tell him he should take a drive to see May Ruth from time to time. She don't live that far from him. But you think he gone make the effort? All right, let's take Charles. Which one is he? Our second—no, third up from Pepper. Used to be Chuckie suited him just fine, but it don't fit him no more. He done left it behind him. Onliest thing is, that ain't all he done left behind. These days he focusing on that good job he got, too. That good money he making. But he don't think about that girl that come up in the family way a couple of years ago. She say that baby was his, but Charles say it ain't. So I go take a look at him myself so I can see the little fellow with my own eyes. And I say he looked a whole lot like Charles to me. Enough to make me a believer. I say, 'Son, don't you wanna know if he belong to you? Don't you wanna know if that's your blood in his veins?' He say, 'He ain't mine.' And that's supposed to be the end of it. Like saying so give him a free ride. Ain't no free ride when you throw your child away. It'll all catch up with him down the road, though. All right, that's Charles. Let's take Martin. He in school in Atlanta. At a fine, fine school, Morris Brown. Grades fall at the top of the mark. But you can't go down there unannounced 'cause if you do, you might ring his doorbell and he might open it, wearing them red hot pants that look like women's pants, and that shiny shirt that's wide open, showing glitter on his chest—"

"Stop it, Herbert. Just stop it. Why you want to make my life such a misery?" I try not to cry, but I can't help it. Herbert comes over and puts his arm around me and I don't feel like being smoothed over, especially by the person, my own husband, who just caused the wrinkle.

"Thelma, baby, last thing I want to do is make your life a misery. But sometimes I just don't know what you're seeing when you look out of them eyes of yours. I want you to see things the way they is, 'stead of the way you want them to be.

care much for talking to these machines, Sweet Baby. This my third time today and it still don't feel natural. Like I'm talking to myself, which is more your auntie's domain than mine. So once again I'm gone be brief. The parade start tomorrow. Everything get under way at about noon. Ain't too late for you to come on down. Hell, I'll drive on up to get you, if you want. That ain't no problem at all. Now, I'm gone hang up now, you hear? This is your uncle Herbert, phoning again. Thank you very much."

As he's walking back up the steps, I think about El and Pepper running through this house. It's like I can feel both of them running through like lightning zipping past, snatching something of Sweet Alma's just for fun and her running after them. I latch on to the quiet in the room and I decide right at that very moment that I'm going to see my son. I grab my shoes that are sitting next to that bag of peanuts and I get my purse and hat.

While I dial for a taxi, my hands shake at the thought of going back out tonight. The phone rings and I think about Pepper's little clean-shaven itchy head and all those books he's got in there lined up next to his cot, making like it's home.

"I need a cab sent to the Hoskins house, please," I say to the dispatcher.

"Will be 'bout an hour's wait," he says. "We backed up for a good hour."

"Never mind, then." I hang up.

El's old ten-speed runs through my mind. I slip out the back door and walk around to the side of the house. I tie my purse straps to the handlebars and start down the hill.

The back tire is a bit flat, but not as flat as my feet. So I don't allow it to trouble me.

Bright lights turning off Old Riley shine onto the driveway. Instead of running into Flossie and May Ruth, I take a horizontal path down a row of sunflowers and cut through a

I know Pepper carrying around a heavy load. We told that boy from the outset last year that if he needed to talk to somebody other than family, we'd pay for it. Whatever he needed we'd be there for him. But he done chose to go it alone. That's his wishes. He the one run off from Pittsburgh. We don't hear from him for a good month. Then come to find out he here. Done met him a girl and shacked up with her. Then he gets her pregnant. One that he hardly knowed from Adam. June is nice and all, but what kind of future they got? He the one dropped out of school. Can't hold a job, if somebody strapped one on his back. He the one getting hisself throwed in jail back and forth: Shoplifting back in January. Shoplifting what? A book, a stupid six-dollar-and-eighty-five-cent paperback he said he had to have. The next arrest was driving drunk. Then whatever else after that. I done throwed enough money his way. Now that boy got to find his own way. So do the rest of our boys. So do Sweet Alma. Listen to me good, Thelma. I'm not saying they don't have a reason to be tore up. They all got one reason after another. But they got to move forward."

"It makes me wonder why peace of mind has to come in drips and drabs," I say. "Why can't all our problems be fixed in one sitting so everything works out the way we want them to? All hell breaks loose in our lives at one time. Especially mine. Why not the opposite? Why not peace?"

"Peace, happiness, all that, come by the inch, Thelma." Herbert stands, brushing flecks of shells off his lap. He starts up the back steps, rubbing his gut with both hands. "C'mon, baby, let's go get some rest. Tomorrow is the start of the festival and we want to be ready for the goings-on."

"I'll be up in a minute, Herbert." I'll be up *by the inch,* I say to myself.

He starts up the steps, then turns back and goes over to the telephone. He dials and after a few seconds he says, "Good evening, this is your uncle Herbert Gray. You know I don't well-worn path in the woods. I'm led by the lights along Old Riley and from what I know of the land. I know this land like the back of my hands, I do. I know where the poison ivy grows down on the far southern edge. I know where all the tracts of Osage orange crawl. That's because I've gotten tangled in all of it enough, and it's grabbed me and skinned my legs enough that I tend to remember, even without intending to. I also know where you can and can't walk around the pond out back because there are places where the mud sucks you in like quicksand. If you're not careful. Yes, indeedy.

I get to the bottom of the property and sit there for a minute to catch my breath. I listen to the power lines humming. And to the music along the river coming from the boats stopped at the pier. I listen to the water, more of that gurgling sound coming from it. Just like in the kitchen sink. I think of El and Pepper and the summers they went swimming out there, tousling along the waves. I think of Pepper being a little more on the timid side about the water and sticking near the bank while El swam so far out I'd always have to call him back.

"Why do you have to go out so far, honey?" I'd ask him. "We know you're a good swimmer. Swim on back this way. Swim on back this way, you hear?"

I come back to myself and start out on the bike again.

It's wobbly at first. My rear end already has tired from having bumped along the path. My dress catches in the spokes. I stop to pull it up and knot it around my thighs. Only a few cars are out on Old Riley, but they whip pass me. I ride knock-kneed on the gravel shoulder over nasty, pushed-to-the-side roadkill, with dead possum and skunk eyes staring up at me, nearly scaring the life out of me, and over rank beer cans and smashed soda bottles. I keep riding through clouds of lightning bugs and people yelling mean things like "Get the hell off the road," and blowing their horns because they don't see me until they drive up on me, which probably unnerves them as much as they unnerve me. Traffic lulls as I pass by a small cornfield. When I was young, this time of year, corn grew so fast I could hear it pulling up from the ground. Only I can't hear the corn now because I'm concentrating on the hills and how my legs ache and my eyes burn from the light-dark-light-dark rhythm of the street lamps—and the head-on cars. That light-dark-light-dark rhythm reminds me of a New York subway ride. Lights flickering on and off. And my nerves remind me of a subway ride, too. Only now my nerves are run down from the firecrackers going off in the direction of the park and the snapping and popping of the Halley's Comet flags overhead on the lampposts. All that noise is the other reason I can't hear the corn.

By the time I cross the bridge, I've lost my hat and all feeling in my fingertips and in my rear end. Another half mile and up ahead I see the two bright white columns of the courthouse and that one little lit window in the basement, which is exactly where I'm gunning.

I park El's bike in the rack in front of the building. I walk a few paces, walking stilted before I remember to unknot my dress.

It's after hours, so I ring the bell. After a while, Mr. Sewell shuffles to the door. I see the peephole wink at me and I know he's looking through it. He opens the door a crack.

"How're you, Thelma?" he says, talking real low. He steps outside the door, pulls it behind him, leaving his heel in the jamb so it doesn't close. "Pepper all right. Pastor Delaware is down there with him now. He's been there for some time. I'm trying to get him to leave since time is up. Now, you go on home, Thelma. And you can see him in the morning before the parade."

"I want to see him now, Mr. Sewell," I tell him. "I know it's past time. But I've just got to see him tonight. Even if for two seconds. One second. I want to peep in on him and see how he's getting along. I just had this urge, you see. I feel like he needs me. I have these urges from time to time, but I'm not normally within shouting distance with us living out East. And I know you aren't supposed to allow me to come in. But he's not really a prisoner and—"

Mr. Sewell raises his hands for me to be quiet. He looks around behind me to see who's there and who isn't. Nobody I can see. But straight up where he looks for the longest is the sky over the interstate. It's layered misty gray and blue. Clouds of gray, like in the movies when God is in the sky and the sky speaks in that deep billowy bass voice like my Herbert's, but it's a white man's bass voice, speaking, giving orders.

We stand there long enough before Mr. Sewell lets me in. I follow him to Pepper's cell. As if I need an escort. I know the way just fine.

I search for the lemon stick-up smell and find it immediately. Pastor Delaware sits on the chair with his opened Bible in both hands. Pepper's lying on his cot, laughing.

I'm so happy to hear laughter I don't know what to do.

"Pepper," I say, "your mama's here."

He looks up from Delaware's Bible, smiling at me. "What you doing here?" he says. But it doesn't sound so mean like it did earlier. "Go on home, Mama, you been here all day. You don't need to be here all night, too."

Delaware says, "Good evening, Thelma. Good to see you. Robert and I have been having a good visit. We've been reminiscing."

Delaware stands and holds the chair out for me.

"What've you been reminiscing about?" I say.

Pepper says, "Mama, you remember last year, I was trying to learn how to drive. I was practicing for my driver's test?"

"I remember," I say. "You're the last one to learn and weren't the least bit interested for the longest." I turn to Delaware. "All the other boys jumped at the chance, but not my Pepper."

"I ain't all the other boys, Mama," Pepper says.

"I know, honey," I say, fearing more wrinkles. "I know that."

"That same evening Mr. Paul mess with that baby, but earlier before everything went down, Daddy was under that party tent in the middle of the yard, eating. He was mad at me 'cause he was trying to teach me how to drive, but I wasn't learning the way he wanted me to. Aunt Flossie come running out to the porch, swiping me upside my head. She said, 'Come on, Pepper, come go with me. I've got to go get some ice.' I wasn't doing nothing. Just sitting on the porch, watching Sweet Alma hugging up with Rena Davies's little baby. Aunt Flossie was lighting a cigarette on her way down the stairs. She turned to say something to me and saw Sweet Alma with the baby. 'Don't that baby have a mama?' she said. 'I'm baby-sitting,' Sweet Alma said. 'Rena had to step out for a while.' Aunt Flossie sucked her teeth. 'She steps out more than she steps in, if you ask me.' Sweet Alma say, 'Well, Mother, nobody asked you.' Aunt Flossie grabbed me by the hand. 'Come on, boy,' she said, 'you baby-sitting, too? Let's go before El comes out and wants to go.' First I thought we was just going down to the mini-mall to get the ice from there. But we went around to the loading area in the back of All-Rite Liquors to that parking area that's wide open back there. The car's reflection followed the length of glass, over FOR RENT signs that hung in many of the storefronts. Aunt Flossie stopped the car. She made me get out and come around to the driver's side. Then she made me sit behind the wheel. 'You ready?' she asked me. I didn't say nothing at first. She said, 'El told me about the fight you and your daddy had. And I'm going to teach you how to drive. It's easy as pie.' I looked at her. 'El said Herbert thought you cussed him, that's why he cut your lesson short.' 'I ain't cuss him,' I said. 'I just told him the hell with it, since he kept ragging on me. He just kept yelling at me to do this. Do that. Naw, don't do that. So

I just say, To hell with it. I ain't never got to learn how to drive. My feet move just fine.' I turned away from her to watch the cars up on the interstate zooming pass. Aunt Flossie said, 'Okay now, watch the road in front of you. I can teach you, if you want to learn. Do you want to learn?' I nodded and wiped my hands on my pants before I turned the key. I looked over at her, just smiling. 'Sit back, honey,' she said to me. 'No need to inhale the steering wheel. Just sit back and enjoy the ride. Calm yourself. Here, take a hit off my cigarette to steady your nerves. Your daddy just gets worked up. Don't mind him.' I took a quick drag and coughed. Aunt Flossie closed her eyes. She pulled a cold beer from her purse and opened it. Took a long swallow. She nodded for me to go ahead. I knew to place my foot on the brake before I put the car in gear. Then I started to move around that loading area, real slow. So slow the engine seemed taxed and Aunt Flossie had to tell me to give that truck some juice. I pressed down some more, then some more, getting the hang of it. And pretty soon we was flying down that dusty road along all that limestone with cars zooming on the interstate to our left. I could tell Aunt Flossie was smiling at me, but I was too scared to look anywhere but straight ahead. Pretty soon them tires didn't feel like they was gripping the road so hard no more and the motor didn't feel so taxed no more. The car's motion was smooth and easy. Humming a sweet little melody. Pretty soon the bumps and the jerks made the two of us laugh, and I didn't, at least for the time being, feel so weighted down. That's what me and Delaware was talking about. We was just remembering the good that happened before Mr. Paul come back to the house that night. We was just remembering the good.'"

21

Thelma

The Festival

THE YEAR BEFORE

Herbert and I were sitting at one of those tables under the tent. El meandered for a while over by the bandstand before coming over to sit next to us. For the longest, he didn't say anything. He just sat watching me piece together my specialty finger sandwiches. Herbert was picking at the sweet potatoes. He doesn't like my finger sandwiches because he says they don't have any smell on account of them being too little to hold a smell. And no taste to speak of, either. But that didn't stop El from pulling about five from the stacked pyramid, mashing them together, and shoveling them into his mouth.

"You got something on your mind, boy?" Herbert said, rubbing El's shoulder.

"Nope," El said over a mouth full of food.

Pepper and Flossie were driving up in her pickup truck. Her light swirled on top. Pepper sat in the driver's seat, smiling wide. Spitting spite more than anything at his father, is what he was doing when he saw Herbert watching him. Spitting spite, more than anything, Herbert said.

Herbert stood. He said to El, "Boy, you must be liking them sandwiches real fine?"

El said, "They all right." Only you couldn't tell "they all right" by the way he was throwing them in his mouth. They seemed more than all right.

When Herbert walked over to the pickup for a driving report on his son, El said, "Aunt Thelma?" By then Pep had jumped from behind the wheel and was walking with his chest poked out toward Herbert. El simply looked over and didn't run after Pep the way he normally did, so I knew something was the matter.

"Aunt Thelma," El said again, "can I ask you a question?" I nodded and sat down next to him.

"How come nobody, not Grandma, not Sweet Alma or Aunt Cora . . . how come nobody will tell me about my daddy?"

"Where did all this come from?" I asked him. The question took my breath a bit.

"I don't know," he said. But I could tell he knew exactly. He just wasn't saying.

"I never knew my father either," I said. "And look at me. I turned out all right."

"But you're a girl, Aunt Thelma. It's okay if you was raised in a house full of women. I need a man who can give me a road map."

"El, honey, who's been filling your head with this foolishness about a road map?"

"Nobody," he said. He looked down into his lap, but I grabbed his chin so he could look at me.

"The important thing is that people love you. It doesn't matter whether it's men or women. You know Sweet Alma is your real mother. And she loves you. You know your grandmother loves you. We all do. Don't be silly."

El's attention returned to his sandwich as he separated the meat from the bread. He ate this particular one piecemeal, licking the side with the mustard first, then the side with the mayonnaise.

I placed my hand on El's shoulder, but it didn't fall right. I knew that it wasn't a steady hand at all. There's no stopper anywhere to fill in the hole left from not knowing who you are. That's what Herbert was trying to tell our boy after that girl turned up pregnant. It's like being split in two, knowing one half and not the other. And the pieces fitting lopsided, never, ever coming together just right. After years of living in my own skin, looking high and low for evidence of who I was, well, I couldn't leave El as empty-handed as before he came to me. Me his own auntie, whom it was clear he trusted and felt some kind of connection to. Even at eleven, he had to have understood we shared a similar lopsidedness.

"El, honey," I said, " we look up to the sky for everything, especially direction. It's where we believe heaven is, and all of its consolation. We see a universe that holds many promises, even though we have no idea exactly what that promise is." I turned to look back over to the driveway. Herbert, Flossie, and Pepper were leaning against the pickup, talking. I whispered, " I only know your daddy's name and that he lived in Chicago. I wrote it down years ago and I've still got it in my bureau at home. I'll mail it back to you next week. It'll be our little secret, okay? Maybe one day when you're a lot older, that will help you find him. I don't know. Maybe Sweet Alma can tell you more later. Both she and your grandma are just trying to protect you, is all."

"I don't need no protecting," El said. He looked up to the porch where Sweet Alma was seated in Aunt Cora's chair, rocking little Jamie. For the longest, El just watched them rocking. Like the sight was trying to lull him, too. Lull him right to a calm place. He said, "I haven't decided what I'd call my daddy yet. Nothing seem to sound right when I practice it."

"I used to wonder that myself," I said. "I used to think about our first meeting. I had it all planned out, what it would be like. Early morning. A bright sunny day. Springtime."

El kept watching Sweet Alma until Pepper ran to the porch with his chest still poked out. When El saw Pepper running, he left me to my fantasy and ran over toward the house.

Earlier, the sun had the tree limbs laid out in gnarled shadows against the porch planks. Day had turned and the shadows were gone. Still, El hopped along the porch like one of the shadow balance beams remained. Like he had been doing all throughout the afternoon. He hopped along till he got over to the front door. Then he jumped down in a pretend dismount with his arms in the air, holding his feet together so that he rocked, off-balance. He then followed his cousin inside.

Day Four

22

Robert "Pepper" Gray
The Festival
THE YEAR BEFORE

I was looking out El's bedroom window that morning when them cops come for Mr. Paul's white truck.

Only reason I was looking out the window was 'cause I ain't slept hardly all night with that truck out there. That truck was so white that when them firecrackers lit up the sky, that truck seemed set afire. Only it wasn't and by morning it was still standing clear into the first of sunlight when they come to get it. Round 'bout six o'clock.

I heard the police car when it pull into the drive. And I saw Daddy walk out to meet that white cop who got out. That cop brought a brother with him to drive the truck back. I saw the brother get out and jump up in the cabin of that truck. His sleeves was rolled up and his black arm hung out the window—making that white look whiter—as he waited on Daddy to finish talking to that cop.

The bedroom window was open wide, but I couldn't hear a lot of what they was saying. They kept moving around. Gravel is what I heard mostly until they moved closer to the porch and that cop said to Daddy, "We're about to move him over to the courthouse in Jasper. The judge can decide later on this morning whether he's getting bond. Probably will, though."

"Do he know he better not look back this way? Do he understand that?"

"I don't know what he understands. How can you tell with somebody like that?"

"Well then, I'll follow behind you and make sho' he understands well enough. He was talking that shit last night about killing my boy. Talking out of his head, is what he was doing. But I just want to make sure."

"We can't have no trouble, Herbert."

"Won't be no trouble," Daddy told him. "Onliest thing I want to do is make sho' he understands not to come back this way."

Daddy said he ought to get his wallet first, so he came inside.

I jumped into my clothes fast as I could. Soon as I opened the door to leave the room, El was standing in the doorway, fixing to enter the room. He said, "I'm comin' with you."

"Nigger, you ain't goin' nowhere," I told him.

"I got to go, Pep, and you can't stop me." He flew past me, going over to his pants. He pulled them over his shorts.

"I can lay your ass out," I told him. "Why you got to go?"

"I just got to, that's all, and if you try to stop me, we both'll be right here. You may beat me, but I'm gone get one good lick in."

He started walking toward the door and I held him behind me as I opened it and peeped out into the hall. I saw Daddy leave his room and head down the back steps. We waited for the front door to close and we was on our way down the back, too, to the side of the house. We jumped on them bikes and waited for that truck and that police car and Daddy's car to pull off. This time no lights flashed or nothing. This time that truck just moved real slowlike down the drive. So as not to disturb the trees or the rest of the morning.

El and me followed behind far enough so they couldn't see us. Wasn't no cars out hardly, so wasn't no need for them to stop when they got to the end of the driveway. They just drove on out onto Old Riley and kept going at a good clip. We followed far enough back. Wasn't no need to get too close since we knew where they was going. I could hear El breathing. We both was breathing hard. Heads down, our legs digging. We knew when to stop pedaling on the declines and when to get going fast again where the road swept up.

The closer we got to the downtown, the more floats we saw lined up along the riverbank. Cops was unloading them sawhorses they place at intersections up and down the street. A bunch of red, white, and blue balloons—must've been about a hundred of them—was tied to the trusses of the bridge. The welcome banner hung zigzaggedy across the way.

We didn't stop for any of it. We kept riding until we made it to the courthouse. We woulda rode around to the back if we'd known that as soon as we'd pull up, Daddy would be coming out. He saw us the same time we saw him. We jumped off our bikes.

He said, "What in the Sam hell y'all doing here?" He looked down at his watch.

"We wanted to see," I said.

El wiped sleep from his eyes. "I got to give Mr. Paul something."

"Y'all don't need to be giving nobody nothing. Go get in that car."

Neither one of us moved at first. We could hear what sounded like Mr. Paul's creepy-ass voice coming from a little basement window. We could hear it but couldn't make out what he was saying.

"I know y'all want to know what happened," Daddy said, "but ain't nothing here that concern you. Now get in that car."

El said, "But, Uncle Herbert . . ."

"Now get," Daddy said.

We both went and got in the backseat. A police car with its lights flashing pulled in front of us. Daddy was lifting the bikes into the trunk when we saw Mr. Paul coming out. El tapped my arm, but I was already looking. Mr. Paul had on handcuffs and that cop was leading him by the arm down the steps. He had a white bandage crisscrossing his head. He looked toward us, but I can't say he saw us. He just got his ass in the car.

"Y'all do the damnedest things, you two." Daddy got some string to tie the trunk down since it wouldn't close over the bikes. "Just won't act right to save your lives."

Before Daddy got behind the wheel, El whispered to me, "You think he'll come back, Pepper?"

"I done told you over and over, he ain't coming back," I told him. "He ain't stupid enough for that."

"I got something for him if he do come back."

El lifted his shirt a crack so I could see the handle of the gun sticking out of his pants and pressing into his stomach.

"Nigger, you must be crazy," I whispered to him. "Where'd you get that gun?"

"It's Grandma's."

Daddy got in the car. He said, "Y'all sho' got a lot of conversation for this early in the morning."

El held his hand on his waist. I grabbed his arm. But he didn't move it. And neither did I. So Daddy wouldn't know, we both quietly stared out the window.

The downtown stores was opening and people was washing their sidewalks, picking at the flowers in the whiskey barrels outside the stores, buffing them windows one last time before the parade.

Near the taxi place, some of the flag bearers in the marching band had on their matching getups and were practicing their steps without the music. The baton twirler—a relief pitcher who had a fastball and a change-up that come closer to Sweet Alma's than anybody else—worked on throwing

her baton. Only she kept missing it when it came spinning
back down. Frustrated, she looked down at her watch, knowing that if she ain't had it right by then, she was in for some
trouble.

Daddy slowed as we passed her. "It's that timing that's
gone mess her up come time for the parade," he said. "It's that
timing that mess us all up."

We got back to the house and Daddy went into the kitchen.
Aunt Cora, Aunt Flossie, and Sweet Alma was sitting at the
table. Me and El ran up the front steps to Aunt Flossie's bedroom. I pulled El inside and locked the door behind us.

"You got to put it back," I said. He looked at me. "I said
you got to put it back, right now, or I will kick your ass."

He opened Aunt Flossie's closet door and crawled toward
the back of the closet. I listened at the bedroom door. When
he came out, I dragged him back to his bedroom.

"You got some explaining to do, boy. What the hell you
doing with that thing?"

He say, "You can't tell nobody, you hear?"

"You just tell me what you got to say."

"Mr. Paul coming back."

"I done told you—"

"I got something that belong to him and I know he coming
back for it."

He felt around under his mattress. He pulled out a baseball
card of Ernie Banks. It was wrapped in plastic. It was much
nicer than the card he had already.

"We had our baseball cards spread out along the porch the
night of the party. Me and Li'l Sidney and Junior. We didn't
have but a few. Just the ones we keep on us. We was talking
about trading up when Mr. Paul say he got something to show
us. He said it was in his room. We followed him up there.
And he went into his closet. He pulled out this album, this

black album, with seem like a hundred baseball cards. He lay it across his bed and we jump on the bed and start to flip through them. Then, just out of the blue, he said if we loved baseball so much, we should get our daddies to take us to the Baseball Hall of Fame in Cooperstown, the birthplace of baseball. He said, By the way, El, where is your daddy? I've been meaning to ask that. The whole time I been here, I ain't seen him. I didn't say nothing. But Li'l Sidney jump in, minding my business. He say, El ain't got no daddy and he don't know where he is. Junior turned over on the bed and started laughing. He pointed to the Ernie Banks card Mr. Paul had in the middle of the album. Last summer, Junior said, El lied and told everybody Ernie Banks was his daddy. El say that's why he play shortstop, to be like his daddy. The coach bust him out in front of everybody, saying, Ernie Banks ain't your daddy, boy. I grabbed Junior around his collar and yanked him so hard I tore his uniform. He pushed me and we got to swinging. Mr. Paul got me off him. Junior got up and ran out and Sid ran out after him. Mr. Paul started shaking his head. He said I didn't have to fool with them. He said he would be my friend. He took the Ernie Banks card out and handed it to me. Said I could borrow it for a while. But I had to give it back because it was worth a good piece of change. A good, good piece of change. I could borrow it, but I had to give it back before he left. He handed the card to me, playing like he was snatching it back and forth. He do that a couple of time, then put it in my hand. He said the only thing about not having no daddy around was that I had to protect these women. Mr. Paul say the only problem is that sometimes boys raised by a house full of women turn out to be sissy boys instead of protectors. I said I ain't no sissy boy. He put his arm around me. Said, I'm not talking about you in particular. He pointed to a baseball he had on the dresser. He said, That ball's got two hundred and sixteen stitches in it. It's stitched by hand. And if you miss any one of them stitches, the wadding falls apart. That's what a daddy is for. To make sure, along the way, you don't fall apart, you don't have too many missteps. That you know what's what, that you got a road map and you can find your way. Mr. Paul said he would take me to Cooperstown since I ain't had no daddy to do it. He said we'd have to convince Grandma. I got mad then 'cause I knew she would never let me do nothing. Then Grandma called me. Yelling all over like she was crazy. She called me to come down for the circle dance and I left his room."

"What the hell Mr. Paul know about what a father do?" I said. I started walking around that room. "And he ain't coming back for no damn baseball card."

"He said it's worth something. A good piece of—"

"He ain't coming back," I told him.

"He could come back and bash in my head for this card or"—El stopped for a second—"or for payment for me bashing in his head."

"Shut up, El."

"I ain't gone tell nobody. I ain't tell nobody yet, have I."

"Shut up," I said.

"But I was the one that hit him, Pep. I'm the one he gone come back after. He said he was gone kill me. You said it yourself."

"I shouldn't've told you nothing."

I walked over to the door, opened it, and looked out into the hall.

"Uncle Herbert sure seemed proud, thinking you the one that whacked Mr. Paul. Uncle Herbert was telling everybody last night about you. He sure was proud. But what if Mr. Paul comes back for me? He won't be coming for you. I had to hit him, Pep. I had to make him stop messing with that baby. I was on my way up there to return this baseball card to him and I opened that door. I had to hit him. Now I know he's coming back for me. I got his card and he gone remember I hauled off and hit him square in his head."

The next thing me and El heard was Aunt Flossie screaming. Me and El ran downstairs. We could hear the screaming coming from the basement. So we ran down there.

Daddy and Sweet Alma was standing around the freezer. Aunt Flossie stood back, staring down at a plastic bag in Daddy's hand. Her face was green with stiff cucumber on it and she was holding a blue liquid mask that Mama freeze up, then use to take the puffiness out of her eyes.

"Oh, it's a dead bat, is all," Daddy said. "Everybody just calm down. May Ruth found the ol' dude out back and was saving him for Animal Control. She ain't mean for nobody to find him. It's just that with bats, they got to be tested for rabies, and when she called Animal Control yesterday, they told her they couldn't get to it until today. So they told her to go on and freeze him since she'd already picked him up and put him in a plastic bag. I guess we ain't expect nobody to be down here. I been the onliest one coming down for the meat. I told May Ruth to tuck him out of sight until them folks come. They got to open up his head and test his brain for rabies."

"May Ruth, you and anybody else for whom this makes sense should have their heads opened up and tested, too," Aunt Flossie said.

"What we need to be considering is how our nerves is shot," Daddy said. He put his arm around El to calm the tremble in his shoulders. Then he put his arm around me. "Now, I want my son and my nephew to sit down. I want everybody to take a breath. Sis screams like she just touched fire and we all taking things out of proportion."

Sweet Alma jumped up on the washing machine and crossed her legs. She said, "Maybe we should cancel everything. Who feels like continuing on with the celebrations now, considering what happened to that poor little baby. Rena's gone. Maybe we all should just leave, too."

El said, "I don't want y'all to leave yet. I don't want y'all to leave. Not yet." El got this real panicky look in his face and his eyes watered up.

Aunt Flossie bent down to look at him. She looked up at Herbert and back down at El. She pressed her cheek against his and got that green cucumber stuff on him.

"Grandma, I don't want them to leave."

Aunt Flossie said, "Baby, it's all right."

Daddy said, "We ain't goin' nowhere, boy. We got a few days yet. We ain't going until we make sure things in order. You ain't got to worry none 'bout that."

Sweet Alma jump down off that washing machine to push El upside the head.

"Now we all got to get ready," Daddy said. "We got to see El in the parade, sitting up big as he pleased on that float. Where's your uniform, Jackie Robinson? Ain't that who you s'pose to be? That uniform cleaned up and ready?" El nodded. "Well, you don't look like you even close to readiness. Nobody's close to readiness. We gone be the last ones at that parade. El, you go on before you're late for your ride. We all gone make this here thing work out. You hear me? Pepper, I'm gone fix you a special breakfast. Your favorite flapjacks. That sound okay?"

I nodded.

"Sis, go finish fixing on your face. El, you go get yourself duded up. Sweet Alma, you can stand putting some of that green stuff on your face, too."

"Oh, shut up, Uncle Herbert," Sweet Alma said.

Aunt Flossie wiped the green stuff off El's face and rubbed it on Sweet Alma's.

"C'mon, now," Daddy said. "Let's everybody get a move on. We ain't got no time for fooling around."

Daddy was acting the way he acted when he used to be the third-base coach for Little League. Clapping his hands, trying to get everybody all pumped and ready for the win.

One thing I can say for Daddy is that he knew better than anybody how to guide the runner home. That was the importance of third-base coaching. He had the right instincts to tell the runner when to keep coming and when to stay put. Then all the little runner had to worry about was pumping his arms, quickening his pace, and heading in the right direction.

But his instincts wasn't working right that morning.

Daddy should've forgot about that sad look on El's face and listened to Sweet Alma about calling the whole thing off. But Daddy never listened to no damn body. Thought he knew every damn thing under the sun.

This wasn't no baseball. And it wasn't no ordinary festival opening. Already everything had been turned upside down. Any fool could tell clapping couldn't right this shit.

But, to tell the truth about it, I think we all left that basement hoping it could.

23

Thelma

I look down at my watch. It's close to noon.

"Thelma," Aunt Cora says, "you're liable to have all those nails that are holding my gallery together lined up crooked by the time you finish all that pacing. Here." She hands me a page from her newspaper. "My crossword has the good fortune of being close to your astrology section. Let Sister Verleane tell you how your life is going. Let Sister Verleane tell you what happens next."

"I don't think I want to know," I say.

"And, honey, take all that mess off your shoulder. Pink has always made me tired and I'm getting weary by the moment watching you lug it around."

"This is my travel case of nail polishes—fifty-five shades," I say. "My foot buckets, Moisturizing Fast Finish, and cool ginseng gel, which relaxes the customer while secretly extracting his or her foot toxins, are inside. I'm afraid that if I put this case down, I'll walk off and leave the stuff inside. I've got to remind Herbert to put it in the trunk. And if I'm going to remind him, I've got to remember to remind myself."

"Neither he nor the trunk is here, so put it down until he comes back. Course, I still don't like the idea of you doing people's feet so close to my food."

I place the travel kit on the porch and move to get the newspaper page. Only I don't make it over because Flossie Jo's truck comes speeding into the driveway.

"Oh, Lord in heaven," Aunt Cora says. "Now, Thelma, let's be civil to one another. Let's try, okay?"

"I don't hear you reminding Flossie about being civil. Does civility include her avoiding me for a full twenty-four hours just so she doesn't have to take care of her obligations? Even though she doesn't consider them her obligations. I went into her room at about three this morning and she wasn't there and her bed hadn't been slept in. Where could she have been at that hour?"

"With an old friend," Aunt Cora mumbles. Still I hear her, even over May Ruth, who's sitting next to Aunt Cora and snoring now. She'd been so quiet that I'd forgotten she was there.

"Whew, Lord, I'm exhausted," Flossie yells as she gets out of the truck. "Just got through putting together all those food baskets for the Sick-and-Shut-in Committee. I've been there since five this morning. Next year they're going to have to find some other slave."

Flossie starts up the steps. I stand at the top, blocking her way.

"Well, good morning, Flossie Jo," I say.

"Good morning, Thelma."

"Did you fix a basket for your nephew? Or do you plan to let him starve as well as rot?"

"Don't start with me, Thelma. My nephew is neither sick nor shut-in. Sick in the head, maybe."

"How do you get off saying such mean and spiteful things?"

"He can leave that jail when he wants to, Thelma. Now please step out of my way. I'm running late. We don't want to be late for the parade, do we? Where's Herbert's car? People already are starting to line up along the river. And I need to dip myself in a bathtub soon."

"Thelma," Aunt Cora says, "come get this newspaper I have for you, honey. Don't you want to know what Sister Verleane has to say?"

"I know what she has to say, Auntie. She says Flossie here is going to take me to see my son, right this very moment. She predicts that we're going to jump in that truck of hers and go over there to see my son so she can forgive him for El."

"Thelma, I'm not going over there and I mean that. He can walk out of that jail when he wants to. And when he's ready, he will. He has to learn how to be a man. That's what his own father says. Pepper needs to learn how to be a man. You've coddled him so much he can't figure his way out of a god-damned paper bag. But that's on you. I'm not going to con-tribute to this craziness."

"I was there last night, Flossie," I say. She tries to scoot around me, but again I step in her way. "And you know what he told me? He told me that he remembers when you took him for a practice drive behind the mall. You see what he's thinking about? His heart is so filled with thoughts of you, honey. He remembers when you took him driving because you saw him feeling low."

"I am determined to have a good time," Flossie says. "That's how I woke up this morning, determined to have a goddamned good time for the next three days. Now please, Thelma, get the hell out of my way before I move you."

"That's enough, you two," Aunt Cora says, walking over. May Ruth's snoring has gotten louder and sounds like a train rumbling through. "You two are more like sisters than sisters-in-law. It's a shame for all this dissention. Enough of this fool-ishness."

"You don't scare me, Flossie Jo," I say to her. "You don't scare me one bit. I'm used to having to take up for myself.

And you're used to closing up, shutting out the world. Tight as a clam. You don't let anybody in. You don't talk to anybody. Not Sweet Alma. Not my son. You think the world revolves around what Flossie needs. Only it doesn't."

"Get out of my way, Thelma."

"Pretty soon you'll have shut everybody out. And you'll be old and alone and shriveled up. And nobody will say boo about you. Not one word of boo."

Herbert blows his horn and the three of us look toward the driveway. I notice June is in the front seat. I'm so taken aback by the sight of June that I step away to see better. Flossie skirts around me, kicking my case of polishes over. She opens the screen door and slams it behind her.

The banging jolts May Ruth. Her arms flail. "I've often found that if you hand-feed, they will follow," May Ruth says breathless as though we know exactly what she's talking about. "The birds." She fans herself. "If you hand-feed them, they will follow."

Aunt Cora hurries inside.

"Don't be following after me," Flossie says over her shoulder.

"Who's thinking on you?" Aunt Cora says. "I don't feel like having to talk to that ol' hard girl that's coming this way."

Herbert helps June out of the car. She's wearing a big white tent top with black shorts. Sweat has shellacked her top to her skin and she's huffing and puffing as she rocks up the porch stairs. Because she's in her final turn, everything on her looks swollen, but nothing more than her feet. I try not to stare at the two loaves of wheat bread stuffed into her sandals.

"Hi, June." I lean forward to kiss her cheek and she turns her head the wrong way. I wind up smashing into her forehead and kissing her lips. We both turn away.

She says, "Hey," in that surly tone of hers.

Herbert helps her sit in the chair next to May Ruth.

"Good morning, dear heart," May Ruth says. She leans over to hug June.

June says, "Hey," again and starts rubbing on that big stomach of hers. Rubbing like Herbert. Only Herbert doesn't look down into his the way June does. She acts like it's a crystal ball and she's searching for her future. I wonder if what's inside includes my son.

Herbert walks back down the porch toward me.

"I see Sis done made it back," he says, looking down at her truck. "She near ready?"

"I'm not talking to Flossie," I say. "She's upstairs. You'll have to ask her yourself."

"Y'all need to stop this shit right now," Herbert says. "Don't make no sense at all. I'm gone in to get the fan so June can get some air while we wait." He turns back around. "How 'bout I fix y'all a service of some of that good ol' lemonade?"

"With lots of ice," June says.

"Coming right up."

"The air is filled with the festival," May Ruth says, immediately striking up a better rapport than I did. "I'm so glad you decided to come on out and enjoy the day with us. I'm so, so glad."

I run over just so I can't be accused of not being eager to see the woman who's carrying my grandchild. Though I run slowly because once again I'm carrying my foot case and it weighs down heavily on me. I fidget and stand over her with my case. "Heat not only makes feet rise, but also stimulates toenail growth, according to my textbook."

They both look at me.

I turn to look out at the sunflowers and I see a fleet of black cars coming down Old Riley and winding in between the trees. They get closer and we can see they're Porter cabs, getting ready for their part in the parade. June sees the cabs, too, which I suppose is why she says, "That man at the cab place offered Robert a job. But Robert say he'd die and go to hell before he'd be caught chauffeuring people around."

"Funny, you didn't mention that last night," May Ruth says.

"I probably ain't mentioned a lot last night. I was too hot, too tired. When Mr. Herbert came by this morning, I was going out of my head. He's been coming by every morning, but I don't know why I couldn't stay in that apartment another minute this morning. He asked me to come along and I told him I was giving birth to myself, even if this baby ain't ready to release me. But yeah, Robert says he'll die and go to hell before he'd be caught chauffeuring people around."

I say to myself, "Die and go to hell?" I say to God, "Lord, forgive him, he didn't mean that." But I don't mention anything to May Ruth or June. I just play like I'm invisible, which is what June seems to be doing just fine. Either that or she makes a habit of damning folks' children right in the very presence of their parents. (Even though he did damn himself first.)

June says to May Ruth, "Pepper mentions all the time that his uncle Solomon is in the business in St. Louis. Says his uncle has done well for himself. I don't know how Pepper come off being so uppity about driving people."

"Solomon has quite a livery service," I say. "When Flossie met him, she was in college. Back then he was chauffeuring the college president and other dignitaries. He hated it and vowed to one day have his own business. It hasn't been easy, but he has done quite well for himself."

Herbert comes out with the lemonade. Aunt Cora comes outside with her newspaper tucked under her arm and a glass of lemonade. She catches June sitting in her chair, but she doesn't say anything about the chair and June isn't the type to offer to move, even for an old woman.

"June," Aunt Cora says, nodding and looking over her glasses.

"Miss Cora," June says back.

"How are you and that baby coming along?" Aunt Cora's back straightens. It's normally ramrod straight, but the sight of June adds starch to her little white dress.

"I'm making it," June says. "Sick and tired, hot, can't breathe, can't hardly walk. I'm on my second yeast infection, and before now I ain't never had one."

Aunt Cora rolls her eyes. "Good to know you're making it at least. There's a stool down the porch for you to prop your feet, if you need." She bends toward the open window behind June. "Herbert, come get this stool for June."

"I don't need it," June says. "But I may have to pee again soon."

"Can't help you with that," Aunt Cora says, turning to go back inside. "It's down the hall."

May Ruth says, "Speaking of peeing . . . You will excuse me, won't you, dear heart?"

May Ruth leaves and it's just me and June out here. Suddenly the porch seems on fire. I get sweat coming from everywhere, like June. I sit down in May Ruth's seat. "June, I've got an idea. . . ."

"I don't want no painted-up toes," she says with complete disregard to my real point, even though she doesn't know it yet.

"No, that's not what I had in mind," I say. "Why don't you and Pepper come out East to live with us once the baby gets here and you get situated? Don't close your mind to it just yet, pretty please." June folds her arms over her stomach and looks off. But I keep going. "We have more than enough room and I've raised ten babies—what's one more around the house? They got good schools out there and nice places for young people to go. You can come and stay as long as you like, and you'd have a built-in baby-sitter."

"I ain't moving," she says. "Pepper can go if he likes. Me and my baby will be fine without him. And won't be need for no public aid, neither. We gone stay put and I'm gone make it, if I have to struggle all by myself."

"I wasn't suggesting you two split up. Alls I'm saying—"

"Miss Gray, I ain't moving." She toots her lips out like she's about to sound a big horn. All the while, she's shaking her head and rubbing on that big crystal-ball belly of hers where my granddaughter, I'm sure, nears the boiling point from the friction. "When I was sixteen, my sister, who was a year younger than me, ran away from home and got herself shot. She was gone for near-about six months. Only word we ever heard of her came from some coroner telling us to come down and identify her in the morgue. When we saw her on that slab, she had two bullet wounds in her neck. Two tiny black crusty circles was what was left after color drained out of her face and life out of her body. And for the funeral? All the undertaker man did was put a patch over both of them crusty circles, hit them with some heavy makeup, and the next thing we knew she was in the ground."

"I'm sorry, June. I didn't know."

"I ain't looking for your sympathy, Miss Gray. Alls *I'm* saying is that you don't see me stumbling around here like a fool. Some nights Pepper cry himself to sleep. I feel sorry for him. I really do. But I can't baby him. I got a baby coming. I don't need two."

A string of paper clips that link one pane to the other and glimmer in the sunlight cast shadows that resemble chain links across June's face. I want to put my arm around her, but any fool would know she's not the type that would allow it. I stand instead. "I'm going inside to see what's taking everybody so long," I say. My heart feels like it's splitting straight up the middle. "Can I bring you something back?"

She stares back, shaking her head and tooting out her lips. This time all that head-shaking simply means no.

· · ·

As usual, everybody is ready and we're waiting for Miss Flossie.

We're waiting and waiting and watching the people down on Old Riley. As is customary for the opening parade, most folk walk to the fairgrounds because walking gives you time to reflect and puts some measure of hardship on you. We see wide-brimmed hats and dresses in pale blues and pinks, bright yellows and oranges; beige suit coats flung over shoulders, exposing pressed suit pants. Long flowy hair ribbons and patent-leather shoes, white and black—all get their due.

Aunt Cora paces before the screen door, peeping inside at the clock on the wall near the phone table. Herbert folds the top down on the car. He starts wiping at the shine on the bumper with his handkerchief.

Finally, Aunt Cora walks over to the screen. "Florence Johnson Penticott, you coming before nightfall?"

"Dear heart, be a little patient," May Ruth says, "we have time. It's only half past eleven. Things don't get under way for another thirty minutes."

Aunt Cora yells up again, "Flossie Jo?"

"Maybe she's stuck in the lavatory, Cora."

No sooner than May Ruth finishes, we hear Flossie coming down the steps. She says, "What're you trying to do? Wake the dead?"

Aunt Cora sees Flossie and her mouth drops. She steps back away from the door so Flossie can exit. "Well, I'll be damned. Looks like the dead has arisen."

Even though I don't look at her long, I do see she's wearing a lemon-colored sundress that hangs off her shoulders, comes in on her waist real fine, and flares out above her knees. Her hair is pulled back under her floppy yellow hat and her face is colored real pretty, too. She wheels around me to May Ruth, plucking a meshy pink hair curler from May Ruth's crown and handing to her. May Ruth laughs and follows Flossie Jo down the steps.

"I am determined to have a good time," Flossie says into the air.

Down on the driveway, May Ruth tosses sunflower seeds a few feet in front of her. A flock of birds, maybe ten or twelve, come nearby to eat.

Flossie says to May Ruth, "If one of those birds shit on my new hat or my dress, I'm coming after you."

"Oh, never fear, dear heart," May Ruth says. "Their little anatomy is such that they don't poop and eat at the same time. Ordinarily."

I let Flossie sit in the front seat with Aunt Cora and Herbert so I don't have to sit next to her.

May Ruth and me, on the other hand, are sardines in the backseat next to June. I hold my travel case on my lap and snuggle in tight as I can.

As Herbert pulls down the driveway, I listen to June's breaths. She's wheezing and struggling, though she's not wanting to wheeze any more than I want to listen to it. I remember those days clearly.

Once on Old Riley, I can hear a Jamaican band starting up on the opposite side of the river. Somebody hits the tin drums and beats the tambourines and the trees grab the sound, shaking it back out over the water. All around the smoke from the pits hangs in the air, pulling everybody toward the downtown, as though there's no other direction within miles of Halley worth turning toward.

24

Thelma
The Parade

At noon, Greater Faith's bells ring out to high heaven, and because we're standing on the steps, the sound moves through me like ripples in water. People fill the sidewalks out to the curb. Once the bells quiet, so do everyone and everything, nearly everything. Balloons bounce against one another and you can hear that. Loose pieces of ticker tape scratch along the church steps and the street.

"Ticker tape reminds me of the war," May Ruth whispers to June, who clearly doesn't understand. "The revolution, dear heart? Propaganda rallies? Pure manipulation, it was."

Flossie stands down on the sidewalk on a patch of grass under a tree. She can't see the lights when they start to flash on top of the two sheriff's cars crossing the bridge. But when the cars start to move, she, like the rest of us, can hear the sigh that escapes from nearly everybody. Young and old, like it's the first time. The first time the cars ever inched forward toward the welcome banner. The first time a little boy has ever accompanied the cars with a patient little drumbeat. *Thrrump. Thrrump. Thrrump.*

Flossie takes her hat off and fans herself, fanning as though she doesn't have a care in the world. As though she's still determined to have a good time. She leans back against the tree, waving off some bothersome fly.

As is customary, the cars pause by the taxi place. A ram horn sounds.

Aunt Cora says, mostly to herself but loud enough for those close by, "'Long toots told you when to wake and break water. Short ones told you when to eat and sleep. When to hit them fields, yoke them steers. Feed. Breed. Die.'"

People who are sitting, stand. Men yank off their hats and place their hands over their hearts. Everybody starts to sing. "Lift every voice and sing till earth and heaven ring. Ring with the harmony of liberty. Let our rejoicing rise high as the listening skies. Let it resound far as the rolling seas."

I lift up on my tiptoes so I can see the paraders coming across the bridge. Herbert takes my pink case from my shoulder and tucks it under his arm.

The paraders are led by the grand marshal, who is dressed in his red three-cornered hat and long red coat, which makes me hot just to look at him. Even from a distance. The grand marshal gets to the ribbon that two young boys hold from one side of the street to the other. He pulls large clown scissors from under his jacket and cuts the ribbon. And the horns sound to high heaven.

The high-school band members come up behind him, playing "The Star-Spangled Banner" at a faster clip to match the quick timing of their steps. That baton twirler tosses her baton up in the air, catching it between her legs and behind her back and between her legs again.

The young actors for the play are next. The kids wear placards on their chests to tell the crowd who they are since you can't really make heads or tails out of anybody, except maybe Frederick Douglass, on account of the cottony white wig, and Abraham Lincoln, on account of the black suit, the beard, and the tall hat. The rest of the signs—I know because my boys have all participated at one time or another—identify the boys as Denmark Vesey, Marcus Garvey, Nat Turner, Dred Scott, Booker T. The girls often include such people as Mary McLeod Bethune, Sojourner Truth, Harriet Tubman, Phillis Wheatley.

The parade stops. Young Abraham comes forward with a microphone. He fixes on that big tall hat of his and says, "I, Abraham Lincoln, president of the United States, by virtue of the power in me vested as commander in chief of the army and navy of the United States, order and declare that all persons held as slaves within said designated states and parts of states are, and henceforth forward shall be, free. . . ."

The crowd roars. I mean *roars*. Everybody waves their hands, or their flags, or their fans, or their hats; they bounce their children on their necks. Jubilee time. Folk pretend to get to shouting. Ticker tape and confetti are released from the tops of the stores and rain down on everybody. Firecrackers sound.

My palms feel sweaty. Ordinarily, Herbert and I hug and dance. But Herbert has June by the arm and he can't be bothered with hugging on me with him trying to steady her. Ordinarily, after Herbert and I hug and dance, I grab Flossie's arm, and even though she never really wants to, she lets me spin her once or twice and we laugh. But not this year. This year we're standing on two different sides of the divide. Too far apart to even begin to think about dancing.

Last year, though, we hugged and danced, even after all that confusion.

Last year Flossie grabbed my arm and we twirled around and then waited, arm in arm, for the marching bands, cheerleaders, specialty floats, and beauty queens to pass so that we could get to El's float.

Pepper climbed a tree to see better. I kept watching him because I knew he didn't care for heights. But he wanted to see his cousin. Toward the end of the parade, El's float finally came. The baseball players, in their caps and crisp uniforms, rode beside a glittery gold ball with a pink cellophane tail, Halley's Comet. Some boys wore the old-timey uniforms that drooped and sagged, with placards saying, JOSH GIBSON, SATCHELL PAIGE, BUCK LEONARD. NEGRO LEAGUE. MEXICAN LEAGUE. CANADIAN LEAGUE. NO NATIONAL LEAGUE. Until you saw the little slugger, our El, with the New York Yankee uniform, Jackie.

The crowd sang out, "Have you seen Jackie Robinson hit that ball? Oh yeah!"

And El took his bat and swung at the air. The crowd roared. Flossie just waved as she took pictures, one after the other, snapping pictures even after the float had passed us and we couldn't see it anymore at all.

Now a white float led by a white Cadillac comes down the middle of the street. The lieutenant governor of Illinois, a Republican, and some Democratic senators and representatives stand aboard. Some of the Democrats hold red, black, and green flags, reading, "Run Jesse Run. Again" and "Register to Vote. Again." Posters say, "More Money for Health Care," "Better Day Care," "Better Housing," "More Jobs."

Reenactors from Company B, 42nd United States Colored Regiment pull up next. They are Yankees, wearing blue uniforms with brass spurs and carrying guns that are just a-shining. They walk ahead of the Elks and the Veterans of Foreign Wars, who walk ahead of the slaves. The crowd gets really quiet at the sight of the barefoot men, women, and children in tattered domestics with chains round their necks. Some wear muzzles. Some are wheeled forward because they're in the stocks. Some are harnessed with rags tied around their eyes or around their mouths. Some of the children have got neck chains, one-eighth-inch thick plates, some a quarter-inch thick. Clinking and clanking. The children are always the hardest to see. I remember Herbert wouldn't ever let any of the boys be slave children. They can play any role up there except that one, he said. The driver is astride his horse, bringing up the rear, cracking his cat-o-nine tails whip and cowhide. When the last float passes under the wrought-iron arch into the fairgrounds, the crowd follows behind. Flossie waits for us as we descend the steps.

Viola Miller jogs over to Flossie with her two dogs.

"Good afternoon, Madam President," Viola says, struggling with the crazy dog's leash. "Well, if you aren't the belle of the ball. Flossie, I don't think I've seen you this pretty in years. Not that you aren't normally pretty. But today I'm going to have to stay far away from you because you might just steal my show."

Viola walks away, pulled backward and forward by the dogs. Aunt Cora takes up her pocketbook and bats it after Viola. They all laugh.

I'm pulling up the rear. May Ruth and Aunt Cora are arm in arm. Herbert has June by the arm. They both rock out of sync. Flossie walks alone, with that switchy walk of hers. I just don't understand how she can be so carefree.

On the way, I can't help but fix on the sidewalk leading toward the taxi place. One right turn at the corner and the courthouse looms. Just one right turn.

The fairgrounds spread out about twenty acres. The Victuals tables and barbecue pits are arranged in the wide-open middle, where the shade is piecemeal, upwind from the smoke. Each pit has a whole hog rotating. Sparks fly up through their ribs. About ten fifteen-foot-long tables are set up in a U-shape, not far from the baseball field, which stretches out to the far south corner. The vendors pitch their small tents around the edge of the fairgrounds, mostly along the canal wall, on the east. The Ferris wheel and the other rides are set up on the opposite side, near the hill that leads to the promontory, where most people believe our comet landed. Beyond the hill, the Hallelujah tents with all those wayward women line the orange grove.

I take my place behind the table. I don't feel like setting up for the pedicures just yet since Herbert has seated June down at the end of the table, where I'm supposed to set up.

"June," he says, "when this baby coming?"

"They say the middle of this month."

Herbert nods and says, "Uh-huh. Seem to me like that baby's got its own notions. And I should know, seeing that I been through this with Thelma leaning on my arm more times than a li'l bit."

I walk over by my shade tree I stake claim to every year. A group of children gather around.

"Miss Gray, can I have a piece of candy?"

"Miss Gray, you got some gum or something?"

"Miss Gray."

I take out a pack of gum and divide it fifty different ways like I used to do when our boys were young. Herbert used to say, "Jesus Christ, Thelma, them boys' mouths ain't gone never know the meaning of a entire stick of gum." That never stopped me before from twisting off piece after piece.

After my last stick of gum is doled out, a little boy walks over. He's one of the slave boys and has a snotty nose to go with his torn nightshirt. It hangs on him like a dress. He walks up, slow and scaredlike, and has the saddest look on his face when he looks at my hands and sees they're empty. I take out my handkerchief and wipe his snotty nose. Then I brace my back against the tree and prop my purse on my knee so I can dig in it properly. Last thing I want to do is send that child off wanting. I all but upend my purse until I find a little piece of lemon cough drop that's still in the box. I shake it loose and hold it up to the light to inspect it before handing it over to the little snot-nose slave boy. He takes it and dashes off through a sideways column of pit smoke over to the Go Karts, where he's too little to get on, so he just stands by, watching and sucking on his cough drop.

I go back to the table and start passing out shallow containers of dry ice at the end near June. I set the cakes atop the ice. The first thing June notices is May Ruth's annual offering: a chocolate cake baked in the shape of a Black Power fist. The arm of that thing is about a foot long and muscular with thick licorice veins. The fist fans out like a misshaped catcher's mitt. Then in tiny tattoolike letters are the words FOR THE BIRDS. After all these years, the cake remains the most deformed-looking thing sitting at the desserts table amid scores of pound cakes and coconut, cherry, and sweet potato pies.

June balls up her face and points to May Ruth's cake. "What is that?"

Aunt Cora says, "It's the ugliest thing intended for consumption within miles."

"Y'all say that before you taste it," Herbert says. "Once you cut into it, you won't think it's ugly. May Ruth say she got the idea at a peace rally in Los Angeles. Them Black Panthers Stokely Carmichael and Bobby Seale was there. But Archibald Clemons, one of the older cabdrivers, think she got the idea from him. Years ago, Archibald tied together a handful of cherry bombs and Roman candles and took a match to the bundle. He got so overcome by the excitement, all that smoke and sparkles, that he held on too long and the whole thing nearly blowed his right hand clear off his arm. Fifty-five stitches it took to make Archibald's hand flush with his wrist again. Skin grafts sort of brought it back to the right color, but despite months of that therapy, them fingers never have worked right. The middle one still stands up in the F-you position while the others fold limply inward. But for as long as I've knowed old Archibald, he ain't never been one to get mired down in the circumstance of it all. He just drive with his left hand now, and his knees when he's busy counting his change. Every year he take so much pride in May Ruth's cake that he's always the first to pose for a picture beside it before slicing into it, right along the thumb area. It would never occur to May Ruth to tell him that her cake ain't got nothing to do with him. No sense is stealing somebody's joy."

June leans toward a clipboard of papers, positioned next to the cake.

"What's that for?" she asks Herbert.

"That's May Ruth's annual petition to get that Johnny's Hunt Club place shut down. Though she been trying for years, she ain't had no success at it. One year she stayed on after the festival just to picket outside the parking lot gates. Had traffic backed up to the interstate. But all she got was arrested."

May Ruth sees us paying her cake so much attention and dances over to jimmy it when the heat causes a knuckle to cave in. She picks at it sure enough before licking the chocolate off her fingertips and going back down the table toward Flossie and the vegetables.

Pretty soon the food is arranged properly. Barbecued hog—only the high-up parts—beef, mutton, lamb, and chicken cover nearly two-thirds of our table. The vegetables, some red soda drink, the desserts take up the remainder.

Pastor takes a microphone to the center of the U. The music near us dies down when Pastor motions for everybody to bow their heads. But music is all over the fairgrounds, so we still hear somebody singing into another microphone south of the baseball field. Naturally everybody's shushing one another, so we hear shushing along with the clanking from a blacksmith in the far-off distance. He's hitting an anvil over and over.

Our Victuals line starts to move almost before Pastor says Amen. Aunt Cora walks up and down our table, making sure everything's laid out right. Two of the interviewers from the college who take down the oral histories come over. One is Indian and has his recorder and notepad; the other is white and has a camera and a wrinkled sheet of paper that doesn't look like it's worth much anymore. The white boy with the camera takes Aunt Cora's picture really fast, takes her name and moves on. The Indian one—he's either that or Pakistani or Egyptian or Ethiopian or one of the Moored-up nationalities, I can't hardly tell because he's as dark as Herbert, but his hair is straight as white folks' hair—well, he's the one with the recorder and he stays behind.

Aunt Cora points down to me and I wave back at her. She points over to May Ruth, then down the table at Flossie, where the men cluster longer than normal around Flossie's collards. Still talking to the boy, Aunt Cora walks over to me and takes my hand without any regard to the coleslaw, sweet potatoes, and fresh pole beans I'm supposed to be minding. Or my ladle, which I use, giving the proper turn so that with each spoonful of vegetables I bring up the right combination of ham and pot liquor, without giving folks too much of the fatty meat or the Penticott business to chew on.

Next, Aunt Cora walks down to get Flossie Jo, looping arms with her, too. Aunt Cora does all the talking. I smile.

In near-rote fashion, Aunt Cora says, "As the years passed during Reconstruction, more people flowed in and one acre grew to two and two to three to well over a thousand, and before you knew it, the railroads had overtaken the canal in transporting commerce, rendering our canal obsolete in its infancy; but that didn't matter much because somebody suggested a seventy-six-year comet had fallen here, and that brought a college professor and a few newspaper men and many others—chasing whimsy—to the newly named Halley's Landing. . . ."

That college boy hangs on Aunt Cora's every word. His head is down, left hand just a-moving on that pad. Left-handed like my Pepper. I'm sure he's wondering why Flossie and I are standing here. Not like Aunt Cora needs us to help her tell what she's been telling for decades.

I look over at Flossie and she's not listening to Aunt Cora at all. She's watching that same little snot-nosed cough-drop boy who now has found his way to the little merry-go-round in the sandbox. He's all by himself, struggling, trying to push it. But he's too little and his ragged shirtdress keeps getting tangled in his legs. What he really wants to do is push the merry-go-round, creating enough speed so he can jump on. The boy is working and working, sweating like a little runt pig, trying to make it happen like he wants it. But he may as well be moving a mountain because he hasn't the strength to make it do anything but move just a teeny bit.

Flossie can hardly fix on the interview, and now neither can I. She breaks away and goes over to the merry-go-round. She takes off her hat and her sandals before dipping her feet into the sand. The boy knows why she's there and he lights on the merry-go-round, sitting right in the center. His arms hug one of the metal supports and his cheek presses hard against it.

Flossie points to the big merry-go-round with the horses down the way, as if to ask: *Don't you hear the music it's making? The* rum-pah-pah, rum-pah-pah. *Don't you see the motor in the middle, which means there isn't a need for straining somebody's back, and the big clear lightbulbs that flicker on and off, glowing yellow and electric white, even in the afternoon sun?*

From what I can see, neither says a thing. They make this connection without even speaking.

Flossie spits on her hands and gives that merry-go-round the biggest shove she has in her power. This sends him and possibly Flossie herself into wondrous, wondrous flight.

25

Thelma

JUST BEFORE NIGHTFALL

I'm sitting at the end of the Victuals table, waiting on June's feet to finish soaking. My cake timer says I've got a good ten minutes left.

Even though the rain has stopped, Viola still has her dogs' leashes thrown against the tree trunk. The same tree I stake claim to every year for my breaks.

The mean dog is hunkered down low to the ground, while the other one, the gimp one, just sniffs around in circles. He doesn't seem to care one way or the other that the rain has stopped, the thundering has quieted. Neither bothered him anyway since his hearing is shot along with his eyesight, so sniffing, I suppose, allows him the use of the one good sense he has left. The mean dog is aware that the rain has stopped but doesn't seem to trust that the quiet will last long.

And Lord knows I understand that feeling. Yes, indeedy. Understand it well.

I want to keep working on June's feet. But there's not much to do while they're soaking. So I line up my nail polishes and foot creams. I get out my pumice stone. I pull out two because her feet haven't had a good husking in a while and they're bound to give my stones quite a beating.

I'm deciding on a polish when I smell baby powder and I know it's not coming from the bottles. When June raises her arms behind her head, looking off into the sky, into what remains of twilight, I see clumped pieces of powder under her armpits. My nose can detect baby powder in a field of sweet alyssum. The smell of baby powder rolls through my head like the tune of an old record. Yes, indeedy.

I look up in the sky and I see some shooting stars. Just a few. Everything and everyone has its own time and its own season, the Bible says. Life has its own cycles. I know it's true. Our comet orbits every seventy-five years. That Leonids meteor shower comes in a big way, every thirty-three years, my professor says. And, as I think about it, there's the Perseids shower that comes every year. It's like the Leonids, but it's got a different name and comes much more frequently. I forget why. But it happens every August around this time, too, when the earth passes through the Swift-Tuttle Comet. Though, like I said, I don't see much of a shower now. Just June's soaking feet.

As we wait, June starts to doze off, so I look around the park. I see Flossie standing next to Ben near the concessions stand. Ben says something that tickles Flossie and she throws her head back, laughing. The breeze snatches that hat of hers and whips it around a few times, looping it like it's attached to one of those funny strings. Ben chases after it. Flossie's hat lands, upends and lands again, toying around the back bleachers where my big brother, Solomon, and three old dudes are ducked under, playing a quick game of craps. They try to scoop everything up when Ben runs past, still trying to grab hold of that hat, missing it and stumbling. Solomon sees the hat and, I believe, automatically knows who it belongs to. The crowd keeps watching Ben, too, and keeps watching Flossie Jo, who's jumping up and down and clapping when he finally catches her hat.

With that hat in his hand, Ben walks back over to the concessions stand. On the way, he flexes his muscles and bows to the crowd. Flossie just smiles at him as he walks toward her. They sit for a few minutes. My cake timer says five more minutes left for June's feet.

Flossie points to the canal, over by the hill. Her arm sweeps in front of her, following the length of the canal wall, then over to the baseball field and behind it, to a wall of trees that spread out dark and thick. I wonder if she's thinking what I'm thinking. I wonder if she's explaining the path my Pepper took up that hill. How he crossed the dance area—near where Sweet Alma was dancing—then tore out running, looking over his shoulders. He stopped before that black wall of trees. But in a few seconds, right in the center, there was this fuzzy gleam of a flashlight, like a big old white star, poking out through the night, coaxing my Pepper up the hill.

I wonder if Flossie's explaining why the canal is so lighted so early in the evening. Not just the lights that the Beautification Committee strings, but the three big arcing lights that shine down on the water, showing tiny white pearls and mist.

When the propane cannons sound, it makes all of us jump. Even Viola's mean dog. He starts to pace in circles. The birds fly up from the canal as though they know we're watching—as though they're expecting all of us to be right here on time.

I look back up at the sky. Only when the night is the darkest can you see the stars.

26

Pepper
The Festival
NIGHTFALL, THE YEAR BEFORE

El told me to give him five minutes. He said, "Give me five minutes and follow me up the hill." I told him his ass should be over on them rides or something.

He said he been over there. He said he was up on that Ferris wheel, seeing all over the park, and that's when he saw him.

"I saw him, Pepper, I swear I did," he told me. "I saw him and I want you to see him, too. You'll see I ain't lying."

I told him, "Nigger, you ain't seen nobody."

He said, "I saw him, Pepper. I swear to God. I know it was Mr. Paul. And I want you to see him. You'll see I ain't a liar. I told you he would come back."

I'd been slipping and drinking that lowdown-ass homemade wine that May Ruth and Aunt Cora and the rest of them old folk mix together every year. Make you sick long before it make you drunk, then afterward, make you sick again. A fight in every bottle, Aunt Cora say. Even when you drink all by your lonesome. A fight in every bottle. I gave El a little taste, just a dab. And yeah, I know I wasn't s'pose to. He copied me all the time and was begging for some with his hands out and his greedy fingers wiggling for it. I ain't gave him enough to wet his lips hardly. But he thought it was a lot and started acting like he was drunk right off. He was squinting his eyes and laughing too much. His eyes ain't squint so much after he thought he saw Mr. Paul, though. They was wide open after that.

I told him all that squinting was probably the reason he thought he saw Mr. Paul in the first place. I told him if he opened his damn eyes right, he wouldn't've saw no damn Mr. Paul.

I gave El five minutes, then I run up that hill after him.

When we met up, El started to run. And we ain't never run that hard in our lives. I was like, Slow down, boy. Slow your big ass down. We ain't run like that before, especially not through them woods late at night in the dark. Not like that. Branches snapping under our feet. Them sticky bugs pricking our legs. The hot night air, heavy and strangling, pressing down.

By the time we got to the top of the hill, I couldn't even breathe right. I was coughing hard, trying to catch my breath. We ran across that open field up there. Them ol' horseflies flew into my nose and mouth. And every time I breathed, I swallowed something, if not a bug, then a piece of brush or dirt or something else El done kicked up. The land sloped into a valley, and that's where them Hallelujah tents set up every year. That's where El was running to.

We stooped down behind a bush, looking on seven or eight of them Hallelujah tents. Pots of grease that was set on fire gave just enough light so people could see what tent they was visiting, but not so much as to draw too much attention to the entire setup.

We stooped down some more. I told him, "You ain't seen no Mr. Paul."

We was watching the people dancing. Most didn't have time for dancing. They was going straight into them tents. But the people dancing, the women, had on short skirts and shit like them *Solid Gold* dancers on TV. Only their outfits wasn't as glittery as them TV dancers, but the moon was and so was the stars and them pots of grease, shooting firing sparks into the air.

El said when he saw Mr. Paul, he followed him up here and watched him go into the third tent from the left. And he pointed to that third tent. We stayed stooped over and jogged to where he pointed.

He said he saw that bald head and everything. Them glasses. That white, white shirt.

El swore up and down Mr. Paul was heading to this particular tent when he left and came back for me. El said the man he saw was the only white man down there. I whipped out my knife and sliced a hole wide enough in the back. We couldn't see shit, but we could tell by that man's talk that he was a brother. Not no Mr. Paul. Talking more shit than a li'l bit. I told El I was going back. I told him I wasn't feeling so good. That rotgut was starting to wear on me.

He whispered, "Maybe the next one." We went over and I sliced another hole.

Like a fool, El flashed the light this time. I almost forgot he had it. El said, "Say, Mr. Paul. That you?"

They was on a pallet, that man and the whore. In seconds, the light traced the man's black pants, which was down around his knees, and up to his round white ass, and then that whore's black face and then up along his white T-shirt, which was still on. The man was white and bald, but he wasn't no Mr. Paul, like I said.

When he jumped up, we shot off running.

This time my stomach felt on fire. Before I knew it, my mouth was watering heavy and I had to heave. I bent over the canal wall and tossed right into the water.

It was so dark we couldn't hardly see a thing down below or all around us. Barely the blue smoke ring hovering above the fairgrounds, now lifting. Just a hint of them dimmed-down lights around the Ferris wheel and the roller coaster. We could hear old Mr. Fortnight and Jesse Bee picking at them old somber notes from their old tired guitars. They couldn't play for shit, but nobody seemed to care.

My head was spinning, so I sat down by a tree. El, playing drunk, climbed up on the wall and started walking it, up and down, doing a soft-shoe, balancing. Wasn't nothing for any of us to walk it. It was wide enough. About a foot wide. We'd walked it before. Mostly during the day. But never at night. The sky lit up with fireworks. The kind that give light and just a little sound at first. El's arms was stretched above his head and I thought, for a second—I thought I saw that gun tucked into the waistband of his pants.

"Boy, get your ass down," I said to him. I was wiping vomit from my lips. "What's in your pants," I said to him. "Nigger, you still got that gun?"

He was laughing hard, dancing. "I ain't gone fall," he said. I could hear he was relieved about that man not being Mr. Paul. Sounded as relieved as he could be.

Down in the park, most of the people was still caught up in Mr. Fortnight's guitar number. We could barely hear that. El stayed up on that wall, holding steady.

Everybody was holding steady. I couldn't move just yet. My stomach was still caught up in my throat.

Everybody was holding steady. Until a shitload of fire-works lit up the sky. For a split second there was no sound again and I could see El's silhouette. He looked like a bat up there, dancing, twirling. For a split second, I was sure I saw that gun again, tucked into this pants. I was sure the metal held the light.

Fireworks went off, sounding like trip-hammers.

El lifted his arms straight up in the air. Then the cannon that scare them damn birds went off. Louder than I could hear it. It was like it was right under us. Like we was standing right on top of it. Them gulls flew up from the canal in a tangled web over El's head.

One second El was there. The next he was gone. One second I could see him dancing. The next I didn't see nothing but black night.

I started blinking my eyes.

I thought he was playing at first. Then I thought I was dreaming. I don't know exactly what I thought. I ran over to the wall, expecting him to climb back up, crawl back up the wall. Wasn't nothing for El to dive in the canal. He was a damn good swimmer, I kept saying to myself. Damn good. At first I wasn't even sure he'd fell back. I thought he'd jumped down and was crawling 'gainst the edge.

I yelled and yelled at him to stop playing.

I said, "Stop playing, fool. Stop playing. Stop playing, fool."

I never heard a splash that night. At least when I think about it or when people ask me, my mind freeze up and I don't believe I heard it. But sometimes I really can't say whether I heard it that night or not because I hear it now. All the time, over and over.

You know what I'm saying?

I hear it now. Over and over. And it seem real enough to me.

27

Alma "Sweet Alma" Penticott

I was dancing with this drunk dude when I saw Pepper running across the baseball field.

It had begun to drizzle, but nobody cared. Especially none of us who jammed the dance area near the stage.

My dance partner kept pulling me toward him and we weren't moving to a fast song. But that's the only kind of dancing his samba hips wanted, despite the rhythm, because he was drunk and wanted me to brush against his hard-on in swipes faster than the music.

Pepper had always been slow and I couldn't believe how fast he was running. But I didn't hardly pay any attention to him at first. I was more concerned with my dance partner's hands, moving down from my waist to my ass. His samba hips directing mine to a samba beat that neither Mr. Fortnight nor Jesse Bee could even imagine, let alone play.

As Pepper got closer to the Victuals table, I could tell he was crying and his chest was heaving. He hadn't stopped running. He grabbed Uncle Herbert first. Uncle Herbert was behind the table talking to my father. Then Pepper started pulling Uncle Herbert, saying something, yelling something.

When Daddy's face and Uncle Herbert's face took on Pepper's, I started to pull away from my dance partner. The man grabbed me around my waist and didn't want to let me go. Everything was so loud that trying to talk would have been futile. I pushed him away. I shoved him as hard as I could and started through the crowd to the table.

Mother was down at the opposite end of the table. She was filling somebody's plate when she saw Pepper, and automatically she knew something was wrong. The plate simply slid from her grasp. I remember it sliding right to the ground. She couldn't hear Pepper, either. But she knew something was wrong because he was crying and pointing back toward the hill, pulling his father.

As I neared the table, Mother, Uncle Herbert, and Pepper were running toward the hill. May Ruth and Aunt Thelma were behind them. Daddy was running toward the church, screaming, "Get help!"

The story changed up and down the line. Somebody said it was an ol' drunk that had fallen in the water, which is why way down the line you could hear some people kinda laughing. Soon they got the word that it wasn't a drunk at all. It was a boy, a young boy. Soon people were gathering up their children, counting heads, lining them up. When they were accounted for, people went to the wall to help in the search.

Within seconds, a group of women enveloped Aunt Cora and started praying. People quieted to let through the chant coming from the huddle. I turned away from the table and started running toward the hill.

At the top of the hill, Mother lay over the canal wall. Uncle Herbert had already dove in. "El!" he called. "El, can you hear me?"

The canal itself churned. We couldn't see a thing. Mother bent over. She'd taken her shoes off to jump in, but Aunt Thelma and May Ruth were holding her, knowing that at any moment Uncle Herbert's splashing around down there wouldn't be enough for her. The music stopped.

"You see anything, Herbert?" Mother yelled down, stretching forward, scratching against the wall. "Can you see anything at all?"

Uncle Herbert didn't answer her, he yelled, "El? Can you hear me, son?"

"El!" I yelled. "El!"

El was a month old when Mother came to visit me in St. Louis. She refused to let Daddy drive up to get her. She never hesitated to remind him that she didn't need a chauffeur. And she made it clear that she was only coming to see me. She would stay the night in a hotel; the next morning she'd leave.

I waited all afternoon for her, and when she arrived, my heart was pounding as I raced down the steps to meet her. I hugged her and quickly searched for El, only to find she'd left him with Aunt Cora. As she inspected me, my T-shirt and blue jeans, my face and hair, she said it was too early for him to travel. Like a fool, I thought she was referring to his age. But I later realized that "too early" referred to our little secret. She needed to make certain our little secret was intact in St. Louis and that there would be no danger in anybody learning the truth about me.

After that first visit, Mother drove down once a month. She often looked tired and she never failed to remind me how tiring it was caring for a baby. She brought pictures of El, but she never brought him. She'd show me the pictures and shove them back into her purse.

"I want to keep one, Mama. If someone asks, I'd say he's a cousin or my little brother."

"There's no need for lying, Sweet Alma. You'd do better to keep it out of the way. No questions asked, no need for lies."

During another visit, my father told her my grades were slipping.

"Sweet Alma, honey," she said, "I know you can do the work. What's your problem? All you have to do is focus. How difficult is that?"

"But I can't focus, Mama," I told her. "All I think about is El."

"That's because you're a little girl, Sweet Alma," she said. "You've got some foolish romantic notion of what it's like to care for a baby. They're hard, hard work, Sweet Alma. Some nights I hardly sleep. You think they cuddle and coo all day and night? They don't. They're not dolls, Sweet Alma. They cry; they need things. And you're left to figure out what at every juncture. I expect you to take advantage of being foot-loose and fancy-free. I don't expect to see these half-assed grades. Sacrifices are being made; lives are being put on hold for you. You haven't told anybody, have you?"

I nodded, biting my fingernails. "I just mentioned it to one of my friends."

Removing my hand from my mouth, she said, "Jesus Christ, Sweet Alma. Whose business is it? Who has to know? Wasn't this the reason you came here?"

"I only told one girl, Teresa. She's in my gym class and she's my best friend."

"You don't have best friends other than me and your father. Do you understand that? Me and your father. You don't have any others."

"Teresa didn't believe me, anyway."

I had also told Teresa that I had changed my mind. I wanted El back. But with Florence, you don't change your mind or your direction without some massive upheaval. Once the course has been plotted out, she expects everybody to keep going straight ahead.

Within minutes, a helicopter hovered over the river, casting a white beam down into the water and onto the riverbanks. Klieg lights shone on the last lock on the canal and the surrounding concrete breakwater that opened out into the river where bloodhounds sniffed near the water.

Makeshift tents were constructed for us to sit beneath. But nobody could sit. We cared even less about the rain. We all stood folded over the wall.

About a half mile down, an officer in a raincoat was directing traffic. Fire trucks with enormous generators sat partly in the grass and partly in the street. The officer used two yellow flares to push cars onto the shoulder, around the trucks.

May Ruth had my mother's arm. Aunt Thelma was on the other side. May Ruth's face had that blank quality, like staring up at a movie screen. In her eyeglasses, I could see the small dot of the helicopter rising again, its light drowning out all the others. The red light on the tail wing, the white cone of light from its underbelly. The colors flickered and bent across her face, across each of our faces.

We stayed on the hill for about an hour. Or it seemed an hour. Afterward it made more sense to follow the current to where the canal's lock met the river. The helicopter was landing on the other side of the lock. Even with all the rain, people continued to crowd the river's edge. I made my way through the crowd until I saw an officer. He was feeding a line from one of the trucks that held a generator.

"Why is the helicopter landing?" I yelled over the hum of the generator.

"The lightning," he said. "It's far more dangerous to have him up there now with all this lightning and with all these people around. Just can't risk it. Soon as the lightning eases up, the pilot'll go back up there."

"Do you know what the boy's chances are? Of surviving?"

"They don't look good, miss," he said, offering me his raincoat, draping it over my head. A voice was coming over his radio. But the static made it difficult to make out what was being said. The man jumped up into the cabin of his truck to talk on the radio.

There was so much water. The rain came down in sheets. Mother stood along the edge of the river with Uncle Herbert and Daddy. She was pacing and waiting. She would stop to point if a wave peaked and the water seemed—even the slightest bit—to offer some hope. "There, over there, I saw something. There. Are you blind? Over there."

An officer made his rounds to all of us. Aunt Cora was sitting under a tent. Aunt Thelma and Pepper stood under a tree, not far from me. Pepper stared out into the water. When the officer suggested to Uncle Herbert that we go home, Mother insisted she wasn't going anywhere. Uncle Herbert took her by the arm and she snatched her arm away. After a while I saw Aunt Cora and May Ruth walking with a couple of police officers to a car along the road. They were going home.

I began to walk along the river. At about midnight I had walked the length. I headed back to Aunt Cora's place.

The light was on in the living room, and as I neared the house, I could see May Ruth standing in the window. Seeing me, she came outside to the porch. Aunt Cora remained seated in the living room. Her eyes were closed and she was petting the top of her Bible. A window fan rustled the sheers and the heat from the motor pushed back onto the porch.

May Ruth extended her hands.

"I don't know anything more," I said to her. "I feel paralyzed. I know I should be down there, but I don't want to go back."

"We're all quite afraid," May Ruth said, pulling me close to her. "We mustn't give up hope. Do you understand? We mustn't. We've got to believe that that silly little boy is somewhere having a time at our expense."

The phone rang. May Ruth ran inside to answer it. There were only two rings, and by the time she reached the phone table, the ringing stopped. As she was walking back toward the living room, the phone rang again. This time just once.

Then, fifteen or so minutes later, Uncle Herbert's car was coming up the driveway, followed by my father's. The helicopter was still down. But now the divers' klieg lights had been turned off. The rain was barely falling. But falling.

Aunt Cora, May Ruth, and I stood on the porch.

Before Mother, Father, Aunt Thelma, Uncle Herbert, and Pepper took one step outside the car, the three of us knew El was gone.

We knew before Pepper, crying, jumped out of the car and ran around the side of the house with Uncle Herbert and Aunt Thelma tearing out after him. We knew before my mother got out and then my father, who grabbed her hand as they walked toward the porch. Mother's legs were covered with mud and her dress was soaking wet. Her purse dragged behind her and she was coming toward us as though a team of horses couldn't stop her.

When Mother got to the porch, May Ruth ran down to her. But Mother held her hand up. She placed her purse at the foot of the steps. My legs felt weak as she tried to speak, fighting back tears.

"El is gone," she said. "His body was found about a mile from where he fell in. His body got caught in the undercurrent and his jersey was snagged on a steel rod jutting from a concrete embankment. He had a gunshot wound in his belly."

"A gunshot?" Aunt Cora said.

"The gun somehow was still wedged in his pants band. The gun must have fired when he hit the water."

"What was he doing with a gun?" May Ruth said.

"Pepper told the police that El had been afraid. But Pepper ain't making hardly no damn sense right now. Pepper said El had been afraid after . . . after Mr. Paul. I don't know. Pepper ain't making no sense. I keep trying to talk to him, to ask him about that gun. I want to know what they were doing up there in the first place. It was that same old gun we keep here.

I don't know. There are more questions than answers right now. But El's gone. I saw them when they dragged him from the water. I saw them. I saw that baby coming out of the water."

"I can't stay," I said. I couldn't look at Mother. I turned toward the door. "I can't stay any longer. I can't do this. I can't breathe."

Aunt Cora took me by my shoulders, wiping my face with her palms. "Everything's so confused right now, honey. You got to stand up, though. I know you can—"

"What do you mean, you can't stay?" Mother said. "You can't simply run off somewhere and pretend nothing's happened here."

"For the last ten years, I've been running away and pretending nothing's happened, Mother. I'm ashamed that I want to leave now, but that's all I can feel. I know I can't stay. Not today. Not for the funeral. I can't do it. I'm his mother, but I don't know what that feels like. I didn't know what it felt like in life, now I don't know in death, either. You know more about losing a child than I do. You know more about being his mother than I do. I feel like I've lost a little brother. It hurts. But even the hurt feels out of whack. Like I'm coming out of my skin. I can't recall five times that I burped him, Mother. I can't remember five that I changed his diaper. I can't remember spending more than a week at a time with him. I do remember him getting on my nerves from time to time and being glad when I jumped back in my car or on some train, going far away from him. Sometimes feeling so grateful that I was footloose and fancy-free."

"Not once did you offer to switch places, sweetie," Mother said.

"You're right. I wanted the best of both worlds. I wanted to see my son every now and then. And afterward I wanted to be able to come and go as I pleased. How do you think that makes me feel now? I'm not blaming anybody. I just know that if I stay, I'm going to go out of my mind."

My purse was in the kitchen. I ran inside to get it. When I came back out, Mother was standing on the top step.

"This isn't about you, Sweet Alma. Don't you fucking walk out of here. You hear me? Now is not the time. Don't you leave here."

Mother started to cry.

"I'm very, very sorry," I said, passing her. I didn't look back. I walked over to my car and got inside. I drove as fast as I could down to the main road.

I refused to look back, even as the house withdrew in my rearview mirror.

Day Five

28

Herbert

DAYBREAK, THURSDAY, AUGUST 7, 1986

I hear that sweeping sound again.

The temperature is steadily rising as I make my way down the steps, out to the porch.

"You can't sleep, either," Sis say when she see me. "I got up this morning feeling like the porch needed to be swept down. Now, what the hell do I care about what the porch looks like?"

I shrug and take a seat on the top step. She sit next to me, swiping at some mosquito or bug nagging her 'round the knees.

She say, "I don't know who's louder, June or May Ruth. They should be roommates or at least figure out how to synchronize their snoring. The entire second floor reminds me of a train station."

The sun ain't even made it up good yet and I hear voices down along Old Riley. Either folk getting up or finally heading home to bed.

I turn to Sis. "How you making it?" I ask her. "Tell me how you really making it?"

"Doing just fine," she say too quicklike. She yank at her cut-off shorts, 'round the crotch area, before standing. "And you?"

I just turn back toward the sunflowers since I don't feel like playing games this morning. Some days you just don't feel like fooling 'round.

"I think I'm gone start breakfast," I say. "You got any special requests?"

"Edible is all I require. That's enough for me. I'll complain about it later." She look up smiling.

Aunt Cora done come down the back steps. We can hear her turning on the faucet and the television in the kitchen. The phone ring and she let everything sit to answer it.

She talking for a few seconds and I happen to know she talking to Viola by her conversation, but Sis don't. And Sis ain't paying Aunt Cora no real attention until she say, "He hanged himself, huh? That's the way you found him?"

Sis's knees near snap backward and suddenly it's like the planks below her feet done dissolved into nothing. That broom fall to the floor and she get to sweating as she slide down the wall. I hurry and pick her up. I take her into the living room.

Seeing us, Aunt Cora rush in. She say, "Did she faint?"

"Fell flat out," I say.

Sis lean her head in her hands and start to cry. She bent over, she crying so hard. I've saw Sis carry on in church before. When the Holy Ghost fall on her, I'm talking 'bout. I've watched her tear up a whole pew row, shouting. I think of that 'cause right 'bout now Sis seem slain in the spirit, as they say. She bent over crying and crying, shaking from top to bottom. Sis put her head on my chest and I pet her like she a baby. You can't pet her ordinarily. But I pet her now. I can feel her trembling. "I'll never, ever forgive myself," she say. "Herbert, I'm so sorry. I never thought . . ."

"You never thought what?"

"I never thought Pepper would try to kill himself."

"Pepper ain't tried to kill hisself, Sis. What the hell you talking 'bout? Mr. Lacey, that dim-witted dog, is the one hanged. Not Pepper."

Aunt Cora sit down next to Sis and take Sis's hand. "Earlier this morning, Viola's dog got tangled up in some vines. The dog, not your nephew. Last night when Viola called Herbert, he told her he'd come over and cut the dog down in the daylight. So Viola's wondering if it's daylight enough for him. The dog's been hanging there all night because your brother-in-law here wouldn't get out his bed." Aunt Cora say to me, "She also wants to know if you'll dig a hole for Mr. Lacey. Viola said the dog tore out running. She knew something was wrong with him. Mr. Lacey normally sits quietly under her porch. But he started to whine and then tore out running all the way down to Old Riley, then back up the hill. Viola said, being half blind as he is, he got tangled in some vines and hanged himself. That other fool dog didn't try to intervene at all."

Slowly me and Aunt Cora start to laugh because laughing allows us to breathe again. And we all need to breathe right about now. I put my arm 'round Sis.

I say to her, "Well, I guess I ain't got to ask again, how you making it. I believe I already know."

"Some days I can't think. I can't sleep. I eat and I don't get full. I'm so angry. I'm mad at God. At the world. It's not just Pepper I'm mad at. I'm mad at the entire goddamned world. I'm mad at your boy and didn't hardly know it. Didn't know I was separating him out at all."

"Nobody's to blame here, Sis," I say.

"My head knows that. But my heart doesn't. I've got things I just don't understand. All those years ago, I didn't want that child. I prayed that he wouldn't come here alive. I didn't want him, Herbert, Cora. Now I can't bear to let him go."

Aunt Cora step back and fold her arms. She close her eyes, then open them again, looking over her glasses. "Herbert, take Flossie down to that courthouse."

"Is that what you want to do, Sis?"

Sis don't say nothing at first. Then she start to nod her head. "I'm ready. I'm ready to go. I don't hate Pepper, Herbert. God knows I don't."

"You've got to tell him that," Aunt Cora say. "You've got to tell Pepper. Now you all go on right now, you hear? Take a second to splash some water across your faces. But go on." Aunt Cora start making her way back to the kitchen. "Course, if I'd known that dog would evoke this type of response, I'd have hanged ol' Mr. Lacey myself months ago."

We get to the courthouse. I don't recognize the ol' dude behind the counter. I assume he's new. He listening to the radio and he turn the volume down when we walk in.

I say, "We got to see Robert Gray."

He say, "The young man who didn't want to leave, right?"

"That's right. He the one."

He scratch behind his ear and say, "He just left, mister. Not more than fifteen minutes ago."

"You know where he was heading?"

"I didn't ask. I was told that as soon as that boy started talking about leaving, to show him the door. And that's what I did. He can't be that far, though. He left with all them books of his. Was gone for two minutes before he came back. Wanted to know if I could lend him some bus fare. To get him out of here? I gave him all the change in my pockets."

We jump back in the car and drive 'round toward the canal and back up the street toward Old Riley. Neither of us can figure on how we missed him. We turn the corner and both of us start smiling 'cause we see him clear as day sitting on the bench at the bus stop. It's that clean-shaved head that made us miss him the first time. I'm hardly able to recognize my own boy.

I turn the corner, then back up to the bus stop.

Sis get out. I stay in the car. She sit next to him on the bench and he start to get up and leave. But she say, "Pepper,

I've got something to say to you. I hope you'll listen. Now I can't make you, but I hope you will." He sit back down.

"Morning, son," I say.

He mumbles, "Morning."

Sis say, "Years ago, when I found out Sweet Alma was pregnant, I thought I would die."

"What you telling me for?" Pepper say, leaning forward. He rest his chin in his hand and look off toward the church.

Sis reaches over and rubs on his back. "If someone had stabbed me in my chest, it couldn't have felt much different from my own daughter being pregnant at fourteen years old," she say. "I thought there was nothing El could ever do to match that feeling. Then he died. And that pain was far worse than anything I'd ever felt before. I still feel it, Pepper, it's as raw as a year ago."

"You think I don't feel it?" Pepper say, looking at her.

Sis say, "I know you do. Only I'm a lot less mature in the way I handle it. I'm old enough to know better. Still, I don't know how to make the pain go away other than to try to disperse it, I suppose. To make other people feel as I do. And I am truly sorry."

Pepper look up at her, but he don't say nothing.

She say, "You and I should go for a walk. Would you walk with me, Pepper? We'll walk for a while, and if we get too hot, we can take a bus or a taxi or hitchhike. Let Herbert gather your things. We've got a few miles ahead of us. Let's just see how much crow your aunt can chew on along the way. Do you know that expression about 'eating crow'?"

"I know it," Pepper say, wiping at his nose.

Sis take a couple of his things and put them in the front seat of the car, like she showing him how easy it is to do. "What you probably don't know is that crow is a tough old bird to chew. Tougher for some than for others."

Pepper's face don't crack a smile or nothing. He stand and stuff his hands in his pockets. He start walking even before

Sis got every book arranged proper. He turn one time to make sure everything's collected. But he don't change his expression. He don't let down that guard. He like some kid who done dragged his hand along the stove. He now 'fraid to go back over to it. He know that stove got its good points, can do him a whole heap of good, but he also know it sho' 'nuff can burn the hell out of him.

I keep a watch over them until they get down pass the corner. I keep watching my boy as he drag hisself along. Them feet of his like they talking to one another. Begging the other's pardon for getting in the way. I'm remembering back when it was nothing for me to lift that boy. For me to take him by the arm, with him laughing his sides out, and hoist him onto my shoulders. Sometimes both of us would be so tickled that I could hardly believe so much laughter could fit inside two people, and I could hardly tell where the most of it came from.

In my head I'm praying for his laughter again. For laughter for all of us. Sometimes it's hard to get that back. Sometimes it's the hardest thing in the world to return.

29

Herbert

Viola Miller and me standing in a small clearing along her side yard.

Them trees behind us teem with old restless blackbirds that don't sing worth nothing. Can't study on singing on account of them being too busy crying out louder and louder as the sun come up and as the dirt darken this here hole.

With the last pat of the shovel, a truck pull up into Viola's driveway. She don't pay no attention to it at first 'cause she leaning on me with her hands covering her eyes. (Naturally her leaning ain't helping my shoveling none, though it's doing her just fine.) Her live dog scrunches down at her feet, moaning and looking sorry at the ground where the dead dog now lay covered over. At first I can't tell which is worse off: Viola or the live dog. But then it become clear as day when that truck pull all the way up to the new fountain—where the water drain down the bosoms of the naked green mermaid lady—and Viola glimpse that truck through the trees. She gather herself mighty quicklike, wiping at her nose and patting at her hair. She pull out a hand mirror from her robe pocket. That robe real frilly with feathery stuff 'round the collar and remind me of something May Ruth would go for. Onliest thing is, I ain't never seen even May Ruth in a getup like Viola's.

When Viola don't like what she see in that hand mirror, she say, "Oh my, " and take to running. She sprint like a antelope or one of them Olympic hurdle jumpers through the woods up to her house. She don't stop for nothing until she make it to a side door. The young man don't see her, which, to me, mean he must be kinda daft. His truck say, EUGENE'S LAWN CARE SERVICES. And I'm hoping he notice more while taking care of folks' root worm than he do while walking from one place to the other. He sho' don't see her, but that ain't the onliest reason I'm thinking he must be kinda daft. He look about eighteen, no more than twenty-two, and must somehow be enjoying taking up so much time with ol' Viola— who's older than old, so old, Aunt Cora say, that Viola's knees done turned in on her; Aunt Cora say "done turned" 'cause she don't remember Viola ever being as knock-kneed as she is now, and I agree, seeing I just witnessed her running on them knock-kneed antelope legs of hers.

That boy get to her front porch and mash on the bell. He swerve 'round to look into the morning and then start to whistle a bit to pass the time.

I decide to get out of the way 'cause I ain't up for no long conversations this morning. Especially with a young man who, from early reports, don't show signs of even a lick of sense. Even though he do have a pretty enough whistle on him.

I also decide that I know now who worst off between Viola and that dog. Far as I can see, it's the dog that's worst off 'cause he ain't moved or barked or nothing all morning. Not when them blackbirds flew in and flew back out, or when that truck pulled up, or when that young man started whistling at the mermaid (that got her lips tooted up, too, like she whistling back at him, or blowing a kiss, even though only water coming through her toot). Ordinarily this dog bark at the world. But not this morning. This morning he ain't got nothing to say on account of his heart being broke in two. And his heart and his bark may as well be connected.

I grab up my shovel and pickax, then move away from the grave and the dog finally get the gumption to lift up. He stretch his hindquarters out, but not enough to really talk about, just enough to reposition hisself on top of the fresh mound. Next he scratch at the top dirt a bit like he'd give anything in this world to dig, but he know he ain't s'pose to. He know it ain't right to disturb nothing, so that scratching turn into patting mighty fast.

"I know, ol' dude," I say to him and I reach down to rub on his head. "You gone be all right. Don't seem like it right now. But you gone be all right."

After a while, Viola open the door. And before I know it, Viola walking arm in arm with that boy back toward the clearing. She telling him what happened to the dog this morning.

When I hear Viola coming closer—and she re-creating a snivel for the young man's benefit—I go on and make my way back to the well-worn path. I done spent enough time with the likes of Viola Miller, and I pity the live dog who's now left all by his lonesome with that woman.

Soon as I cross over to Aunt Cora's property, I see Thelma standing on the porch, pacing back and forth. She see me and come running down the porch steps. She lean forward looking at me coming as if leaning forward give her a better view than simple looking.

"Where've you been, Herbert?" she say. "And where are Flossie and Pepper? Aunt Cora said you took Flossie to see Pepper this morning. I've been waiting for you to come back. I've been waiting to see how they're getting along."

"I 'spect they getting along just fine." I stomp black dirt off my feet. I take my knife out and start to pick at the dirt under my fingernails.

"What do you mean, you suspect they're getting along? Where are they?"

I look down at my watch. "Let's see, it's about nine o'clock. Oh, I'd say they should be along shortly."

"Herbert, how could you leave that woman alone with my son?"

"Thelma, that woman is your sister-in-law. She ain't no stranger. And your son is a grown man, or near about. When we got to the jail this morning, he'd already left. Don't know where he was heading, but he was sitting at the bus stop. I want to say he was coming here, but I can't be sure. Anyhow, Sis told Pep that she needed to talk to him and that they could walk and talk. They on their way, walking. They may walk all the way. They may walk part of the way. They may see a taxi and flag it down. They may stop and get some breakfast. They may take a boat. Hell, I don't know, but we got to let this thing run its own course."

"There are nearly six miles between here and the downtown," Thelma say, untying her apron strings. She pull the apron 'round so she can chew on the knot she done made.

"If it don't matter to them, why should it matter to us? Pepper done rested good enough. Sis accustomed to walking more than that every day delivering mail. And you and me both know this ain't got nothing to do with walking. Six miles won't begin to cover half the distance that's sitting out before the both of them."

Thelma look faint, but she ain't got time for fainting. She march 'round to the side of the house for the bicycle. I follow after her.

"Now, Thelma, we can go looking for them. Or you can trust that everything gone be all right and we can wait for them to arrive. Will you trust me on this one? Will you?"

She stop short of the bicycle and drag herself back 'round to the porch.

"Besides, you ain't asked me one thing 'bout how my back is getting along after digging that hole for Mr. Lacey. C'mon upstairs with me for a second. I can shower and you can give me one of them massages. What do you say to that?"

"I don't feel up to it right now, Herbert."

"Waiting on this hot porch won't get them here any faster. We may as well spend some time together this morning."

I take her hand and she follow, looking over her shoulder until she can't see what's out the door no more or who's coming up the drive. She ain't got the safety net of seeing, but she following just fine.

We get up to our room, and all of a sudden that dog next door start to bark. We both look out the window, wondering if he barking at Sis and Pepper coming up the drive. Turns out he ain't. He just barking at the sky or them birds. Something or another.

I start to undress for the shower. And it occurs to me that dog's got to know now that he ain't tied to nothing. Surely, he got to know he can run wherever them legs of his take him. Could be that means he gone wander off. But considering what happened to that other dog last night, it could be that that live dog ain't going nowhere. He gone stay put and give a whole lot of thought to every move he make. Least now we know he got choices. Maybe that's the important thing.

30

Flossie
NEARING NOON

At the top of the hill, Pepper and I see Cora and Thelma sitting on the porch.

Thelma sees us and starts to run down the steps, but she stops as though yanked by a cord. She sits back down.

"The way I see it," I say to Pepper, "we can pretend to be fighting and throw your mother into a tither, just for sport, or we can just keep on along the way we are."

Pepper looks over to me. "Mama's heart probably can't handle this hardly," he says.

We keep on up to the porch. "Hey, Aunt Cora," he says, waving.

Cora adjusts her eyeglasses. "Son, I'll sure be glad when your hair grows back."

Pepper smiles, rubbing his head. He kisses his mother, then sits beside her, leaning back on his elbows. Thelma was polishing her toes and has one foot completed.

"I hear June is here," he says.

"Yes, she's in the kitchen, eating," Thelma says.

"She ain't been no trouble, has she?"

"None at all," Cora says. "She's been a delightful houseguest." I look up at her. She rolls her eyes back toward her newspaper. "She's going to have that baby any day now, Pep.

We noticed last night that her stomach is dropping. That's why she stayed with us. I told her she's got to be ready at any moment. I've been praying that she has it tomorrow. What a wonderful gift that would be. Yes, Lord, what a wonderful thing that would be."

I tap my leg, gesturing for Thelma to put her foot on my thigh. She hesitates at first, looking at me as if I might chop her toes off. I grab her foot and then the nail polish. I finish painting her remaining toes.

Inside, I can see May Ruth and June sitting at the kitchen table. "Hey, June," I say to her. "I brought you a visitor."

I push against Pepper's knee and he gets up and goes inside. I sit next to Thelma.

"I'm going to visit Sweet Alma," I say. Cora folds her newspaper. "I'd been thinking about it all week, but I officially decided it while Pep and I were walking. I'm going to try to get her to come back for the last day of the festivities tomorrow. I don't know if she'll come, but I'm sure as hell going to try."

"She may not come," Cora says. "You know that, Flossie Jo. She, like you, is as stubborn as a mule. I'm all for you going, but I'd hate to see you disappointed."

"If she doesn't come in time for tomorrow, then that's fine, too. But I won't leave Chicago until we talk. I've recently learned some techniques to get people to do what's right." I turn to Thelma. "Haven't I, Thelma? I'll stare at her, stare her down until she can feel it on her insides, or I'll block her way so she can't go around me. I know how to get to her. But for now I'm going up to shower. I'll have lunch, then leave after that. Thelma, you'll take care of my collards for today, won't you?"

"Of course I will," she says as I stand. She grabs my arm. "What did you two talk about, Flossie? What did you say to Pepper?"

"We talked about the sun and the trees, the water. That old asphalt road down there. We talked about El and that new baby Pepper has coming. Suffice it to say that we both are going to try living again. Emphasis on *try*. We both got things to look forward to. Funny how easy it is to lose sight of that."

June and Pepper are in the living room. He's got his head to her stomach, listening.

I start up the front stairs when I hear May Ruth humming in the kitchen. It sounds like an Irish dirge or a whiny wheel. I walk back to the kitchen, but she doesn't see me because she's too busy staring out of the window.

"I prefer your snoring," I tell her. "In the fall, when the trees are bare, you can see straight through to Viola's bedroom window."

"Really? Then you must get yourself a pair of high-powered binoculars and wait for her man friend to visit so that you may get some pointers for Ben."

"I don't need any pointers."

"Does Ben?"

"I don't know. It's too early to tell. And who says I'll ever know?"

"Will you let me know if you ever know?"

"I most certainly will not. I'm going to see Sweet Alma—"

"What an absolutely splendid idea."

"But I may or may not make it back before you leave on Saturday. Here's my point: I want you to come live here in Halley. I'll fly out within a week or two to help you get your affairs in order. And you can come back here with us. I'm sure Cora will agree."

"Flossie, don't be such a soppy sentimentalist. It's so unbecoming."

"You think about it. You, yourself, said how much you love this place. You're closer to us than your family abroad. Imagine all the bird-watching you can do. And you'll be here in the fall during hunting season, which means you can get yourself arrested as many times as you want. Have you told the others about your cancer?"

"Not yet, dear heart. Not yet. The festivities aren't over, now, are they? In due time I shall tell everyone. In due time."

The teakettle on the stove starts to whistle. May Ruth drys her hands and takes the kettle off the eye. She pours tea for both of us.

"Promise me you'll think about it."

"I promise only to consider Halley and its many curative powers. Nothing more."

"I don't want you to be alone. You don't have to be, May Ruth. You really don't have to be."

May Ruth puts her cake batter in the oven, then twists the timer on the stove. She picks up her binoculars from the table and places them around her neck. She then removes her bracelets and her earrings because they make too much noise and would frighten the birds away. She pulls her Thermos from her slouchy purse along with her field guide and a few note cards.

"I'm off for a swim, dear heart," she says as she stuffs her hair beneath her straw hat. She looks up at the clock on the stove and synchronizes her wristwatch. "I don't suppose you have time to join me for a quicky?"

"Not a chance, sister," I say, hugging her.

"Very well, then."

"Don't forget to think about what I said."

"I shall think of nothing else, dear heart," she says. "You know what? Sometimes grief opens up a window. Sometimes grief opens it wide enough for something wonderful to fly in."

As she leaves through the back door, I stand at the kitchen window, looking out. I think about the picture Pepper showed me earlier this morning as we sat along the river.

In the picture, El is standing next to Pepper, somewhere along the banks. Where exactly, I couldn't tell. The sun hits both boys so that their faces are aglow. El is noticeably taller. Pepper noticeably lifting a bit to eliminate the height difference.

They wear blue-jean shorts and their feet and bony chests are exposed. The bills of their Halley's Comets baseball caps jut from side pockets—El's from his left pocket, Pepper's from his right. And they are straining to hold up a large fish, while competing to see who can smile the broadest. Behind the boys, fishing rods lay out on the grass, and I can see the hull of a boat in the water.